Escape to the Hummingbird Hotel

by

Daisy James

Cover Design by Berni Stevens

Edited by Laura McCallen

ISBN:978-1-914304-09-5

As this is my twentieth book – wow, how did that happen?
– I'd like to dedicate this book to all my wonderful readers.

Contents

Chapter One	1
Chapter Two	13
Chapter Three	31
Chapter Four	43
Chapter Five	53
Chapter Six	61
Chapter Seven	73
Chapter Eight	87
Chapter Nine	103
Chapter Ten	113
Chapter Eleven	127
Chapter Twelve	139
Chapter Thirteen	155
Chapter Fourteen	165
Chapter Fifteen	179
Chapter Sixteen	191
Chapter Seventeen	203
Chapter Eighteen	213
Chapter Nineteen	223
Chapter Twenty	237
Chapter Twenty-One	245
Chapter Twenty-Two	259
Chapter Twenty-Three	269
Chapter Twenty-Four	281
Chapter Twenty Five	291
Chapter Twenty Six	299
Chapter Twenty Seven	309
Chapter Twenty Eight	321
Acknowledgements	335
Also by Daisy James	337

Chapter One

Abbie's Attic Flat in Wimbledon
Flower: Innocent Heart Iris

'How do I look?'

Abbie performed a theatrical twirl in front of Emily, the hemline of her floaty, scarlet dress rising above her knees, the wide sleeves rippling at her wrists when she leaned towards the mirror to fasten her pearl earrings in place and complete her outfit.

'You look amazing.'

'Oh, Em, I'm so excited.'

'I know you are, darling, but…'

Abbie turned towards her best friend, confusion swirling.

'But what?'

'It's just, well, are you sure this is really what you want?'

'We've been dating for over a year, Em.'

'I know, but it's so sudden, so unexpected… so unlike Dan.'

Abbie could hear the anxiety in Emily's voice, and yet the determined jut of her chin was evidence that despite the awkwardness of the situation, she still felt she needed to express her concern, needed to make sure her friend wasn't making a mistake, and for that her heart blossomed with affection as she reached out to touch her arm.

'You're right, and I admit it *was* a bit of a shock. I genuinely had no idea Dan was even thinking of proposing. He's never been the best at keeping secrets and he hasn't dropped *any* hints, which is why I'm so glad I spotted him through the window of Tiffany's when my cab got caught up in the rush-hour traffic. When he told me that he was taking me out for dinner at the Sky Garden – the *Sky Garden*, Em, my favourite place in the whole of London! – well, I just thought it was so we could celebrate him winning the British Florist Association award last month.'

As soon as the words left her lips, Abbie wished she could have snatched them back, especially when she saw Emily's eyes narrow and her smile vanish. She groaned inwardly; they'd been over this ground before and she knew exactly what was coming next.

'You mean the award *you* should have won?'

'Em, please…'

'Sorry, Abbie, but that design was yours, not Dan's. Your style is so distinctive, infused with such originality and flair, that I'm surprised the judges didn't query his entry. Everyone knows you're the creative genius behind

FlowerEssence's fabulous success, that it's your special touch that all your celebrity and VIP clients are swooning over. You know, I still can't quite believe that Pierre Fontaine – *the* Pierre Fontaine, the famously fiery French fashion designer – booked your boutique to dress his spring/summer catwalk show last month. That event was absolutely one of the highlights of my entire life.'

'Mine, too!' Abbie laughed, relieved to see the smile had returned to Emily's face. She checked her watch, performed a quick final check in the mirror, grabbed the silver evening bag her friend Pippa had lent her, and snatched up her fringed wrap to ward off the surprise chill of the late June evening. 'Okay, shall we—'

But Emily wasn't listening; she was clearly on a roll, and Abbie had learned from past experience that it was quicker to let her say her piece than to prolong the conversation by arguing. She just wished she hadn't chosen that particular moment – ten minutes before the taxi was due to arrive to take them from their tiny attic apartment in Wimbledon to the restaurant at the top of the spectacular Walkie Talkie building – to press her case.

'What I can't understand is why Dan insists on taking all the credit. Why can't he share it? Why doesn't he invite you up onto the stage to accept the accolades with him? Acknowledge in front of everyone that it was a joint enterprise? He's not just your boss, Abbie, he's your boyfriend – soon-to-be fiancé – so you'd think he'd be proud of your achievements, shouting about your amazing talent from the rooftops. I know I'm biased, but it's your expert knowledge and innovative use of every flower, plant and piece of exotic foliage known to the world of botanical artistry that has propelled his business into the highest echelons of floral decorating.'

'Emily, I really don't—'

'You're a qualified botanist, not a lowly florist's assistant, which is how Dan still treats you after being there, demonstrating your skills on a daily basis, for three long years. I know for a fact that before you joined *FlowerEssence* the blossom-bedecked grapevine was humming with gossip that the boutique was on the verge of bankruptcy. All I'm saying is that he should give you the credit you deserve.'

'I—'

'I've known you for a long time, Abs. Before you met Dan, you used to wax lyrical about one day landing a job at Kew Gardens or the Eden Project. You need to chase your dreams, not sacrifice them on the altar of Dan's desire to be labelled "Florist to the Stars".'

'I love Dan, Emily. We're chasing our dreams together.'

'But your dreams are so different. He loves the crazy celebrity lifestyle, all the glitz and glamour of the A-list parties, the must-have backstage passes to opening nights, not to mention the accolades dished out at the award ceremonies. You, on the other hand, want a cute little cottage with roses around the door and a garden big enough for a greenhouse and a lily pond. Tell me, how are you going to persuade him to move from his minimalist bachelor's pad overlooking the Thames to a quiet leafy suburb? And what will he do when you leave the boutique to take up your dream job as head botanist at Kew Gardens?'

'We'll work something out.'

'I can predict how that will go…' Emily muttered darkly.

Abbie smiled, filled with gratitude for Emily's unerring loyalty. They had been friends since Abbie had packed up her life in Devon and headed for a fresh start in London, hoping that a complete change of scenery would alleviate even a modicum of the grief that had overwhelmed her after her mother had passed away. She knew the director of fate had been smiling on her the day she spotted Emily's hand-written ad in the newsagent's window seeking a flatmate to share her tiny top-floor apartment with the fabulous roof terrace. They had hit it off right from the start, but what had sealed their friendship was the fact that Emily was also running away from her previous life, albeit for wildly different reasons.

'The guy can't even arrange a surprise proposal without getting found out.'

'Em, can we not do this right now? I'm on my way to what I hope will be one of the most momentous nights of my life. Okay, so it won't be the total surprise that Dan wants, but I'm actually delighted it's worked out this way.'

'Why?'

'Well, first of all, it means I've been able to have my hair tamed so I won't look like Medusa on steroids in my engagement photos, *and* I've got to wear this unbelievably gorgeous dress that Pippa managed to snaffle from Pierre Fontaine's spring/summer capsule collection, not to mention these shoes, which she wore to her best friend Lexie's Christmas Extravaganza fashion show.'

'They *are* stunning shoes,' Emily conceded, almost drooling at the ivory silk stilettos.

'And secondly, if I hadn't caught a glimpse of Dan

choosing my engagement ring, then I wouldn't have been able to share this magical moment with you and all our other friends. I'm so excited that you're all going to be there at the Sky Garden, watching from behind that bamboo screen, just waiting for the moment Dan slides the ring onto my finger so you can all leap out and shout *Surprise!* I can't wait to see his face! Promise you'll have your camera ready, Em?'

'Of course I will.' Emily met her gaze, her hazel eyes filled with contrition. 'I'm sorry, Abbie, I didn't mean to put a dampener on things for you. I just wanted to make sure you'd thought things through and this is what you truly want.'

'It is, it really is, and thank you.'

'What for?'

'For looking out for me.'

Just as Abbie reached forward to give Emily an appreciative hug, her phone buzzed and she glanced down at the screen.

'Okay, the taxi's here. Come on, time to go.'

They clattered down the five flights of stairs – the lift was always out of order – and jumped into the back of the black cab. Now that she was actually on her way to meet Dan, Abbie's stomach began to churn as the nerves kicked in, and she was grateful for Emily's attempt to distract her, although not for her choice of subject matter.

'Hey, by the way, did you ring that lawyer back?'

'No, not yet.'

'Why not?'

'Well, what with designing, arranging, and delivering the flowers for Dianna and Jacques' wedding tomorrow, and then getting everything sorted for tonight, I'll admit it slipped my mind. Anyway, I didn't even know my aunt. She left Devon before I was born to go and live in California and Mum never talked about her. Something happened between them, that much I do know, but every time I tried to broach the subject with Mum before she passed away, she would get this sad, distant look in her eyes and divert the conversation. I didn't want to upset her, or bring back unhappy memories, especially after she got ill, so I eventually gave up.'

'Maybe your aunt's left you something in her will?'

'I doubt it. Why would she?'

'Perhaps a family portrait?'

'Or a collection of silver spoons?' Abbie laughed.

'Or a wad of cash. Yes, I reckon it's a small bequest, just enough for you to put down a deposit on that little country cottage with a garden full of flowers that you've been going on about for so long.'

'I think you're getting a bit carried away, Em.'

'Well, you won't know until you make that call.'

'I promise to ring the solicitor first thing tomorrow morning, okay?'

'Great.'

Abbie stared out of the window at the dense urban sprawl flashing by. Even on a drab, drizzly evening, the streets were teeming with people on their way to see a West End musical, or a play, or a movie, or to enjoy a cocktail or two with friends, and a fresh burst of elation whooshed through her chest. She was excited about getting engaged. She adored Dan; tall, handsome, bronzed, with a penchant for regular manicures, but, most important of all, a fellow lover of all-things floral – the perfect person to spend the rest of her life with.

The agonising emptiness, that unsettling sensation of being cast adrift without an anchor she had harboured since her mum had passed away, was about to be replaced with the feeling of safety and security she craved, of knowing that there was someone by her side who would catch her if she fell. Emily was wrong; Dan didn't take her for granted. Okay, so it might be nice to be recognised for her floral flair every once in a while, but she was more than happy to share the knowledge and expertise she had gained while studying for her degree in botany, and she hoped – one day – to introduce an even wider range of flowers and plants to the business. Maybe tonight would be the time to talk a bit more about not only their personal future, but their professional future, too.

'We're here! We're here!' Emily squealed as she jumped out of the cab, linked her arm through Abbie's, and dashed across the pavement into the lobby of the Walkie Talkie building, her short flower-bedecked dress revealing more than a little thigh. Abbie followed her to the bank of elevators and paused.

'Have you got the paper streamers?'

'Check.'

'And the confetti?'

'Check.'

'And the party poppers and rainbow whistles?'

'Check.'

'And you'll make sure there's an extra bottle of Champagne on ice for the toast after you've all jumped out from behind the screen?'

'Check!' Emily giggled as she blew the ends of her

fringe from her eyes before stepping into the lift and reaching into her bag to look at her phone. 'Okay, there's a text from Martha, she says that everyone is in position, and Dan is already sitting at your table and has absolutely no idea that twelve of your best friends and colleagues are spying on him.'

The elevator pinged, and as Abbie stepped out into the Sky Garden restaurant, her heartrate increased and a sudden wave of breathlessness ambushed her.

'Are you okay?'

'Oh, Em, I'm so nervous.'

'Don't be, darling. Just go over there and enjoy every single minute.'

Emily leaned forward for one last hug, and then shot off to find their friends. Abbie took a moment to compose herself and marvel at the magnificent bird's eye view of London that was spread out in front of her. Then her gaze landed on Dan, sitting at a table next to the huge floor-to-ceiling windows, scrolling through his phone, so unbelievably handsome in his designer suit with the lilac silk lining, pale pink Jermyn Street shirt, gold cufflinks, and one of the chunky watches he seemed to collect, and a blanket of calm descended.

'Hi, Dan.'

'Oh, Abbie, there you are.'

Dan stood to drop a kiss on her cheek and pull out her chair. As she sat, she caught a whiff of his favourite cologne – one he sourced from a specialist boutique in Paris – that sent her already swirling senses into overdrive and she was grateful when the waiter came over to welcome them and hand them the wine menu, a glint of knowledge in his eyes as he waited for their order.

'I thought as this is a special occasion that we'd treat ourselves to a bottle of Champagne. What do you think?' said Dan.

'Sounds wonderful.'

Abbie grinned and couldn't help risking a glance over her shoulder to where a woven screen had been positioned, behind which she knew a dozen of their friends were waiting with bated breath for the signal to pounce. She hoped it wouldn't be too long; she could almost taste the electricity of expectation vibrating through the airwaves towards them, and she was relieved when the waiter returned mere seconds later with a silver ice bucket and two crystal glasses. He proceeded to pop the cork with panache before leaving them in peace.

'Okay, so you're probably wondering why I've asked you here tonight,' Dan started.

Abbie smiled as innocently as possible, hoping he wouldn't see the anticipation in her eyes. She didn't trust herself to speak, knowing her voice would sound like she'd inhaled a mouthful of helium, so she simply sipped her Champagne and waited.

'There's something I want to ask you.'

This was it!

Her breath quickened and she gave Dan her most encouraging smile, noting that he didn't appear nervous at all. All the other diners in the restaurant seemed to fade away into the background and she felt like they were the only two people in the whole world, sitting there, together, in such fabulous surroundings, about to change their lives forever.

'I want you to come to Paris with me.'

'You want…' She stopped. Had she heard correctly? 'Sorry?'

'I want you to come to Paris with me. Oh my God, Abbie, this is absolutely a dream come true for me. You'll never guess what's happened. Pierre Fontaine has asked me to decorate his apartment in Paris for his fiftieth birthday party at the end of next month. It's a huge opportunity for me to showcase *FlowerEssence*'s merchandise to a wider – and more discerning and sophisticated – clientele. Maybe this will be the catalyst to us opening a branch over there! I've always wanted to live in Paris, be part of the glamorous jet set – weekends on the Riviera, skiing in the Alps, drinks on a yacht moored at St Tropez. So, what do you say? Will you come with me?'

Abbie saw that Dan's pale blue eyes were shining with delight, but her thoughts had frozen and she was struggling to compute what he had just said. She knew she was staring at him, her jaw loose, as she waited for her brain to reconnect to its modem, and when realisation finally dawned it brought a wave of unassailable shock.

'You… you want me to go to Paris with you?'

'Yes.' Puzzlement stalked across Dan's expression. 'Why are you so surprised?'

'I thought…'

Abbie scrabbled around in her brain for something, anything, that she could say to Dan that would mask her mistake, but she wasn't quite quick enough and he read her mind perfectly, his own mouth gaping in astonishment at her misunderstanding.

'Oh my God, you thought… you thought I was going to…'

'I…' Her stomach curdled when she saw the abject horror in Dan's eyes and it took all of her strength not to howl out loud at the pain that caused, so instead she blurted 'I saw you in Tiffany's… last week.'

'Tiffany's? Yes, I was there to collect a necklace for my father to give to Mum for their thirtieth wedding anniversary next month, not… well, you know, not to pick out an *engagement* ring!'

Heat rushed into Abbie's cheeks, tears gathered along her lashes, and she was filled with mortification. She grabbed her napkin from her lap, but her hands were shaking so much that it fell to the floor. Dan jumped from his seat and had just crouched to collect it for her when a cacophony of joyous voices burst forth.

'*Surprise!*'

Chapter Two

Abbie's Attic Flat in Wimbledon
Flower: Love-Lies-Bleeding

When Abbie woke the next morning, the whole mortifying incident came flooding back to her like a particularly disturbing nightmare. She couldn't remember anything about her journey back to the apartment, or how she had ended up in bed, but she could recall with absolute clarity the gut-wrenching minutes after the celebrations had died down and her friends saw the mortification on Dan's face and realised for the first time that something was wrong. In fact, not only was it the most embarrassing moment she'd ever experienced, but that image of Dan's complete incredulity would be seared on her heart for the rest of her life.

How could she have got it so wrong?

Fortunately, Emily had been on hand to handle the situation. Along with their friend Martha, she had ushered everyone from the restaurant with promises of cocktails at the wine bar next door, and, eventually, the gobsmacked diners at the *Sky Garden* had realised the impromptu dinner show was over and returned to their pan-braised halibut with oyster emulsion, though now with a new topic of conversation to enjoy. Emily had then fixed Dan with one of her trademark glares, linked her arm though Abbie's, and marched her from the restaurant.

Abbie pushed herself out of bed, dragged on her dressing gown, and performed an involuntary double-take when she caught a glimpse of herself in the mirror. She was used to sporting the haystack-esque hairstyle, but not the swollen and bloodshot eyes, and tramlines of mascara down her cheeks.

She looked a mess.

However, it was what going on *beneath* the surface that whipped her breath from her lungs. She felt like she'd been walloped in the solar plexus by a particularly bad-tempered heavyweight boxer. She was dizzy and nauseous, and her heart was pounding so fast she thought it might leap out of her chest and head for the hills if she didn't make a concerted effort to calm down, so she forced her wobbly legs to take her into the kitchen and set the kettle to boil.

'Oh, Abbie, you're awake. Darling, I'm so sorry, I really am.'

When Emily drew Abbie into her arms, she almost lost the grip on her emotions. Tears threatened and she had to swallow several times before she could speak, and even then, all she could manage was a hoarse croak.

'Thanks, Em.'

She didn't sound like herself, which wasn't surprising because she felt as though she was inhabiting someone else's body, that everything she'd experienced over the last twelve hours had happened to someone else and she was simply an innocent bystander watching the heart-wrenching events unfold.

'Here, drink this.'

Abbie accepted the mug of strong black coffee Emily handed to her with a smile of thanks, and dropped down onto the sofa that had seen more than its fair share of heart-to-hearts over the years – mainly the forensic dissection of why her friend persisted in dating fellow members of the acting profession when every one of them seemed to be intent on playing a role other than themselves; macho racing car driver, muscular superhero, dishevelled but cheeky romcom lead, broodingly handsome aristocrat.

And yet, no matter how many disastrous dates Emily went on – with Josh, or Patrick, or David, or Karl – she simply put the lack of connection down to experience and moved on to the next, with optimism and an unshakeable belief in the power of love. But Abbie wasn't like Emily. She couldn't simply parcel up her relationship with Dan, store it on the shelf labelled "Didn't Work Out" and move on. Even if she wanted to, that wasn't who she was.

'So, what are you going to do?'

'I don't know, Em, I really don't know.'

'Are you going into the boutique today?'

'How can I? How can I face Dan after what happened last

night?'

'You can't just give up your job, Abs.'

'I don't want to, but can you imagine what it's going to be like, seeing the embarrassment, the awkwardness, the *pity*, scrawled across his face every single day?'

Abbie cringed at the thought. She placed her mug on the coffee table and picked up her phone to glance at the screen, surprised to see she had over twenty text messages, but also a voicemail from Dan.

'Oh…'

'What?' asked Emily, leaning over her shoulder for a peek. 'Oh.'

Abbie dialled into her voicemail, her heart pounding out a concerto of distress as she listened to Dan's message, and this time she couldn't hold on to her emotions any longer. Hot tears flowed down her cheeks, and once again, Emily gathered her into her arms and held her, waiting until she finally calmed, wiped her eyes, and inhaled a steadying breath.

'What did he say?'

'That my services at *FlowerEssence* are no longer required.'

'What? He's fired you!?'

'Well, he didn't quite put it like that, but he suggested it was best for both of us if we made a clean break and I looked for another job.'

'Oh my God, the absolute and complete utter… Abbie, I'm so, so sorry. But you know what? Dan has just made the biggest mistake of his life, and I'm not talking about the "proposal-that-wasn't" because, take it from me, I know there's someone else out there much more…

Anyway, what I mean is that you are *the* best florist in the whole of London. I know I've said it before, lots of times, but it's your talent, and yours alone, that has made *FlowerEssence* what it is. It's *you* who landed all those corporate contracts, *you* who won all the accolades and should have collected those silver trophies that Dan's displaying in those ridiculous glass cabinets at the boutique. This is his loss, and your gain, because now you can start to chase your dream, and do what you love.'

'Oh, Em, I wish I had even half the confidence in myself as you have in me.'

'Well,' said Emily, waiting until Abbie met her gaze. 'Maybe this is your chance to fly without Dan holding your strings.'

Abbie sighed. She'd had the same conversation with Emily before, many times, and each time she had refused to accept what her friend was saying was true – that she craved the security of a relationship so much she was prepared to put all of her dreams on hold to keep Dan happy. But what was wrong with that? She loved him and he loved her – or so she had thought – and everyone knew that for any partnership to work there had to be compromise.

However, she now had to concede that Emily was right; she *had* been living in Dan's shadow, a follower never a leader, and his persistence in refusing to acknowledge her talent had constantly undermined her already shaky self-belief. Nevertheless, the origin of that particular psychological issue could not be laid at Dan's door; the reasons went far, far deeper than anything he'd done or said, and Emily knew that.

'Em, I—'

'Okay, so, I've called in sick at the pâtisserie. What do you say we break out the Ben & Jerry's and indulge in a marathon session of cookery and fitness porn?'

'Sounds like a plan.'

Despite her misery, Abbie couldn't help but smile. Watching re-runs of cookery and baking shows – Nigella, MasterChef, Bake Off, even old episodes of Delia for her, and exercise videos on YouTube for Emily, whilst indulging in a profusion of sugary treats, usually ice cream, but also triple chocolate fudge cake, or white chocolate and lavender-infused profiteroles, or a selection of macarons Emily brought home from the pâtisserie where she worked – was their go-to prescription for those occasions when life tossed a random grenade into their path.

What made their choice of remedy all the more ironic was that, despite their binge-watching, Abbie still couldn't even boil an egg, and the one time she had attempted to cook a meal for Emily when she had first moved into the flat, she had set off the fire alarm and the whole building had to be evacuated in the middle of a snowstorm. A couple of the residents still refused to speak to her when they passed her on the stairs, and, for the sake of their friendship, she had promised Emily not to try again and to stick to her preferred means of sustenance – the local Italian deli.

Emily, on the other hand, was a confirmed fitness-phobe, but with an unhealthy addiction to viewing every kind of exercise class that the internet had to offer the connoisseur; from Ashtanga yoga to boxercise, gymnastics to Tai chi, Pilates to step aerobics and all

fitness fads in between. Abbie often came home from work to find Emily sitting on their sofa, completely mesmerised as she watched a group of willing participants being put through their paces by muscular and tanned instructors, her hazel eyes sparkling with delight, exhilarated and uplifted without having to move a single muscle.

'Fab.' Emily strode into the kitchen and removed a huge white confectionery box from the fridge. She collected two spoons from the drawer, dropped back down next to Abbie on the sofa, and opened the lid.

'Wow!' said Abbie, her mood edging up a notch.

'Looks amazing, doesn't it?

'You are a culinary maestro, Em.'

Abbie stared at the morello cherry cheesecake, hardly able to believe someone could produce something so aesthetically pleasing and yet mouth-watering at the same time. She grabbed the remote, switched on the TV and selected the Food Channel, heaving a sigh of contentment to find a repeat episode of Nigella Bites. At least the TV gods were on her side today.

She settled in next to Emily, aware that her friend was casting regular glances in her direction, making sure she was okay, and her heart gave a nip of gratitude for her good fortune at having such an amazing cheerleader in her corner. They knew each other's pasts, understood each other's pain, supported each other's decisions, and delivered sage advice whether asked for or not. She decided that too much time had been spent on her problems and it was time to swing the spotlight.

'This is one of the most delicious cheesecakes I've ever tasted.'

'Thanks, it's a new recipe I've been working on with André.'

'Em?'

'Mmm?'

Emily's cheeks bulged with an overload of cheesecake, her eyes fixed on the way Nigella was grating nutmeg onto a pomegranate and cous-cous salad, a look of absolute wonder on her face. Abbie's resolve wavered, but she pressed ahead because it was her turn to be supportive.

'You need to talk to your parents, you know. You need to tell them that you've found a new passion; one that you love even more than acting, one that makes you happy – truly happy. And not only that, one that you are extremely good at it.'

Without taking her eyes from the screen, Emily wrinkled her nose.

'I can't, Abs, you know that. They've spent thousands and thousands of pounds putting me through drama school, and you have no idea how many battles I fought, how much disappointment I've witnessed in order to do that instead of going to law school. How can I now tell them I've changed my mind again, that I don't want to be a lawyer, *or* an actor, I want to be a pâtissière? Dad would have a coronary, and I don't even want to think about what Mum would say.'

Abbie smiled in sympathy. Emily's whole family were lawyers – her mum, her dad, her sister and her brother, two uncles and *three* cousins. After their initial horror at their daughter's career choice, her parents had generously indulged her desire to become an actress by supporting her through stage school. And she had initially kept to her

side of the bargain by landing several high-profile roles in West End theatre productions, the meagre salary she earned supplemented by a part-time job at a tiny pâtisserie which was how she'd realised that what she truly wanted was to be a pastry chef. She was now in the process of learning the required skills from a sexy French pâtissier and loving every minute.

In a strange quirk of fate, Emily now only took on acting roles so she could pay her share of the rent, but she hadn't yet had the courage to inform her family that all the money they'd spent on her education had been in vain; she wasn't going to be the next Emily Blunt – although not only did she share her name with the actress, she also looked a little like her – because she couldn't bear to see the disappointment on their faces. So, she kept up a constantly manic schedule of working at the pâtisserie during the day and the theatre at night.

'I will tell them, eventually. I just need to pick the right time, that's all. Hey, talking about family…'

Abbie met Emily's eyes and the bottom dropped out of her stomach. Just the word "family" caused a painful jolt of electricity to slice through her heart. She had shared her story with Emily, just as Emily had shared hers, and her friend understood that she still nursed an unextinguishable ember of agony that had lodged itself deep in her soul after the loss of her beloved mum.

She had been fortunate to have an extremely close bond with her mum – best friends as well as mother and daughter – which had been inevitable as her father had left before she was born, and neither of them had heard from him since. She knew her mum had been devastated by his abandonment, but had stitched his rejection of her and her unborn child into the fabric of her life and got on with raising a caring, generous, and well-balanced daughter. Her much-too-soon loss had left a crater-sized hole in Abbie's life – a void she had dared to hope would be filled by Dan as they built a new foundation, perhaps a new family even, together.

Although she would admit this to no one, not even Emily, she had briefly held out a faint hope that perhaps her father – whoever he was, and wherever he was – would contact her to express his condolences and suggest they got to know each other. She didn't really know whether she wanted that, but anyway it didn't matter because he never did, and now that her Aunt Liz had joined her mum, she felt even more adrift. She had no safety net; no living relatives, no *family*, and that terrible, heart-shattering word "orphan" had passed through her thoughts on more than one occasion before being banished into the dark crevices of her brain, buried but not eradicated.

'Abbie? Are you okay?'

'Yes, I…'

But tears had started to roll again. Emily laced her fingers through Abbie's and they sat for a while in comfortable silence, simply staring at the screen while Nigella chopped, sliced, whisked, and sprinkled, the rest of the cheesecake left forgotten on the coffee table.

She knew Emily was simply biding her time, that there were things she intended to say as soon as she thought Abbie was ready to hear them. One of the many things Abbie loved about Emily was that she had a sensible streak running through her veins, a characteristic that allowed her to slice through all of life's extraneous confusion and chaos and burrow down into the core of any problem. She had lost count of the times she'd listened to Emily's straightforward, sometimes blunt advice, knowing that whilst the truth might hurt for a few moments, it was dispensed with the best intentions and was always, without exception, exactly what she needed to hear.

'You know, Abbie, this might be a good time for you to do what you've been promising to do since the day I met you.'

'What's that?'

'Start to make a few inquiries about… well, about your past.'

'I really don't…'

Abbie intended to politely push the suggestion away, just as she always did, but her assertiveness reserves were so depleted at the moment she didn't have the strength to say anything that wasn't the truth, so – to Emily's evident relief – she changed her mind and nodded instead.

'I know.'

'That's great, and you have some spare time now, while you're preparing your CV for that dream-come-true job at Kew Gardens.'

'Or the Eden Project.'

'And for surfing the estate agents' websites for that cosy little cottage with a huge garden.'

'And an orchard.'

'And an orchard. And I know exactly where you should start!'

'Where?'

Emily's scooted to the edge of her seat, picked up Abbie's phone and handed it to her.

'You have to call that lawyer. I know you didn't find anything in your mum's personal documents, but maybe your aunt left some sort of clue in hers!'

'Em, they hadn't spoken in almost thirty years. I doubt I'll find anything about Mum, or me, in Aunt Liz's documents.'

'Well, you won't know that for sure until you call her lawyers, so call them.'

Emily leaned back against the sofa and folded her arms, her eyes filled with resolve not to let Abbie off the hook this time.

'Okay, okay.'

Abbie rolled her eyes at her friend and quickly scanned the rather formal email she had received from a Mr Toby Thompson of Lumley & Thompson, Solicitors and Commissioners for Oaths.

'Oh, I really hope she's left you a piece of jewellery, or a cute Triumph Stag – a red one. Hey, what if it's a Ming vase? Or a Canaletto?'

Abbie laughed as she dialled the number on the email and waited for someone to pick up.

'Don't hold your breath… Oh, yes, hello there. I wonder if I could speak to Mr Toby Thompson, please? Oh, okay, yes, I'm Abigail Coleman. Yes, please, I would like to speak to his assistant, thank you.'

Emily gave her a thumbs up and went to re-boil the kettle, switching the Food Channel to one of her favourite Pilates workout videos on the way past.

'Oh, hello, I'm Abigail Coleman. Mr Thompson

emailed me a couple of weeks ago, maybe three, about my aunt's estate – Elizabeth Harris?'

'Yes, hello, Miss Coleman, thank you for calling. I'm sorry to say that Mr Thompson isn't available at the moment, but if you'd like to bear with me for a few moments, I'll try to locate your aunt's file.'

'Thank you.'

To Abbie's surprise, the young woman sounded as though she'd just dashed up several flights of stairs and was very flustered. As she waited, she could hear her opening and shutting drawers and rifling through papers before she returned to their conversation.

'I can't seem to find… never mind, I do actually recall your case. Mrs Harris, your maternal aunt, left you a property.'

'A property?'

'Yes, now where was it?'

A wave of shock rolled through Abbie and she was grateful she was sitting down whilst she listened to Mr Thompson's surprisingly ruffled assistant scrambling through still more papers.

'No, no, the file's definitely not here, so, all I can tell you is that it's in Napa Valley.'

'Napa Valley?'

Abbie's jaw dropped as she met Emily's equally shocked gaze.

'Yes, but look, I'll get Mr Thompson to call you back as soon as he's free. Is this your preferred number?'

'Erm, yes, yes, this number is fine.'

Abbie sat motionless, staring at the now blank screen of her phone. Her head had already been full to bursting with everything that had happened to her in the last few hours, and now this?

'Did I hear right? Did the lawyer just inform you that you've inherited a property in Napa Valley? As in *California*?'

Abbie nodded. 'I knew my aunt left Devon to go and live in America, but I have no idea what she did when she got there, or why she went there.'

'Wow, just wow! Isn't Napa Valley where all the vineyards are?'

'Yes, they make some of the best wine in the world.'

'Maybe she left you a winery?'

'I don't think so, Em.'

'But what if she has? It's a bit more than a cosy cottage garden!'

A kaleidoscope of emotions assaulted Abbie's brain. She didn't know what to think. Unlike Emily, she didn't want to express her excitement because that felt disloyal to her mum. Having been estranged for so long, she was uncertain how her mum would have reacted – if she was still around – when she heard that the sister she'd not seen or heard from for twenty-eight years had left her daughter a property in America. It all felt a little surreal, like she was living in some kind of parallel universe, but thankfully her spiralling thoughts were interrupted by the buzz of her phone before she lost her grip on her sanity.

'Hello? Yes, this is Abigail Coleman. Hello, Mr Thompson. Yes, I did just speak to your assistant. Is it true? Has my aunt really left me a place in California?'

'California? What gave you that impression?'

Abbie wrinkled her forehead and exchanged a glance

with Emily who was sitting on the edge of the sofa, clutching her mug of fresh coffee, oozing unfettered excitement.

'Isn't that where Napa Valley is?'

'Not Napa Valley, *Ropa* Valley!'

'Ropa Valley? But I thought… Where's Ropa Valley?'

'Greece. Corfu, to be exact. It's where your Aunt Elizabeth lived for the last ten years, after the passing of her husband.'

'Her husband?'

'Yes, but it's not just a property, it's a small area of land, too, with a few vines.'

'Vines?' Abbie gasped. 'In Corfu?'

'Yes, as well as the hotel.'

'What hotel?'

'The Hummingbird Hotel.'

'The Hummingbird Hotel?'

Had she fallen down a rabbit hole or something? Was she in the middle of some kind of weird dream? Had Dan's rejection caused her to have some kind of relapse?

'Are you okay, Miss Coleman?'

'I'm sorry. I… well, I didn't know my aunt, I never met her. All I knew was that she'd emigrated to California before I was born, and she never came back, not even for my mum's funeral, so this has come as a bit of a shock, to say the least.'

'Well, she left you everything. The hotel, the vines, a small sum of money, and all of her personal effects. I had hoped you'd call a few weeks ago when I sent you my letter and email. I've made you an appointment to meet with her Greek lawyer in Corfu Town, and—'

'Her Greek lawyer?'

'Yes, Alex Stephanopoulos. Your flights are booked and

have been paid for out of the estate so there's no need to worry on that score. While you're there, you can sign the paperwork, sort out your aunt's personal effects, and then I assume you'll want to put the hotel on the market. If that *is* your decision, then it's probably best you do so without any further delay. I'll email you the details. Good luck, Miss Coleman.'

'But Mr Thompson, I—'

But he'd already rang off and Abbie found her limbs were refusing to obey her request to move, so she sat there, still staring at her phone as though it had been beamed down from outer space, trying and failing to unravel the information she'd just received and put it into some kind of order. When she eventually managed to meet Emily's eyes, she saw she was almost as shocked as she was.

'You've inherited a hotel in *Corfu*?'

'Looks like it.'

'Wow, I mean, just wow.'

'But, Em, I can't just up sticks and fly off to Corfu.'

'Why not?'

'Because I have too much to do here.'

'Like what?'

'Like talk to Dan.'

'He's just fired you by text!'

'Like apply for jobs.'

'You can do that from Corfu. It's the twenty-first century; they have internet there.' Emily smiled and placed her hand gently on Abbie's arm, waiting until she met her eyes. 'After everything that's happened, don't you think it's the perfect time for you to have a break, especially when you've worked so hard and Dan's been taking you for granted, and—'

'Dan didn't take me for granted, Em.'

'Yes, he did. How many holidays have you had since you started working at the boutique?'

'We had a weekend in Amsterdam last spring.'

'To visit the *flower markets*; that's not a holiday, that's work. Anyway, all I'm saying is that this is a gift from heaven – so to speak. It's a free trip to a sun-drenched paradise! There's nothing like a bit of sunshine to cheer a person up, and a little distance might help you to gain a fresh perspective. You can fly over there, meet the Greek lawyer, have a look at the hotel – loving the name by the way – and maybe…'

'Maybe what?'

'Maybe you'll find what you've been searching for since your mum passed away. Maybe you'll be able to unearth a few of those pesky family secrets that she, for whatever reason, chose not to share with you. Perhaps your Aunt Liz wasn't so secretive? Perhaps, finally, you'll find out what happened all those years ago and you'll find peace, serenity, and…' A mischievous glint appeared in Emily's eyes. 'And move on to a new life as a hotelier in gorgeous Corfu!'

'Emily, I don't think—'

'Joking, just joking. What I meant to say was that you can sell up and buy that little cottage you've been dreaming of. And if nothing else, you can send me a hundred photographs of all the gorgeous Greek guys you'll have falling at your feet when they set eyes on those crazy blonde curls of yours.'

Abbie laughed. 'The last thing I want to do is to embark on another relationship, especially with someone who lives in a different country. I don't know the first word of Greek

– they don't even use the same alphabet. I might be heartbroken, Em, but I'm not a complete masochist!'

'So you'll go?'

'I don't see that I've got much choice, but I'm not staying long, just long enough to talk to the lawyer, sign all the legal documents, sort out my aunt's personal effects, and then put the hotel up for sale.'

'And also maybe kiss a few bronzed Greek gods?'

Abbie rolled her eyes at her friend. Nevertheless, she had to admit that her spirits had risen from the depths of the doldrums to hover somewhere between trepidation and anticipation, and if she was honest, a smidgeon of hope. Hope that at long last she may be about to get answers to the questions that had been hounding her for most of her life.

Chapter Three

The Hummingbird Hotel, Ropa Valley, Corfu
Flower: Frilly Pink Bougainvillea

Abbie paused on the pavement outside Corfu Airport's arrivals building, closed her eyes and took a moment to appreciate her good fortune. She had swapped a dank and drizzly London with hordes of unsmiling, harassed-looking people rushing to their destinations, prodding each other with umbrellas whilst inhaling a medley of toxic fumes from the nose-to-tail traffic, for this sun-kissed paradise. There wasn't a cloud in the sky, the air was hair-dryer hot, and there was a distinct whiff of jasmine floating on the light breeze. The only downside was that her hair had ballooned into a halo of curls for which even the words "unkempt bird's nest" would be an understatement.

Right up until a few minutes before she'd jumped onto

the Gatwick Express, she had oscillated between assuring Emily that she was excited about her approaching trip to Greece, and telling her that she had no intention of leaving London, that surely any legalities could be dealt with over the telephone or via a Zoom meeting, or, when she was feeling at her lowest ebb, that maybe Mr Thompson could take a couple of days out of his busy schedule to fly out there on her behalf – a suggestion that had caused Emily to blanch when they calculated how much that was likely to cost.

'You need to do this, Abbie. It's not simply a legal transaction, it's a personal journey that you have to undertake yourself. You know that, deep down, don't you? Whatever happened between your mum and your aunt, your aunt deserves to have a family member sort out her personal effects and not some random stranger who's being paid to do it.'

When Emily had put it like that, Abbie had stopped searching for reasons not to go and started to pack her suitcase. Her friend was right; her Aunt Liz didn't deserve to have her lawyer rake through her private possessions, and the very thought actually caused her to squirm on her behalf. So now, here she was, standing on a cracked marble pavement, waiting for the driver that Alex Stephanopoulos, her aunt's Greek lawyer, had promised he would send to collect her and take her to the Hummingbird Hotel. Much to her and Emily's disappointment, when they had scoured the map of the pretty holiday island, they had discovered that the hotel was nowhere near the sparkling Ionian Sea but instead nestled inland amongst the rolling hills and vineyards.

Abbie wondered what her mum would have thought if she knew she was there, and a ripple of guilt rolled through her chest. She had no idea whether her mum had known that her sister had relocated from California to Greece, or that she owned a hotel, which she had gone on to leave to her niece, someone she knew nothing about and had never met. She hoped the formalities would be wrapped up quickly and without fuss so she could return home and make a start on finding a job, and, once the hotel was sold, investing in a cottage with a small garden where she could work on banishing her demons and filling the void deep in her soul that had widened further since Dan's rejection. In the meantime, perhaps she could use the time in Corfu to think, to take a few moments away from the high-speed conveyor belt her life had become, to smell the roses and nurse her broken heart over several glasses of ouzo, and, maybe, to find some answers about her past.

After a further twenty minutes of fruitless waiting, Abbie surrendered to the inevitable; the driver was not coming for her. She looked over to her right where there was a large sign announcing the availability of a taxi service, her heart sinking when she saw the length of the queue. She had just decided to return to the terminal and seek out a car hire company, when a movie-star-handsome guy with smouldering dark brown eyes, tufted mahogany hair accentuated with a smidgeon of gel, a smattering of designer stubble and a pair of navy-blue dress shorts that hugged his impressive thighs like a second skin appeared in front of her, gifting her with a blast of lemony cologne.

Could this be her driver?

'Are you Abigail Coleman?'

His voice was just as she had expected from his appearance; rich, smooth, with only a slight hint of an accent which made him sound even sexier, and to her absolute surprise after everything that had happened over the last two weeks, she felt a tingling of attraction. How could that even be possible? Her heart was frozen; but it wasn't her heart that was in charge of the situation.

'Yes, yes, I am, but please, call me Abbie.'

'Oh, I thought…'

She saw his eyes flicker over her body from head to toe, his forehead creasing in confusion.

'What? What did you think?'

'Nothing, nothing, just… Well, I thought you would be much older, that's all. Alex said Liz's sister was coming to sort things out.'

'Oh, I'm her niece, not her sister.'

Abbie started to smile but to her amazement the man standing in front of her did not smile back. In fact, he almost seemed irritated by her presence, which she thought was a little unfair as he hadn't even introduced himself yet, although she assumed he was the driver Alex had promised, which was confirmed when he grabbed the handle of her suitcase and strode off towards the car park.

'Well, better late than never, I suppose.'

'What do you mean?' she asked, jogging after him.

'We've been waiting for you to come over and sort out the Hummingbird Hotel for weeks.'

'Well, actually, I've only just heard of my aunt's passing.'

'It was three months ago.'

Abbie stopped abruptly. With all the turmoil and

heartbreak, and then rushing around to organise her trip, she was embarrassed, and more than a little ashamed, that she didn't know this essential detail and she could feel heat spreading through her cheeks that had nothing to do with the rising midday temperature or the fact that she'd almost been sprinting to keep up with the Greek version of Usain Bolt.

'Really?'

'You didn't know?'

The still-unnamed guy paused in his marathon to survey her for a moment. His lips parted as though he was about to say something but he appeared to decide against it. Then, to her surprise, he turned his back on her and instead of racing for the horizon as she had expected, he opened the rear door of a very beat-up old Peugeot, tossed her jam-packed suitcase into the back seat like a sack of old potatoes, and climbed into the driver's seat, slamming the door shut and sending a dribble of rust onto the street.

She remained on the pavement, completely non-plussed, until he wound down the window and fixed her with those gorgeous chocolate-brown eyes, framed in the longest lashes she'd ever see on a man. Despite his completely uncalled for attitude, she felt inexplicably drawn to him, like there was an invisible length of elastic pulling them together. There was something captivating about this man, an energetic, exhilarating vibe, and yet for those who took the time to look – or had suffered a similar fate – there was a shadow of sadness hidden behind the external armour he wore.

'Are you getting in or do you just want me to take your suitcase to the Hummingbird Hotel?'

'I—'

Once again, she glanced over her shoulder at the taxi

queue, but it was even longer than before and the passengers that had been on her flight were now wiping their foreheads with handkerchiefs and drinking from bottles of water. For a brief moment, she toyed with the idea of joining them, then walked round to the passenger door and got in. They hadn't even made it out of the confines of the airport carpark before she wished she had decided to join them.

'So why haven't you visited your aunt here in Corfu before?'

'Oh, I—'

'Don't worry, I get it. Your career in London is more important than your family.'

She was so shocked at the directness of his question, and his totally unreasonable assumption, not to mention the tone in which it was delivered that, to her surprise, she felt her emotions rise for the first time since her world had imploded. Until then she had felt numb, her thoughts and senses dulled, and nothing had been able to drag her spirits out from the doldrums – not even a session of back-to-back cookery shows with Emily.

'Well, no, I—'

'But you *are* over here for a few days to sort through your aunt's personal effects, put her hotel on the market and sell it to the highest bidder, before rushing back to your wonderfully cosmopolitan life in one of the world's most vibrant cities. Am I right?'

Abbie gasped at his totally unwarranted character assassination of someone he'd just met. And why on earth was her driver asking such personal questions? Why couldn't he stick to the usual conversations about the weather? And how did he know so much about her? She assumed he must have got his information from her aunt's lawyer, although it wouldn't have been that difficult to reach the conclusion that he had come to by himself.

'I… Actually, my aunt's lawyer, Mr Stephanopoulos, did tell me that the sooner the hotel is up for sale, the better.' She grimaced at the defensive note in her voice; why couldn't she have sounded more assertive?

'Well, permit me to burst your bubble, Abigail.'

'It's Abbie, just Abbie, and I'd—'

'Well, *Abbie*, let me burst your bubble. You might get top dollar for a hotel on the coast, overlooking the ocean, but the Hummingbird Hotel is not one of those. It's so much more than a place where tourists lay their heads for a week of sun, sea and beach activities. It's a place of calm contemplation, of peace and tranquillity, where guests come to relax and recharge their batteries, and appreciate the natural beauty that Corfu is famous for.'

For the first time, Abbie saw her chauffeur's features ease as he talked about the island that he clearly loved; the tightness in his jaw disappeared, the creases in his forehead vanished, and his eyes took on a sparkle of enthusiasm, and who could blame him? She glanced out of her window, taking in the pink, white and honey-coloured facades of the buildings of Corfu Town, their balconies dressed with pots of vibrant geraniums, their shutters closed against the bleaching afternoon sun, set against a magnificent backdrop of the sapphire-blue Ionian Sea – picture postcard perfect.

'Corfu is more than just a holiday destination; it's my home.'

Her heart softened briefly for her handsome, straight-talking chauffeur, and she wondered what had happened to make him so off-hand with random visitors to the island, until he torpedoed his next question into the conversation.

'How can you decide to sell the hotel without even seeing it?'

'I do have a life in the UK, you know. I can't just drop everything!'

She didn't know why she had said that, but the guy was irritating and was making assumptions without bothering to get to know her. Okay, she *hadn't* visited her aunt before she'd passed away, and that might look bad, but there was a reason for that. Then again, her aunt *had* left her a hotel, so clearly she must have thought a great deal about her. And it was true, she did intend to pack up her aunt's belongings, sign whatever legal documents were necessary, and then head back to civilisation where she had to make a start piecing her life back together and chase down the various job applications that Emily had made her send out. Her taxi driver didn't need to know that she'd lost her "big fancy job" and the embarrassing reasons behind it.

'So, what exactly do you do over there in London?'

'I'm a celebrity florist.'

Oh God, what was the matter with her? She *never* said that; that was what Dan called himself. She cringed, especially when she saw her driver's eyes light up and his lips twitch into an amused smirk.

'What's a *celebrity* florist?'

'We supply floral architecture to the homes of TV stars, theatres and film sets, and catwalk shows – most recently to the Pierre Fontaine Fashion House.'

'Never heard of him'

'He's… never mind.' Abbie realised it was time to switch the direction of the interrogation spotlight. 'So, enough about me, you still haven't told me your name.'

'I'm Nikos Angelopoulos.'

'Pleased to meet you, Nikos,' she said, before muttering "not" to herself. 'And how long have you been a taxi driver?'

To her surprise, Nikos burst out laughing, transforming his already attractive features into drop-dead-gorgeous as he showcased a set of perfectly even white teeth, cute dimples that bracketed his very kissable lips, his movement sending another waft of his cologne in her direction.

'Why are you laughing?'

'I'm not a taxi driver; I own and run my family's vineyard and winery.'

She felt as though she'd been hit by a runaway juggernaut; that *wasn't* what she had expected him to say.

'You make wine?'

'Yes, that's generally the idea. Our estate is in Ropa Valley, next to your aunt's hotel. We were neighbours, actually. Alex asked me to collect you from the airport as a favour. Liz was well-liked in our little community, so we feel her loss sharply, even if you don't.'

'Oh, I—'

God, this man!

Abbie sighed and decided that it was pointless continuing their conversation as she didn't seem to be able to say anything right. Instead, she sat back in her seat and enjoyed the scenery flashing past her window; drinking in the surprisingly lush green countryside, resplendent with cypress trees, olive groves, lemon and orange trees, the hedgerows decorated with multicoloured hollyhocks swaying in the breeze, the tiny villages nestling in the hillsides, the tavernas peeking out from behind flowering magnolia trees.

Twenty minutes later, Nikos took a sharp right-hand turn onto a bumpy track and they travelled for another fifty metres or so before coming to a halt outside a pretty, white-washed building with blue painted shutters, a huge garland of frothy pink bougainvillea around the front door, and a large wooden sign welcoming her to the Hummingbird Hotel.

'Wow.'

If Abbie were honest, the hotel was not what she'd been expecting. She'd thought it would be bigger, more rustic, careworn even, but instead the building had an aura of luxury about it, from the glossy marble steps leading to the front door to the pristine paintwork and the blue ceramic pots crammed with flowers – the Hummingbird Hotel had clearly been lavished with love.

'Your aunt was an amazing hotelier,' said Nikos, as he jumped from the driver's seat, his mood mellowing as he stuck his hands into his pockets and gazed at the picturesque building in front of them. 'Guests return year after year to explore the area, to walk in the hills, or to simply relax and soak up the serene ambience. As you can see, the villa's authentic exterior had been maintained, and yet you'll find that the guest rooms are equipped with all the modern conveniences a discerning traveller requires; there's even a small swimming pool. It's the perfect retreat except for… well…'

'What?'

'Your aunt was no gardener.'

'What do you mean?'

But Nikos didn't respond as he was in the process of liberating her suitcase from the back seat of the Peugeot and heaving it up the marble steps to deposit it at the front door, where he paused and handed her a large brass key.

'Alex told me to give you this, and said he'd be in touch after you've had chance to settle in. Oh, and just to let you know, your first group of guests will be arriving on Friday.'

'Guests? What do you mean, guests?'

'This *is* the Hummingbird *Hotel.* The clue's in the name.'

'Yes, but…'

Nikos clearly wasn't going to hang around to answer the myriad questions that were flying through her brain like lemmings, and before she could stop him, he'd dropped back into the driver's seat and turned the key in the Peugeot's ignition. Panic surged and propelled her towards him before he made his getaway.

'I'll have to cancel the booking.'

'Do you have the cash to refund them?'

'No, but—'

'So there's your answer.'

Nikos revved the engine, but Abbie placed her hand on the open window to stop him.

'How many guests?'

'Five, I think, or maybe six.'

'Six guests!'

'Oh, and it might be a workshop.'

'A what?'

'Liz offered various activity programmes for her guests,

especially during the quieter months before the school summer holiday season starts. They were very popular.'

'What kind of workshops?'

'Painting, yoga, creative writing, cookery.'

'And this week's is…?'

But she knew what he was going to say; it was just the way her life was at that moment.

'Cookery.'

'Oh my God, no, Nikos, there's no way. I can't… I can't…'

She stopped and narrowed her eyes at him.

'You're joking, aren't you? God, please, tell me this is a joke.'

Nikos slammed the car into gear and performed a speedy one-hundred-and-eighty-degree turn, the tyres crunching on the loose gravel. She thought he was simply going to drive away, but he paused next to her and she detected a hint of mischief in his eyes.

'It might be. But I know for sure that Liz was planning to run a yoga retreat at the end of the month. You'll find the reservations book on the reception desk in the foyer, so you can check out the details for yourself. Good luck.'

And with that he drove away, pebbles flying in his wake like confetti at a wedding, as Abbie stood there on the Hummingbird Hotel's driveway watching him go, struggling to come to terms with what exactly she'd let herself in for.

Chapter Four

The Hummingbird Hotel, Ropa Valley, Corfu
Flower: Naked Man Orchid

Abbie climbed the steps and inserted the brass key into the arched oak front door, an uptick of excitement invading her chest as she stepped inside and took her first look around the Hummingbird Hotel. Again, it was not what she was had been expecting.

Everywhere she looked was bright, airy and modern; the smooth white walls were freshly painted, as was the magnificent vaulted ceiling, the floor was fashioned from cool grey marble tiles, and what she assumed was the reception desk was a pedestal of carved white granite upon which sat a sheet of toughened glass and the reservations book Nikos had mentioned. She abandoned her suitcase and strode through a door to the right, which led to some kind of communal lounge filled with elegant white furniture and glass and marble coffee tables, the walls showcasing a rainbow of original watercolours, each one featuring an image of a vibrantly coloured hummingbird.

She opened the French doors and walked out onto a terrace overlooking a gravelled courtyard, complete with central fountain – also in the shape of a hummingbird – and home to a collection of pretty wrought-iron bistro table and chairs where guests clearly took their breakfast each morning in the shade of a resplendent magnolia tree. The left-hand side of the courtyard was bordered by an impressive colonnade of arches that provided access to a row of single-story guest rooms, four in all, sporting terracotta-tiled roofs, white-washed walls, and pale blue painted doors, windows, and shutters. To the right was a high wall with a wooden gate – also painted in what Abbie assumed was the Hummingbird Hotel's branded colours.

She decided to investigate further and skipped down the steps into the courtyard and across to the gate, turning the old brass handle – which to her delight had also been engraved with an image of a hummingbird – and stepped through to the other side, stopping in her tracks.

It was as though she had entered a different world – this one the Amazon rainforest. She seemed to be standing beneath a pergola, in an emerald tunnel of tangled foliage with leaves and flower petals caressing her cheeks and low-level ferns brushing against her ankles. The air felt heavy and humid, with an almost overwhelming fragrance of sweet jasmine and frangipani, and a strange top-note of chlorine.

One step and the path forked; each route offering the

tantalising promise of more exotic flora and fauna to discover. She felt the familiar upsurge of excitement when faced with the opportunity to spend time amongst the things she had loved since she was a small child, helping her mum maintain their tiny garden at their Devonshire home, planting seeds and marvelling at how such a small, inconsequential thing could grow into something so beautiful.

She removed her phone, keen to start cataloguing the unfamiliar plants growing around the pergola, when she heard a loud splash of water from behind the arboreal screen on her right.

'What the…?'

Her jungle expedition over, she made her way through a stone archway that led to a wide paved terrace, surrounded by a brigade of blue ceramic Greek urns bursting with scarlet geraniums, in the middle of which was the hotel's rectangular swimming pool, filled with aquamarine water, its surface glinting in the early afternoon sun.

But the pool wasn't empty.

Before she could step out of the shadows of the archway and reveal her presence to her unexpected guest, the swimmer completed his final length and climbed from the pool and, to her absolute astonishment, he was completely naked.

'Oh my God!'

The words burst forth louder than she had expected and her hand flew to her lips. The only word she knew in Greek was *efharisto* – thank you – and she didn't think that was the most appropriate greeting in the circumstances. Heat rushed into her cheeks, but when the swimmer's eyes eventually met hers, far from being embarrassed, he simply strolled towards one of the Hummingbird Hotel's blue and white striped sun loungers, collected his rather tiny towel, and secured it around his waist before stepping forward to offer her his palm.

'Hi there, I'm Felix Morgan, pleased to meet you.'

She took in his tousled blonde curls, still damp from his swim, his baby-blue eyes and the fact that every inch of his toned, muscular body showcased a smooth golden tan – no tan lines for Felix!

'Hi, Felix, I'm…'

For a moment Abbie couldn't remember who she was, still flustered after being gifted an unexpected front row seat to the Greek version of the Full Monty, although from the sound of Felix's accent, he was more Sydney than Sidari.

'I'm Abbie, Abbie Coleman. I'm Liz's niece?'

'Ah, yes, Liz did mention you.'

'She did?'

'Sure, and I knew we were going to meet today.'

'You did? How?'

'My horoscope said I was going to meet a bubbly blonde from foreign shores.'

Abbie hadn't thought Felix could shock her any more than he already had, but she was wrong. To her surprise, he gave her a wide smile, showcasing his brilliant white teeth, then promptly turned his back on her, dropped his towel, and proceeded to pull on a pair of the most figure-hugging Lycra cycling shorts – in an eyeball-scorching psychedelic yellow – which left very little to the imagination. Clearly, he didn't harbour any body-image issues, and a spasm of jealousy shot through her veins;

she wished she had even a quarter of Felix's confidence.

'I take it you've already met Nikos?'

'Yes, I have,' she said. 'He picked me up from the airport.'

'How did you get on?'

A faint smirk of curiosity appeared on his face.

'Well, if you want the truth, I happen to think he's abrupt, rude, and a little mean.'

'Yes, it has been said.' Felix grinned with delight at her reply. 'But I can assure you that he's actually one of the good guys. His family owns the Angelopoulos vineyard and winery next door.'

'Yes, he told me. So, Felix, can I ask why you…'

'Oh, yes, sorry. Liz, your aunt, let me swim here whenever I want, in return for doing a few odd jobs around the hotel.'

'I take it that didn't include the garden?' she smiled.

Felix threw his head back and laughed, then ran his fingers through his hair before securing it with a hairband. With the jumble of wooden beads around his neck, and pleated leather thongs around his wrists, he looked like he should be crashing out at an Indian Ashram, not floating around on a Greek island, spouting astrological predictions.

'Mainly painting, maybe a bit of pool maintenance, but I can help you with the garden if you like, although it's just that pergola really, unless you include the vines. I'm actually a qualified yoga instructor, but there's not much going on this time of year so I pick up other work where I can. So, what's your vision for the pergola?'

'I don't have a vision as such. I don't think the state of the garden will affect the value of the place very much.'

'You're not planning on staying?'

The disbelief on his face might have made her giggle in

other circumstances.

'Of course not, I don't know the first thing about running a hotel, and, more importantly, I have a life back in London.'

She knew Felix didn't believe her. For some reason, he seemed to see straight through her – as though he knew she had no job, no partner, no life to get back to – and she blushed at having been caught out telling a little white lie. However, unlike Nikos, he was sympathetic enough not to push it, although she didn't like the look he gave her, which said he thought she was a little crazy.

'Well, if you change your mind…'

Then something occurred to her.

'Actually, Felix, I don't suppose you can cook?'

'Cook?'

'Yes.'

'What kind of cooking? I can rustle up a decent barbie, if you like.'

'I was thinking more along the lines of presenting a workshop, here at the Hummingbird Hotel, on authentic Greek recipes to half a dozen discerning foodies.'

'Oh yes, I'd forgotten about that. Liz loved running those retreats. In fact, I think they're what kept her going over the winter months and early spring. She would have loved to know that her niece is picking up the baton – or should I say wooden spoon – from her and taking over the task of delivering the courses she loved.'

'No, no, I won't be doing that. God, no. I can barely boil an egg.'

'Have you asked Nikos for help?'

'No.'

'Why not?'

Felix gave her another of his strange looks but she moved swiftly on.

'Well, he makes wine for a living, and anyway, I'm not sure he'd help me.'

'Okay.' Felix grinned, packing away his towel and goggles into a luminous green sports bag and slinging the handles over his shoulders. 'I'll leave you to ponder the meaning of life, the planet, and the universe. Oh, and just to give you a heads up, Liz probably had a few other courses planned, too. It might take you a while to sell the place, you know, it *is* a little off the beaten track – although that's a big part of the attraction, of course – so why don't you stay here awhile, Abbie? Align your chakras?'

'Align my chakras?'

'You're tense, man, I can feel the negative vibe throbbing in your aura.'

'I'm fine, totally fine.'

'You're a Gemini, aren't you?'

'Actually, yes, I am.'

She stared at Felix; how could he possibly have known that?

'Thought so. If I remember rightly, *your* horoscope said "When the smoke clears, you will see the light".'

'What on earth does that mean?'

'Whatever you want it to mean, but I think you should stay, at least for a few weeks, maybe a couple of months and see what happens when the emotional fog clears. And you wouldn't want to let anyone down, would you? Wouldn't want to tarnish your aunt's memory?'

Abbie saw the mischievous gleam of challenge in Felix's

eyes as he smiled at her before he placed his palms together in front of his chest and lowered his head.

'Go softly, Abbie. *Namaste.*'

Abbie watched him leave, his flip-flops slapping on the stone tiles, so laidback and free from stress that he almost floated on air, and at that moment she would have given everything in her bank account – granted, it wasn't much – for even an ounce of his confidence and serenity. As she followed in his footsteps, a surge of exhaustion ambushed her, and she decided to leave her exploration of the rest of the hotel's grounds, including the vines Felix had mentioned, for another day.

She checked the hotel's front door was locked, grabbed her suitcase and dragged it up the stairs to the landing, surprised to see that there were only two bedrooms to choose from, the first of which had clearly been her aunt's. She pushed open the second door and saw a light and airy guest room with white-washed walls, decorated in the muted blues and yellows of a seaside theme, and a large double bed with wispy white voile curtains surrounding it. French doors led to a small balcony, and when she went to investigate, she was gifted with the most jaw-droppingly beautiful view of the whole valley.

Dusk had produced a tangerine sky, washing the neat rows of vines with a sepia splash, the hills had morphed from dusty olive green to a rich dark emerald, and the cicadas were already well into the second verse of their rhythmic evening sonata. To her left, she could see a collection of white-washed buildings with terracotta roof tiles surrounded by cypress trees, outside which she could just about make out a scruffy red Peugeot. She knew it must be the Angelopoulos residence and winery.

Suddenly, she understood the reason for Nikos' attitude towards her – he was clearly worried about a change in ownership of the hotel, what plans any new owner would have, and whether they would adversely affect his family's vineyard.

She chastised herself for not being more sympathetic. After all, she was on her own in a foreign country where she couldn't speak the language, and, most of all, she could really do with a friend.

Chapter Five

The Hummingbird Hotel, Ropa Valley, Corfu
Flower: Flame Lily

The next morning, Abbie woke to cheerful birdsong instead of the persistent rumble of traffic she was used to. Not only that, when she stepped out onto the balcony, the air wasn't filled with toxic fumes, but was crisp and fresh, and the sun shone down from a clear aquamarine sky. She closed her eyes and inhaled slowly, stretching her arms above her head and relishing the sweet fragrance of honeysuckle emanating from the pots beneath her window. She took a moment to appreciate her good fortune; whilst she was still upset about the way things had ended with Dan, she couldn't fail to be grateful that she wasn't nursing her broken heart under the grey skies in London.

She grabbed her towel and toiletries and jumped into the

shower, scrubbing away the last vestiges of sleep and the grime of the previous day's travel. She then smoothed a generous dollop of coconut oil through her curls, pulled on a pair of white capri pants and one of her favourite blue and white striped tee-shirts, and skipped downstairs in search of a coffee.

She peeked into the first room, smiling when she saw another bright, high-ceiling lounge filled with overstuffed white sofas and elegant cane chairs softened with powder-blue throws and embroidered cushions, and several glass coffee tables piled high with glossy magazines. Every wall sported an elegantly framed, hand-drawn illustration of a hummingbird in flight, its iridescent plumage beautifully depicted. The shiny marble floor led to a set of French doors and out onto a wide veranda of sun-bleached decking that offered a further selection of tables and chairs, even a hammock, upon which to take in the most spectacular view of the Greek countryside. There was no shortage of inspiration – whether that be for painting or writing or photography – and she could clearly envisage the lucky participants of her aunt's retreats enjoying their time there.

A flash of panic shot through her chest.

What was she going to do?

There was no way she could afford to reimburse the guests if she cancelled their booking, and whilst she could probably still offer them the benefit of their rooms for the duration of their stay, she couldn't do the catering or present any kind of course, so if she didn't want to "tarnish her aunt's reputation" as Felix had so kindly put it, she would have to come up with something – or someone – else.

She exhaled a sigh and decided to ponder the conundrum further after she'd had her first coffee of the day to help kickstart her brainstorming session. She found the kitchen, a huge light and airy room opposite the lounge, with high-gloss white cabinets topped with white marble counters, and a large central island unit surrounded by chrome bar stools. She located the coffee mugs in the first cupboard she opened, but was surprised, and a little confused, when she saw the shiny silver kettle didn't plug into the wall as she had expected but instead sat on a hot plate on top of a handsome, rather hi-tec, pale blue and silver stove.

Oh God, surely not?

Her body was screaming for its caffeine fix, so she googled instructions on how to light a stove, rolled up her sleeves and set to work, utilising the chopped wood she found in a basket next to the back door. After ten minutes, she had accomplished the task without any difficulty – much to her astonishment – and allowed herself a smile of satisfaction. She washed her hands and, while she waited for the kettle to boil, decided to go in search of the reservations book Felix had mentioned to see exactly how many visitors were due to arrive – and when – before taking a look at the guest rooms to see if anything needed doing.

She found the leather-bound book on the marble and glass table in the lobby, and ran her finger down the list of bookings to see that five guests were due to arrive on Friday afternoon for an alternative-style hen weekend – featuring rest, relaxation, and an abundance of Greek food and local wine, just as Nikos had said – rather than the more usual party-until-you-drop celebrations.

With a twist of anxiety, she made her way to the courtyard to undertake the second of her morning tasks – checking out the guestrooms – keeping her fingers crossed that everything would be in order. Tentatively, she opened the door to the first of the four rooms on the long colonnade, a smile tugging at her lips as she stepped inside. She needn't have worried; her aunt had clearly known what she was doing because the suite was fresh and luxuriously appointed, with the expected white-washed walls – showcasing photographs of hummingbirds, of course – a king-sized bed with crisp, white linen, and an en suite bathroom with high-end fittings and a selection of luxury toiletries and hair products that smelled like crushed rose petals. She made a note to grab a bottle of the branded conditioner from the boxes she'd seen stored in the cupboard under the stairs to see if the more expensive product would transform her hair from bird's nest to Sunday best.

After checking the other three guest rooms and finding them all spotlessly clean and exuding a faint smell of lemons, Abbie paused to wonder about her aunt's life and what she had done when she had emigrated to the United States. Why she had left the UK? And why had she chosen to come to Corfu and open the Hummingbird Hotel? Her aunt had clearly developed a love of hummingbirds while in California – which Abbie knew were native to the Americas – and she had obviously wanted to bring a bit of home with her to Greece.

She glanced at her watch, surprised to see that a whole hour had passed since she'd lit the stove and her spirits nudged upwards in anticipation of, at last, enjoying her very first coffee since arriving in Corfu. She was halfway across the courtyard, smiling at the tinkle of water coming from the hummingbird fountain, when she heard the screech of brakes on the gravel at the front of the hotel, a car door slam, and footsteps sprint up the steps, followed by urgent hammering on the front door.

'Abbie, Abbie, are you there?' More hammering. 'Abbie?'

She heard a much harsher tone in Nikos' voice than the previous day and she wondered what she had done this time.

'Abbie!'

She made her way quickly back into the hotel and through to the lobby area, wrinkling her nose at the rather heavy aroma of charred wood lingering in the air as she pulled open the front door with a smile.

'Oh, hey Nikos, I—'

'Are you okay?'

She saw his face was suffused with concern, his eyes wide with panic as he pushed past her and headed towards the kitchen.

'I'm fine, thanks, I… Oh!'

As soon as Nikos opened the door into the kitchen, she realised what he was talking about. The whole lobby filled with a balloon of smoke and she rushed forward, her hand over her mouth and nose, coughing and spluttering as she joined him, dashing to open the French doors to let the smoke escape while Nikos dealt with the stove.

'Did you open the flue?'

'What's a flue?'

'Really?'

She saw his incredulity and – now that it was clear any real danger had been avoided and the smoke had quickly dissipated – she couldn't help but switch to defensive mode.

'Well, most of the ovens I'm familiar with have dials and knobs and switches!'

'Ah, so you know what an oven is?'

'Of course I do. I—'

'What were you actually trying to do?'

'All I wanted was a cup of coffee, but I hadn't factored in that I'd have to slip into the role of Bear Grylls's cousin every time I fancy an expresso, or a latte, or a frothy cappuccino!' To her annoyance, she saw Nikos's eyes crinkle and his lips twitch at the corners in amusement. 'What's so funny?'

'Have you tried the coffee machine?'

He pointed to a partially concealed recess in the kitchen wall where a large silver, hi-tec coffee machine was stored and her indignation evaporated like a pricked balloon.

'Ah, I didn't see that.'

Thankfully, Nikos seemed to take pity on her.

'Why don't you go and sit on the veranda while I fumigate the place? Actually no, better still, there's a taverna at the bottom of the drive. Why don't you go and grab yourself a coffee, and maybe some breakfast, there before you burn the whole place down? That would *seriously* deflate the price you can get for the hotel.'

She stared at him for a beat, her thoughts switching between heartfelt gratitude for his timely arrival and assistance, and frustration at the way he assumed she was totally incompetent – although hadn't she just demonstrated how right he was? She decided to take his advice and accept his offer of help.

'Thank you, Nikos.'

She gave him a quick smile, grabbed her satchel, and made her way down the track, her head spinning with everything that had happened since she had arrived on the island. She wondered whether she should just call a taxi to pick her up at the taverna and take her straight over to Corfu Town where she would sit in the waiting room at Alex Stephanopoulos' office until he could see her. She could sign whatever paperwork was necessary to put the hotel on the market, offer him some sort of power of attorney to act on her behalf, and then leave everything in his capable hands and catch the next flight back to the UK.

Why had she thought she could hide out here while she decided how she was going to spend the rest of her life? She gasped at her audacity at thinking she could actually still offer the hotel to guests – good grief, she couldn't even boil a kettle without help!

Chapter Six

Taverna Sofia, Ropa Valley, Corfu
Flower: White Jasmine

By the time Abbie arrived at Taverna Sofia, the maelstrom of emotions from her brush with calamity had calmed. She walked through a gazebo decorated with white jasmine, and made her way round to the other side of the wooden, cabin-like building where, once again, she was presented with the most spectacular view of the whole of the Ropa Valley, a swathe of early morning mist still lingering between the vines and olive groves.

She chose a table in the far corner of the raised balcony, in the shade of an ancient magnolia tree, and sank into a chair upholstered in jolly pink-and-white striped fabric. She was relieved to see that she wasn't the only person seeking a fix of caffeine, and her tastebuds tingled as she caught a waft of their freshly ground coffee along with the deliciously fragrant breakfast omelettes. She leaned back in her seat, listening to the rhythmic chirp of the cicadas, the low hum of conversation from the other diners, the faint tinkle of Greek music that emanated from the direction of what she assumed was the kitchen, and the tension in her temples eased.

'Hi there, what can I get you?'

Abbie smiled at the waitress with the copper-coloured hair held in an up-do by what looked suspiciously like a paintbrush. She guessed they were around the same age, and, judging from her pale skin and the generous sprinkle of freckles across the bridge of her nose and cheeks, not to mention her strong west country accent, it was clear she was also an escapee from the rat race, although she had clearly decided on a more lengthy stay in the Greek sunshine than Abbie.

'I'd love a coffee, please, and maybe one of those breakfast omelettes?'

'Sure, coming right up. I'm Rachel, by the way.'

'Hi Rachel, I'm Abbie.'

'Are you staying around here?'

'Yes, well, no, actually.'

'Sorry, sorry, I didn't mean to be nosey. It's something I'm working on… Hey, can you smell burning?'

'No?' mumbled Abbie.

'Sorry, what did you say you wanted?'

'Just a coffee would be fine.'

'Right.'

Abbie watched Rachel meander towards the kitchen, her mind clearly on something else. She wondered why she was in Corfu, and how she had ended up working in a taverna so far off the beaten track and not in one of the tourist hotspots over on the coast. She had to smile at the irony of her last thought – who was being nosey now?

'Here you are, one espresso. I take it that's what you've ordered?'

'Thank you, yes.'

She grinned at the woman with the wonderfully mellow Greek accent who had set down a double espresso on the table in front of her, before proceeding to gulp down half the cup in one go, relishing the immediate injection of caffeine that helped to invigorate her lagging energy levels and made her feel almost human again.

'Looks like you needed that, and there's an omelette on its way.'

'You're a life saver. I'm starving!'

'Do you mind if I ask you something?'

'Okay?'

'Are you Liz's niece? You have the same features; the same blue eyes, the same tip of the chin, and, of course, that hair is a complete giveaway.'

Abbie took in the woman's friendly face, her thick bob, the colour of butterscotch, her soft, kind eyes, and the laughter lines around her carefully lined lips. She had clearly taken a leaf out of Felix's book in her choice of attire – the colours, not the Spandex – sporting a voluminous bat-winged blouse in a vibrant emerald and turquoise, paired with white jeans and a chunky gold chain around her neck, and favouring a rich, floral perfume which Abbie recognised as one her mum used to use.

'Yes, I'm Abbie Coleman. I'm over here to sort out her

affairs.'

'I'm sorry for your loss, Abbie. If there's anything I can do to help, please don't hesitate to ask. I'm Sofia Diakos, and my husband and I own this taverna. Your aunt and I were good friends, and, like you, she used to come down here and sit on this veranda – at this particular table – and contemplate the view when she didn't have guests at the hotel to look after.'

Abbie finished her coffee, placed the cup back on the saucer, then she met Sofia's gaze, an idea forming in her head.

'Actually, Sofia, there is something you can help me with, if you don't mind.' She paused unsure whether she should ask or what she would do with the response – whichever way it went – and her confidence almost failed her, but she forced herself to press on. 'Apparently there's a group of people coming to stay at the hotel this weekend, expecting to indulge in home-cooked Greek food and…'

'Oh, yes, Liz really loved to run the retreats. I'm so pleased you're planning to continue her legacy.'

'Erm… no, that's not what I…'

She cringed when she saw the disappointment wash over Sofia's face, but she had to make her position clear; she had to be honest so there was no misunderstanding. She just hoped Sofia wouldn't react the same way Nikos had when he'd collected her from the airport – she could do with a friend, especially one who had known her aunt.

'I'm not a cook, or a hotelier, and I've never worked in the hospitality industry. I'm a botanist, actually, but I've worked for the last three years as a florist at a small boutique in London until… well, until I…'

Warmth flooded her cheeks. Sofia smiled, placing a gentle hand on Abbie's shoulder, her eyes filled with understanding. 'I'm sure a few weeks here will smooth out all your emotional wrinkles. Just ask Rachel, she's also an escapee from heartbreak, and look at her now.'

They both glanced across to where Rachel was perched cross-legged on a bench at the far end of the veranda, a glossy magazine on her lap and twirling a strand of her hair between her fingers, staring at the barman with a dreamy smile tugging at her lips. She couldn't make her feelings any more obvious if she started prancing around that taverna waving pom-poms and shouting "I love you, I love you, I love you" at the top of her voice.

When Abbie looked back at Sofia, she realised that her new friend was the village's Keeper of Secrets – including those of her aunt – and if she was going to have any chance of understanding what had happened in the past, Sofia was the person she had to ask, but she needed to think carefully how she was going to do that.

'I'm not staying for a few weeks, Sofia, I'm here for ten days, that's all, just enough time to sort out my aunt's affairs, sign whatever papers are necessary for the hotel to be put on the market, and then I'm heading back home.'

'It could take a while to sell the hotel, you know.'

'I know, I know, I—'

'So what do you plan on doing with your inheritance?'

Abbie was surprised at the directness of the question – just as she had been at Nikos's forthright questions. She wondered if it was her; whether she had been far too reticent in her conversations and social interactions. Had her lack of self-confidence, particularly after losing her mum, been causing her to tread lightly when asking people about their lives? If she shied away from more intimate enquiries, how could she go on to offer her support if it was needed? She stored that nugget of insight away for later dissection.

'I'm not sure, it was all so sudden. I've not had a chance to think about it properly.'

'Don't you have a dream? Something you've always wanted to do? Something that fills your heart and soul, your every waking moment, as you plan out all the details, adding to the list every day? That's what I did when I was young and dreamed of owning a taverna one day.'

Abbie smiled, surprised she was so comfortable in Sofia's gentle presence. She felt like she was talking to an old friend, someone she had known for years, who knew everything about her, who could see straight into her heart and know exactly what she wanted, what she craved, and, probably, what she needed to do to achieve it. Now she understood how Sofia had become the keeper of secrets – she had an innate knack of attracting confidences whether her hapless customers wanted to share them or not.

'My dream is to own a cottage in the country, with a white picket fence and a small garden where I can grow whatever I want, where I can experiment with native and exotic species of plants, shrubs and flowers, but also cultivate my own fruit and vegetables, too. I think probably Devon, which is where I grew up, and where Mum lived before she passed away – she used to open her garden every year as part of the RHS Open Gardens scheme – and because the growing season is longer there.'

'Dreams can change, Abbie.'

Abbie met Sofia's eyes and saw something there she didn't understand, but before she could ask what she meant, Sofia changed the subject.

'We actually have quite a few interesting plant species here in Corfu. Maybe you'll get the chance to explore a little of the area before you leave. Our island is so much more than the beach resorts.'

'I'd love to do that, I really would, but it looks like all my time will be taken up preparing for the holidaymakers to arrive. To be honest, I'm terrified; I'm ashamed to admit I'm a useless cook, and… well, actually, I've just nearly burnt down the hotel and I've only been here for one day. Imagine what I can do in a week!'

'Ah, I thought I could smell smoke.' Sofia laughed.

'And even if I *could* cook, there's no way I could produce authentic Greek food.'

'Practise makes perfect.'

'In three days?' Then a thought pinged into her head and the words were out of her mouth before she engaged her brain. 'I don't suppose you could help, Sofia? I'd pay you, of course.'

Abbie realised she'd offended Sofia and remorse flooded her veins.

'Sorry, I didn't mean… Oh, God, I'm so sorry.'

'It's okay, I—'

'Hey, you know who you should ask, don't you?' said Rachel, putting down a fresh coffee in front of Abbie.

'Who?'

'Nikos.'

'Why?'

'Because he's a qualified chef.'

'He's not just a chef,' Felix interjected, arriving on the taverna's veranda and causing Abbie to do a double-take when she saw his lithe, yoga-toned body encased in fluorescent orange cycling shorts, a pink sleeveless tee-shirt that showed off his impressive biceps to perfection, and his wayward curls almost, but not quite as frizzled as her own. When he dropped down onto the seat next to her, she was treated to the most delicious waft of fresh, minty cologne.

'What do you mean?' asked Rachel.

'He's a *Cordon Bleu* chef who used to work at a fancy high-end restaurant in Paris.'

'I thought he ran his family's vineyard and winery?' said Abbie.

'He does,' said Sofia, shooting Felix a warning look that piqued Abbie's curiosity. 'What Felix means is that Nikos *used* to work as a chef before he came back to Corfu to take over the family business. Abbie, leave it with me, I'll have a word with Panos' brother who owns a restaurant over in Sidari. I'm sure he can come up with someone who might be available to come over to prepare a few meals for your guests.'

'Oh, thank you, that's really kind of you.'

Sofia smiled, stood, and shooed Rachel back to the kitchen.

'Hey, can you smell smoke?' said Felix, wrinkling his nose.

'No, I can't.'

'Funny, I thought I got a whiff and I remember your

horoscope from yesterday.'

'I don't…'

'Want to know today's?'

'Not really,' mumbled Abbie, before giving Felix her brightest smile. 'How come you're here so early?'

'Oh, I live here.'

'I know you live here, but…'

'No, I live *here*, I have a cool studio above the taverna. I'm sort of its guardian angel.'

'You're the taverna's guardian angel?'

'Sure, we all need one, don't we?'

'Well, the way my life's been going recently, I could certainly do with one.'

'I accept the position!'

'No, I didn't…'

Oh, God.

'Oh, wow, I knew this was going to happen. This morning my horoscope said I was going to take on a new, more invigorating challenge which would lead me towards blissful enlightenment. Say, fancy joining me for a yoga session? I've got five ladies coming over from Nissaki in an hour to perfect their palm tree pose and maybe, later, spend a few moments communing with nature.'

'Communing with nature?'

'Yes. You know, Abbie, if we listen carefully, we can hear the earth's inherent rhythm.'

'Erm, thanks for the offer, Felix, but I think I'll give it a miss.'

Abbie couldn't prevent a smile from forming on her lips when an image of Emily floated into her mind – her friend would have loved a seat on the veranda, a cool cocktail in her hand whilst she watched Felix lead a live yoga class.

'No worries. *Adio*, Abbie.'

Felix sauntered away to find a peaceful spot, or maybe just peace, and Abbie tipped her head back, closed her eyes, and enjoyed the warmth of the sun on her face as she replayed the conversations she'd just had. It seemed there was more to Nikos Angelopoulos than met the eye, and she wondered what had led to him giving up an exciting career in the food capital of the world to return to Corfu.

She had just conjured up an image of Nikos, his dark brooding eyes staring into hers, the sexy vibe he seemed to exude from every pore in his body, relishing the pleasurable sensation his unexpected attraction instilled, when the man himself interrupted her thoughts.

'Okay, so the kitchen is sorted – ready for your next catastrophe. I know how adamant you are about not wanting to switch careers from celebrity florist to hotel owner, but burning down the hotel is a bit extreme don't you think?'

'I didn't—'

Again, she felt her temper spark, but she refused to allow him to rile her. She pushed back her chair and stood.

'Thank you for your help, Nikos. It's very kind of you, and I really appreciate it, but if you'll excuse me, I've got a few things to do; guest rooms to check, sweeping, scrubbing, cleaning, dusting…'

'And lawyers to meet with?'

She stared at him, irritated by the way his eyes lingered on hers as though issuing a challenge to her to react, to argue with him, to vociferously state her case for the decision she had made. But that wasn't her. She rarely if ever argued with anyone, preferring the path of least resistance, and anyway, she refused to give him the satisfaction by succumbing to his challenge.

Chapter Seven

The Courtyard at the Hummingbird Hotel, Ropa Valley, Corfu
Flower: Scarlet Geranium

Abbie strolled back down the gravelly track, feasting her eyes on the hedges and plants, the orange and lemon trees heavy with ripening fruit, enjoying the tranquillity and the way the sun caressed her skin, the clarity of the air around her, the sound of the birds and the insects as they went about their daily chores.

To her left were the vineyards of the Angelopoulos estate, stretching across the hillside as far as the eye could see, the vines resplendent with tiny bunches of green grapes, the leaves fluttering in the light breeze, and her botanical interest surged. Maybe she *would* take Sofia's advice and spend a day out in the countryside, but only when she was certain that everything was in hand for the arrival of the Hummingbird Hotel's guests.

When there were jobs to be done, there was no time like the present to get started, so she rolled up her sleeves and spent the next few hours with a mop and a bucket, and then a damp cloth and a feather duster she'd unearthed from a cupboard under the stairs, cleaning the ground floor of the hotel; the lobby, the communal lounge, and the kitchen, before moving out onto the veranda and sweeping away the fallen leaves.

She was surprised that a place like the Hummingbird Hotel didn't have a garden, only the gravelled courtyard and the pergola that connected it to the swimming pool terrace. To make up for that, her aunt had amassed a huge variety of ceramic and terracotta pots, tubs, and urns, each one bursting with scarlet and white geraniums and dotted around the pathways, the veranda, and the steps leading to the front of the hotel. Abbie found a pair of gardening gloves under the kitchen sink and got to work with a trowel, digging out weeds, removing past-their-best petals from the potted plants, shrubs and herbs; the physical, repetitive work clearing her mind of all extraneous jumble, which was what she loved the most about gardening; there were no deadlines, no fussy clients to satisfy, and she got to spend a few hours outside in the fresh air.

For every hour she spent with her fingers in the soil, her spirits edged up a notch. As she inhaled the unfamiliar perfume of the indigenous herbs, her thoughts scooted back to her time at university when her life was filled with the study of plants; their structure, their function, their evolution, their biological diversity, their distribution around the world.

She had loved every minute of it, and, along with her fellow would-be botanists, had dreamed of spending her professional life immersed in all-things botanical, arboreal and horticultural either at a country estate, a commercial nursery, or the ultimate dream, for her anyway, Kew Gardens. She loved the kaleidoscope of colours she encountered – muted, vibrant, variegated – as well as the endless variety of perfumes and fragrances, the velvety feel of a rose's petal, the spikiness of a palm tree's foliage, the sound of autumn leaves rustling in the breeze, of woodland animals scurrying through the undergrowth as they prepared their homes for the long winter months.

It was one o'clock and the sun was now at its strongest. Abbie could feel her cheeks burning, so she returned to the – thankfully, now smoke-free – kitchen and fixed herself a coffee using the coffee machine that Nikos had ostentatiously left out on the central island unit as if underlining her uselessness, and went to sit at one of the bistro tables in the courtyard.

As she relaxed and listened to the tinkle of falling water from the fountain, a surge of accomplishment suffused her chest at what she had achieved in a few short hours. At least there would be no risk of the guests leaving negative reviews about cleanliness; all four of the courtyard guest rooms were ready, the hotel's communal areas were clean and polished, and the pool area was tidy. She planned to offer the guests as much tea and coffee as they wanted via the coffee machine, and to arrange with Sofia and Panos for them to take breakfast at the taverna, which she would pay for out of their booking fees. All that was left to do was to find someone who could come over and cook their evening meal.

Then an idea popped into her head.

It was a long shot but if she didn't ask, she would never know the answer. She grabbed her phone, and saw there was a response to the email she'd sent to the person who had booked the weekend retreat. She quickly scanned the contents, noting with relief that one person had dropped out and there would now be only four people in attendance – the bride-to-be, Savannah Cooper, her best friend and chief bridesmaid, Bree, and two friends who worked with Savannah at her Knightsbridge hair and beauty salon – which meant each guest could have a room of their own. She smiled with relief, then dialled a number that was as familiar as her own.

'Hey, Em, how are things?'

'I'm fine, I've just finished a shift at the pâtisserie. How are you? What's the hotel like? It looks absolutely adorable in the photos you sent through. Oh, Abbie, you're so lucky to be over there, relaxing in the sunshine, eating all the wonderful food, sunbathing by the pool.'

Abbie laughed. 'Actually, I've just spent the last five hours up to my elbows in soapy water, mopping floors, wiping down units, polishing windows, making sure every guest room is pristine and has its quota of luxury toiletries – which I can tell you smell absolutely divine – weeding plant pots, sweeping up leaves. Glamorous, it is not!'

'And what about romance? Are you surrounded by gorgeous, sexy, tanned and toned Greek guys throwing plates at your feet and asking you to dance with them in the moonlight, before taking you to swim naked in the sea, then kissing you, madly, passionately, deeply, until dawn?'

'Sadly not.'

Abbie paused, wrestling with the invisible mischief-maker on her shoulder that was urging her to ask the question that had been rotating through her brain since she left London. She knew she shouldn't ask, but she had to know.

'I don't suppose Dan's been round to the flat?'

'Sorry, he hasn't. Has he returned your calls?'

'No.'

'You need to move on, Abs. Forget Dan, he's ancient history now. Why not take advantage of a fresh start, in a new environment with a laidback holiday atmosphere – it doesn't have to be anything serious, just a bit of light hearted fun.'

'You know I'm not like that, Em. Anyway, all I can think about is the look of horror on Dan's face when he thought I wanted him to spend the rest of his life with me.'

'I don't think—'

'You saw him; you know what happened. I can't go through that again. I'm steering well clear of all romantic dalliances, especially of the Greek kind.'

'Not all guys are like Dan, Abbie,' Emily said, gently.

'Anyway, I was ringing to see if there was any chance, any chance at all, you could take a few days off from the pâtisserie?'

'Why?'

Could she really ask her friend to drop everything and dash to her aid? She knew Emily was an amazing pastry chef, but would she be able to create authentic Greek recipes? She doubted it. And whilst she had no intention of changing her mind about selling the Hummingbird Hotel, she didn't want to do anything to jeopardise her aunt's good name by letting down a group of holidaymakers – she assumed her guests wouldn't want the traditional crazy capers of a hen weekend to be laid on by the hotel owner!

'Sorry, Em, just ignore me. I miss you, that's all.'

'And I miss you, too.'

She chatted to Emily for a few more minutes and after she'd said goodbye, she felt strangely bereft and lonely – homesick, even. The Hummingbird Hotel was an amazing place, surrounded by stunning countryside, with a gorgeous swimming pool, and lots of shady nooks and crannies to while away a few peaceful hours with an ice-cold drink and a good book, but without anyone to enjoy it with, those things held no attraction.

Abbie knew from past experience that the only way to keep her demons at bay was to keep busy, so she returned to the kitchen, refilled her bucket with warm soapy water, and made her way to the communal lounge. She was about to start washing down the coffee tables when she noticed a partially concealed door draped in a floral curtain to the right of the stairs, and decided to abandon her mop and bucket to investigate.

She understood immediately that this had been her aunt's private space. The whole room was filled with a hoard of mismatched comfy chairs that didn't fit with the smart pale-blue-and-white colour scheme of the rest of the hotel, and was clearly a place where she could come to escape her hostess duties. Wooden shelves – crammed with an eclectic mix of books and ornaments – and pictures of pressed flowers and more hummingbirds lined the walls, and there was an ambiance of peace and calm; a true sanctuary.

And then she saw it.

A clearly beloved framed photograph standing in pride of place on a polished wooden chest of drawers. Abbie's heart gave a squeeze. She was about to come face-to-face with her Aunt Liz – albeit in a photograph – for the first time. She picked up the silver frame, her emotions churning, her breath catching in her chest as she saw what Sofia had seen – an older version of herself, with out-of-control blonde curls, piercing blue eyes, and what her mum had called "a cute ski-slope nose". Her aunt had clearly shared the same taste in clothes, too, having chosen a wide-sleeved saffron-coloured tee-shirt and a pair of cream linen palazzo pants for the photoshoot.

She feasted her eyes on the relative she had never known, then moved on to scrutinise the man standing next to her, his arm draped loosely around her shoulders, a wide All-American smile on his face. He was tall, over six foot, broad-shouldered, with blue-grey eyes, thick sandy-blonde hair combed back from his forehead, and a dimple in his chin, and looked incredibly handsome in a pair of black jeans and a pale pink shirt, the cuffs turned back at the wrists to reveal a glimpse of Paisley pattern. They were an attractive couple, clearly at ease with one another, and Abbie was happy that her aunt had found her soulmate, unlike her mum who, as far as she knew, had never ventured into the dating arena since her father had left.

What had gone wrong between the sisters?

She had asked her mum several times as she'd grown up but had never been able to get a straight answer. Sometimes she understood that her mum hadn't wanted to resurrect difficult issues; sometimes she'd been disappointed and a little annoyed that she didn't feel she could confide in her. Every time she broached the subject, the barriers would come up and the conversation quickly diverted so that Abbie had eventually stopped asking, and now it was too late; her mum had passed away five years ago, and now her aunt had joined her. She had wondered why her aunt hadn't contacted her after her mum had passed, and the only conclusion she'd been able to come to was that she just hadn't been interested.

But, if that was right, why had she left Abbie the hotel?

Yes, her aunt had no children of her own, but she still felt uncomfortable, undeserving of the generous gift, and she couldn't help thinking about what her mum's reaction would have been if she had been around. She knew there were people in the village who didn't want her to sell the Hummingbird Hotel, but she had to, there was no other alternative. How could she contemplate making a life here, running the hotel and the various retreats, living the same life as her aunt? What would her mum think of that after everything that had happened?

No, she couldn't do that.

However, there was one thing she *could* do while she was there and that was talk to Sofia, to ask her about her Aunt Liz and maybe learn a little about her life there, and the reasons she had ended up in Corfu, and maybe, just maybe, learn something about her own history along the way.

***

Abbie woke with a start. She couldn't believe she'd fallen asleep, although after the riot of sweeping, scrubbing, and cleaning, she'd engaged in, it wasn't that much of a surprise. She pushed herself up from the very comfortable chintz-covered chair – her aching muscles screaming their objection at the excess of physical activity they were simply not accustomed to – and jogged upstairs to her room to change, choosing a pair of wide-legged linen trousers and a tangerine tee-shirt with ruffled sleeves.

She ran a comb through her hair, grimacing when she glanced in the mirror, and decided she needed a stroll in the fresh air to chase away the sleep fairies. She grabbed a bottle of water and made her way to the courtyard, through the stone archway and the pergola, and this time she turned left, on a mission to inspect the pocket-sized vineyard her aunt had created and tended so lovingly instead of cultivating a garden for the hotel's guests to enjoy.

She knew a little about vines, just enough to recognise a Bordeaux grape when she saw one, and clearly not as much as her aunt. The plants in her mini-vineyard were flourishing, and already the hard green grapes were starting to turn into plump purple clusters, protected from the scorch of the sun by the lush, frilly leaves. She walked the short length of the first row, pausing occasionally to snag a weed or remove a dry leaf, inspecting the soil, taking note of the orientation of the rows, the twist of the trellis, the space between each vine.

When she reached the low fence marking the boundary between the Hummingbird Hotel and the Angelopoulos estate, she leaned forward to pluck one of the ripened grapes from a nearby vine and popped it in her mouth, surprised at the sharp acidic tang – but then, even she knew it was much too early for the fruit's sugars to develop. She experienced a familiar uptick of excitement that spending time with plants of any kind engendered, and she suddenly couldn't wait to read up of the cultivation of vines, but also about the wine-making process – a subject she didn't know much about, though she certainly enjoyed the end result.

She exhaled a sigh of contentment as she surveyed the acres and acres of commercial vineyards that covered the valley, basking under the afternoon sunshine as bees danced between the foliage to the cicadas' serenade. She was about to turn around and return to the hotel when, to her astonishment, the peace was broken by the sound of a man singing what sounded like an Italian aria at the top of his voice, and she decided to wait and see whether it was Pavarotti's Greek cousin.

'Ah, *Yassou*!'

'Oh, hi.'

'You must be Abbie.'

'Yes, I am. Abbie Coleman.'

She took in the ruggedly handsome guy with the wide, friendly smile, chocolate-brown puppy dog eyes, and a mop of curls almost as unruly as her own – except his were dark mahogany. Probably the same age as Abbie, he sported a white figure-hugging tee-shirt and a pair of sturdy leather boots, but what really drew her eye was the fact that he was waving a penknife in the air as he spoke, its blade glancing in the sun.

'Sorry, I didn't mean to disturb you. I'm Dimitris; it means earth-lover, which is pretty apt.'

'Why is it apt?'

'Because I'm the Angelopoulos vineyard's estate manager.'

'Well, it's good to meet you, Dimitris.'

She held her hand out to greet him, shocked when instead of the expected shake, he grasped her palm, pulled her towards him, and gave her a hearty hug – and a sociable slap on the back for good measure – all whilst brandishing his penknife worryingly close to her face.

'You too, Abbie, Nik has told me all about you.'

'Oh, did he? Not all good, I assume?'

'Well, he did say you'd almost burnt down the hotel.'

Dimitris laughed, a sound that caused Abbie to giggle, especially when he tried to lean casually against one of the fence posts but lost his balance, stumbling back a few feet before managing to right himself, but slicing through a branch with his penknife in the process.

'So, Dimitris, how long have you worked at the Angelopoulos vineyard?'

'Only since Nik took over, so about two years. We went to school together. We were inseparable until he jetted off to Paris to train as a chef. I'm not like him; I've never wanted to leave the island to seek my fortune elsewhere. Corfu is an amazing place to live – everything I want is here; my family, my friends, my dog. Why would I want to go anywhere else? Do you have a big family, Abbie?'

'No, not really.'

'I have four sisters and a brother – I'm the youngest.'

That didn't surprise Abbie in the least. She could see him being fussed over by his sisters and indulged for his sunny temperament and cheeky grin.

'Did I hear you singing before?'

'Yes, I was singing to the vines; it works you know.'

'Oh, I agree.'

'You do? You don't think I'm crazy?'

'Of course not.'

Abbie liked Dimitris – he was the complete opposite of Nikos. Open, friendly, laidback, a smile on his lips and with an upbeat, happy vibe. She was suddenly visited by an image of Emily smiling, just like Dimitris, and she knew they would make an attractive couple. She wondered if he had a girlfriend.

'Is it true you're selling the hotel?'

'I'm afraid it is. I don't know the first thing about running a hotel.'

'Well, I don't know the first thing about running a vineyard, but I haven't let that stop me. My dream is to be a professional singer, to perform in the bars and restaurants and night clubs around the island, and until that happens, I'm happy to support Nik here. He couldn't do this on his own, but he's learning, and you can, too.'

'I'm not sure, I—'

'You know, the Hummingbird Hotel is the best thing that's happened around here.'

'What do you mean?'

'Well, before your aunt bought the place, the house was an Athens billionaire's second home. The guy and his family spent two, maybe three, weeks of the year here, and the rest of the time it stood empty until ten years ago when he had to sell it after his divorce. Now that it's a hotel, the guests who stay here spend money in the village; they use the supermarket, they drink in the bars, they eat at Sofia's taverna, they take one of Felix's classes.'

Abbie's stomach gave an uncomfortable lurch. Could this be another reason Nikos had been so snippy with her? Surely any new owner would keep the place as a hotel or a B&B and there would be minimum impact on the community. But there was no guarantee, of course – maybe the new buyer would convert it back to a second home.

Did that mean Sofia, and Felix, and everyone else's businesses would suffer? Would that be her fault? How could it?

Nevertheless, she felt awful, so she said a hurried goodbye to Dimitris and strolled back through her aunt's special vineyard, her head spinning with so many unanswerable questions she thought it was about to explode. How could she ask Sofia to provide her guests with breakfast and then repay her kindness by selling the hotel to some wealthy property investor before disappearing off into the sunset clutching her cheque? She couldn't live with herself.

What was she going to do?

She couldn't change the situation she found herself in, nor how Nikos felt about it. She also couldn't stay in Corfu; she didn't *want* to stay in Corfu now that her long-held dream – that little cottage in the country with the roses around its door – was within touching distance.

But was Sofia right? Could dreams change?

Chapter Eight

The Angelopoulos Vineyard & Winery
Flower: Pale Pink Water Lily

Abbie returned to the hotel hot and sticky, and desperately in need of a cold drink and maybe something to eat. Of course, when she arrived in the kitchen, the cupboards were bare and so she decided it was time to go on a shopping expedition. She grabbed her satchel, locked the door and skipped down the front steps, then stopped.

What was she thinking?

She had no idea where the nearest town or village was, and perhaps more importantly, she had no means of getting there. She plonked herself down on the top step, and dropped her head in her hands, suddenly overcome by everything that had happened to her over the last few weeks. If one of Felix's horoscopes had foretold all the incidents that had delivered her to that moment, she would have laughed out loud at the outrageousness of it all.

But here she was, in Corfu of all places, sitting outside a hotel that she now *owned*, with four guests about to descend in less than two days' time, and not a crumb of food or drink in the house nor the transport to acquire it.

How on earth had she thought she was equipped to do this?

She didn't have the skills, or the know-how, and if she was honest, she was completely out of her depth. It was all just too much to contemplate. An upsurge of emotion threatened to overwhelm her and tears prickled at her eyes. As usual, when she was feeling at her lowest ebb, an image of Dan floated through her mind, and she indulged in a few moments of despondency.

What would it have been like if Dan had been there with her and they were doing this together? She had loved him; she missed him so much, and it hurt that he hadn't even attempted to contact her since that fateful night at the Sky Garden – apart from the voicemail telling her that her time at *FlowerEssence* was over – not even an acknowledgement of the message she'd left telling him she was heading to Greece to handle her aunt's affairs.

A seed of indignation agitated at her chest at his dismissive treatment of her. After all, they had been a couple for over twelve months, and even before that she had worked hard to help him build up the floristry business that his parents had bought for him when he dropped out of university, sometimes putting in fourteen-hour days when they had a special order like a catwalk show, or a film première, or a gallery opening, or a photography exhibition. She had willingly headed over to the wholesale flower market in Covent Garden at four in the morning when Dan had wanted a lie-in, and utilised every ounce of her creativity to produce unique, cutting-edge designs, focussing on colour, texture, form and scent, and had received little praise – or even thanks – from Dan for her effort.

He'd ditched her because she'd wanted to take their relationship to the next level, and now here she was over a thousand miles from home, and she felt more alone than ever. Everywhere she looked, there were couples or families – she had been the only solo traveller on the plane and she had seen more than a few sympathetic glances tossed in her direction and that hurt.

However, feeling sorry for herself wasn't going to get her something to eat for dinner. Okay, so she was alone. That just meant she had to make more of an effort to meet new people, to form new friendships, new relationships – just not of the romantic kind.

She jumped up from the step, dusted herself down, and was about to make her way down the driveway to the taverna to ask Sofia to point her in the direction of a supermarket, when she spotted a small wooden shed she hadn't noticed before, its door and tiny window painted in the Hummingbird Hotel's signature blue. She decided to investigate, her spirits rising as she anticipated discovering a cute Fiat 500, or one of those quirky Citroen 2CVs – her aunt had to have had some way of doing the shopping for the hotel guests.

She was not surprised to see there was no lock on the door. She grabbed hold of the brass handle and gave it a sharp tug, stumbling backwards as the door opened more easily than she had anticipated. She peered inside, and when her eyes became accustomed to the gloom, she was disappointed to see there was no vehicle of any kind.

However, there was a bicycle. She took hold of the handlebars and wheeled it outside so she could inspect it more closely, smiling despite her disappointment when she saw its frame had been painted powder-blue – of course – and sported a large woven basket up front. She couldn't remember the last time she had been on a bicycle, or whether she still knew how to ride one, but she decided to throw caution to the wind and give it a go.

Nothing ventured, nothing gained, as her mum used to say to her when she was growing up.

She dropped her satchel into the basket, cocked her leg over the well-worn saddle, and took a firm hold of the handlebars, then she pushed herself off, slowly at first, weaving and wavering as she made her way along the driveway, the pedals a little stiff from lack of use. The further she travelled, the more her confidence grew, and so did her balance, until she rounded a bend and almost collided with a motorbike coming the other way, swerving drastically to her left in order to avoid a head-on collision which meant she ended up on her bottom in a shallow ditch at the side of the road.

'Oh my God!'

'Hey, Abbie, are you okay? Here, let me help you.'

She rolled her eyes at the inevitability; of all the people to be coming round that bend at that precise moment, it had to be Nikos. She pushed herself up, dusted the dirt from her knees, picked a stray leaf from her hair, and went over to inspect the damage to her bike, which thankfully didn't seem to be any worse for its unexpected detour.

'What were you doing on my side of the road?'

'Your side?' Nikos gaped at her, his dark eyes flashing. '*You* were on the wrong side!'

'I was not!'

'You're in Greece, we drive on the right here.'

'Oh, oh yes, I—'

Her bubble of indignation popped and heat rushed into her cheeks when she saw the satisfaction written across his face; it seems she couldn't do anything right in front of Nikos Angelopoulos and for some reason that made her defensive.

'Why are you here?'

'Well, I knew you wouldn't have much food in, so I thought I'd organise dinner.'

'Dinner?'

'Yes, it's where people sit at a table and eat food that somebody else has made, maybe with a glass or two of wine, and then round it off with a coffee and a glass of ouzo or brandy.'

'I know what dinner is!'

She knew she sounded ungrateful, and a little peevish, but she was standing in front of him, covered in dirt and dust, her hair sprouting random blades of dried grass, having just entertained him by performing a comedic turn on a bicycle. Why couldn't he have met her sauntering down the country lane with a smile on her face, humming a random tune, and wearing a pretty summer dress and strappy sandals, her hair tamed into a neat chignon?

'Sorry, sorry, that's actually very kind of you.'

Nikos was smiling at her, clearly enjoying her discomfort,

then he took pity on her again and pointed to his motorbike which, unlike the red Peugeot he'd used to collect her from the airport, was shiny and new and rather sexy.

'Come on, I've got an idea.'

'You want me to… to ride on that?'

'What's the matter? Have you never ridden on a motorbike before?'

'No, I haven't actually.'

'Well, you're going to love it, I promise.

'I'm not so sure.'

'Well, you won't know until you've given it a go, but if you're too frightened then I'll completely understand.'

Abbie saw the twist of his lips and the challenge in his dark come-to-bed eyes and her stomach performed an unexpected somersault of attraction, but she ignored it and forced herself to gift him with her brightest, most confident smile, and climbed on the seat behind him, unsure what to do with her hands.

'Hold on!'

Nikos revved the engine, and to her surprise, he reached round to grab her arms and guide them around his waist, then they shot off down the lane and she had no choice but to hold on for dear life. However, after thirty seconds of pure panic, she experienced a pleasurable whoosh of exhilaration as the warm breeze whipped her hair high into the air and she leaned into his muscular body, the powerful engine humming, and the fragrance of his citrussy cologne tickling her nostrils.

Instead of pulling into the car park at the side of Taverna Sofia as Abbie had expected, Nikos continued on for another fifty metres and then took a right-hand turn, slowing down as they glided along a wide tarmacked road that ran parallel to the bumpy track that led to the Hummingbird Hotel, this one bordered on each side by a parade of cypress trees like an arboreal guard of honour. They came to a stop next to a magnificent pink marble fountain in the shape of an angel frolicking in the surrounding pond, decorated with floating pink water lilies and looking like something from a Monet painting.

'Welcome to the Angelopoulos estate. Want a tour?'

'I'd love a tour.'

'Shall we start with the vineyard?'

'Of course.' Abbie smiled; the fact that Nikos had run her off the road already a distant memory.

'Hang on a minute, I just need to collect something.'

She watched him sprint across the driveway and disappear through the front door of the house – a handsome rustic building with a garland of white jasmine twisted around the terracotta eaves where she assumed Nikos and his family lived – reappearing within seconds sporting a rucksack and two bottles of ice-cold water, one of which he handed to her.

'Thank you.'

She drank half the bottle in one long gulp, and then followed Nikos through a pair of huge oak gates sporting a polished brass plate announcing that they'd arrived at the Angelopoulos Vineyard & Winery.

'Wow!'

She took in the two enormous outbuildings – both equally as handsome and charming as the main house – which obviously housed the winery operations, then stood open-mouthed at the panorama spread across the valley in front of her. The view was mesmerising; the vines running up and down the hillside like serpents, luscious green, the soil between the rows a dry dusty brown and free of weeds, the white-washed villages nestled amongst olive groves, the random clusters of cypress trees, and the whole scene watched over by an endless blue sky.

'This vineyard has been in our family for over a hundred years.'

'How many people do you have working here?'

She noticed Nikos hesitate, his eyes fixed on the far horizon, his thoughts elsewhere for a moment before he forcibly dragged himself back to the present to answer her question.

'Just myself and Dimitris, but I call in the services of an expert when it's time to prune, which is a skill that has to be learned over many years. Poorly pruned vines will not produce high-quality fruit, and without high-quality fruit we will have poor quality wine. We also have many willing helpers when it's time to harvest the grapes – another decision I take expert advice on – so we do okay.'

Abbie had little knowledge of what it took to run a successful wine business, but that seemed like an awful lot of work for two people to handle, especially as one of them was Dimitris who didn't look like he was the most committed of employees when it came to the cultivation of grapes, unless the fruit appreciated his efforts to serenade them.

'What about your family, do they help?'

She couldn't see Nikos' face because he had crouched to inspect the lower branches of a particularly straggly vine, twisting a loose section of twine into place, but she saw his shoulders and neck muscles tighten at her question and she wondered if she'd strayed into difficult territory.

'My mother moved over to Athens last year to live with my sister, Helena, and her two grandchildren, so for the time being there's just me and Dimitris, and he lives with his family over in Nissaki.'

'He told me they were close.'

'You've met him?'

'Yes, when I was taking a stroll around by aunt's own tiny vineyard. I'm not an expert in vines in particular, but they seem to be really healthy and well cared for, not that there's enough to make more than a few bottles of wine, I assume. I'm not sure why she decided to plant them, to be honest, especially when the hotel has no garden to speak of.'

'Well, Liz and her husband owned a vineyard and winery in California – Hummingbird Valley Wines, it was called, and it was very successful. She obviously wanted to plant something here in Corfu to remind her of what had been her home for over twenty years, or maybe it was to honour Greg's memory.'

Abbie stopped and turned to stare at Nikos, questions flying around in her brain, totally oblivious to the bucolic scenery that was now bathed in a rich golden glow as the sun sank slowly behind the far horizon. Her heart pounded against her chest, and she suddenly felt the need to confide a little of her story in Nikos in the hope that he could tell her more about her aunt's past.

'I'm afraid I don't know much about my Aunt Liz. There was a… a family estrangement years ago, before I was born, so all I know is that she left Devon to go and live in California. So, I don't know how or why she ended up here in Corfu, nor do I have anyone to ask.'

'I know that Liz sold up and left California when Greg died ten years ago. She wanted to make a new start, so she bought the villa from an Athens businessman who in turn had bought the building from my grandfather thirty years ago for a pittance, and then renovated it into a luxury holiday home, which he used a couple of times a year until he sold it to Liz. You should talk to Sofia about your aunt; the two of them were good friends so she'll likely know more.'

They had walked in a full circle and had arrived at a lawned area at the rear of the main house. A cherry tree and two ancient olive trees provided shade from the dying sun, but beyond them, the rest of the garden was a tangled mess. Stem upon stem of colourful entwined petals, and not just flowers and shrubs, there were herbs, too – rosemary, camomile, fennel, borage, marjoram, oregano and sage – providing a myriad of different fragrances to tantalise Abbie's nostrils.

Abbie didn't have to be a genius to realise that Nikos spent all of his time caring for the vines and therefore had nothing left over to give to the garden, and her fingers itched to dive in and explore, but before she could ask his permission, Nikos dropped down onto the grass and started to unzip his rucksack. To her absolute astonishment, he produced two real china plates embossed with the Angelopoulos estate logo, a set of knives and forks, and a fabric napkin each, and proceeded to open numerous boxes filled with slices of *spanakopita*, triangles of *tyropita*, home-made *tzatziki*, *kordalia*, and hummus, and a selection of salads and cheeses.

'Wow, this looks delicious.'

'Help yourself.'

'Thank you for doing this, Nikos.'

'No problem.'

Silence ensued as they both savoured the mouth-watering food. Abbie had always thought food tasted better when it was eaten al fresco, and she relished the taste of the zingy tomatoes, the crunchy cucumbers, the creamy feta drizzled in rich extra virgin olive oil and sprinkled with fresh oregano from the garden.

'Would you like a glass of wine?'

'Is it Angelopoulos wine?'

'It is, although I should warn you that it's not one of my father's. We only have half a dozen bottles of the wine he produced left and we are saving them for an extra-special occasion, although to be honest I have no idea what that might be.'

Abbie saw a complicated emotion flash across Nikos' face as he produced a bottle of red wine – sporting the now familiar Angelopoulos logo – from his rucksack, poured out two glasses, and handed one to Abbie to try.

'I'd like to know what you think.'

'Well, I'll tell you now that I'm no connoisseur. I'm more of a white-wine-kind-of-girl – with a generous splash of sparkling water and a handful of ice.'

She took a moment to inhale the aroma, detecting black cherries, green pepper, and a hint of vanilla, but when she tasted the wine, she was surprised to discover it had a rather harsh aftertaste. However, as Nikos had just told her that he'd been responsible for producing this wine and not his father, she didn't want to offend him, especially after his generous picnic gesture, and so she smiled and nodded her approval.

'Mmm, it's delicious. Thanks for doing all this, Nikos. When you ran me off the road—'

'I didn't run you off the road!'

'—I was on my way to throw myself on the mercy of Sofia for some provisions. As you probably know, there's nothing in the cupboards at the hotel, and I haven't had a chance to find out where the nearest village or town is let alone find a supermarket.'

'Okay, come on. A trip to the supermarket can be our next adventure. You know, it seems like there's a never-ending conveyor belt of tasks to accomplish with you around.'

Nikos jumped to his feet and held out his hand to pull Abbie upright, too. Without thinking, she took it and found herself stumbling forward into his arms, a wisp of his warm breath caressing her cheek and sending flashes of desire cascading through her body, followed by shock at the strength of her reaction to their proximity. She pulled away quickly, a gesture which caused Nikos to smirk in amusement, but she ignored him and began to make her way back to where he'd left the motorbike.

'Actually, do you think we could use the car?'

'Sure, just hang on while I'll get rid of the rucksack and find the keys.'

While Nikos was away, Abbie perched on the circular stone wall that surrounded the pond, and took the opportunity to study the house. She wondered who lived there with Nikos; a girlfriend? A fiancée? A wife? And if so, where were they? And would they mind that their partner was spending so much time in the company of the newest hotel owner in the area?

She was so distracted by the crystal-clear image of Nikos with his arm hooked around the shoulders of an attractive brunette, strolling through the streets of Corfu Town, that she didn't notice that he had returned and when he spoke to her, she jolted in surprise and, to her horror, tumbled backwards into the pond.

'Argh!'

Fortunately, the water wasn't deep, ten inches at the most, but it was filled with water lilies and the bottom was so slippery that when she tried to stand, she stumbled and fell in again, just in case there was any part of her that wasn't absolutely soaked to the skin. She heard laughter, and then a strong pair of arms reached over the wall to lift her out of the pond and set her on the ground where she stood, her arms out wide, her jaw loose, as droplets of water dripped from her hair, her chin, and the tips of her fingers. Her tee-shirt clung to the contours of her body, as did her linen trousers, and she was soaked through to her underwear.

'Gosh, you certainly like to keep a guy on his toes! Is this some kind of reality show? Are there cameras pointing at us at this very moment? I hope I'm through to the next round because, in the space of two days, I've saved you from hunger, drowning, a serious road traffic accident, and a burning building. Tell me, Abbie, what else do you have up your sleeve?' Nikos combed his fingers through his hair, making it stand in spikes, and then took pity on her. 'Come on, let's get you dried off.'

Unable to vocalise her thoughts, she followed him into the house and he pointed to a door at the end of a wide corridor where she found a downstairs cloakroom. She quickly towel-dried her hair, trying to smooth down the halo of curls, and reapplied her makeup. Fortunately, the air was still warm and her clothes were, if not dry, only slightly damp when she re-joined Nikos who was waiting for her on the terrace overlooking the untidy garden at the rear of the house.

'Thanks.'

'Still want to go over to the supermarket?'

'Of course.'

'Do you have any more calamities planned? Do I need to bring my bulletproof vest, or hire a suit of armour, or spray myself with bug-repellent?'

'Very funny.'

She saw Nikos' eyes twinkle with amusement. She sat on the seat opposite him, and for some reason she couldn't understand, experienced an overwhelming urge to explain to Nikos how out-of-character the incidents had been.

'I know you won't believe me, but until I arrived on this island, I led a very uneventful life. After my mum passed away five years ago, I made an extra-special effort to tread carefully, to avoid arguments and evade confrontations, and I was successful. The most excitement I had was a night in with my best friend, Emily, watching re-runs of cookery shows with a tub of ice cream and a plate of pâtisserie. Clearly, I've done something to anger the Greek gods because ever since I got here, I seem to have been battling one catastrophe after another, and I'm sorry you've been dragged into that.'

Nikos jumped up from where he'd been lounging in a deck chair, his foot hooked over his thigh, looking so handsome and polished – not to mention clean and dry – that he might have been about to stride down a catwalk.

'Come on, let's go shopping!'

Later, when she collapsed into bed, her brain rotating through all the things that had happened that day, she felt as though everything had happened to someone else, someone who preferred to live life outside her comfort zone, someone who looked for excitement and relished it.

However, the thing that surprised her most was the emotions that swirled through her body when she conjured up an image of the person who had come to her aid and whom she had shared these exploits with. The man with the brown spiky hair, the tanned and toned body, the mischievous smile, and the dark brooding eyes that couldn't conceal the shadow of sadness that lingered deep within and which he evidently thought no one noticed.

Chapter Nine

The Swimming Pool at the Hummingbird Hotel
Flower: Heart-Flowered Orchid

The following day, Abbie was up and about just as the sun poked its head above the horizon and cast its golden rays wide across the valley floor, melting the last of the mist clinging to the trunks of the olive trees. Even at that early hour, the air was warm and fragrant with jasmine, and as she stepped out into the courtyard with her mug of rich, dark Greek coffee, she felt a blanket of serenity descend.

For the first time since she'd made the move from her home in Devon to London, weighed down by the mantle of grief, her thoughts had calmed from swirling to composed, and so too had her body. It was only in that moment that she realised she had been carrying a heavy burden around with her for years, her muscles taut and tense under the strain, her head crammed to the brim with everything she had to deal with. She had loved working at *FlowerEssence*, but it was hard work, with lots of early starts and late finishes, and whilst there were many satisfied clients, like every other business there were also disgruntled customers for whom even her most creative floral architecture would never be enough.

Now that circumstances had forced her to take a break, the tension in her neck had abated, her appetite was back with a vengeance – she'd just had three, yes, three croissants for breakfast – and when she'd stepped from the shower and looked in the mirror, she had been delighted to see her skin possessed a healthy, sun-kissed glow.

Her visit to Corfu hadn't only improved her physical well-being, but also her emotional well-being. Without trying too hard, she'd gained some perspective on her relationship with Dan, and she could understand what Emily had been trying to tell her before she dashed to their rendezvous at the Sky Garden. Dan had rarely, if ever, acknowledged her flair for all-things floral and it was true that he'd taken the credit wherever possible. Awards and accolades had never been her thing, but a simple thank you would have been nice – she had been his girlfriend, after all, didn't that mean he should have been happy to sing her praises to anyone who asked, to boost her confidence, which was low even at the best of times, at any opportunity?

She finished her coffee, rinsed the mug in the sink, and her heart gave a nip of excitement. She planned on spending the morning on one of her favourite pastimes;

getting up close and personal with the climbing plants and flowers that decorated the pergola, trying not to be too jealous of the wonderful – albeit unkempt – garden over at the Angelopoulos estate.

With a trowel, an old bamboo basket, and a pair of gardening gloves, Abbie got stuck in, starting with the terracotta pots surrounding the fountain, enjoying the faint tinkle of water and marvelling at the kaleidoscope of colour on show; red, white and pink geraniums, dark purple irises, a profusion of chamomile and lavender, and a whole host of different orchids – the bumble bee orchid, the horse shoe orchid, the pink butterfly orchid, the heart-flowered orchid – and some so rare she had to google them.

As the sun gained strength, perspiration prickled at her temples. She tried to brush her curls away from her eyes with the back of her hand, only to have them fall straight back again. She put down her trowel, removed her gloves, and sauntered through the stone archway towards the swimming pool terrace, its rippling turquoise water so inviting in the midday heat.

A picture of Felix emerging from its depths made her smile, and she suddenly decided to throw caution to the wind. She stripped off to her underwear and launched in with a splash, shrieking out loud as the cold water hit her body, then pounded through several lengths before swimming to the shallow end and simply floating on her back, her arms and legs outstretched, her eyes closed, her face turned towards the sun.

Bliss, pure bliss.

'Hey, don't you have guests arriving tomorrow?'

'What—'

She quickly slipped under the water to hide from her unexpected visitor. Typical! She should have guessed that if she put herself in the embarrassing situation of swimming in her underwear, Nikos wouldn't be too far away.

There was no way she was going to climb out of the pool in her bra and knickers, so she fixed him with a stubborn stare that made him laugh out loud, a wonderful deep, rich, infectious sound that almost had her joining in – almost, but not quite.

'Would you like me to fetch you a towel?'

'Yes, please, that would be great.'

She waited until Nikos had disappeared through the stone arch and quickly clambered out of the pool, pulling on her white cotton tee-shirt and navy-blue shorts, knowing they would be dry in no time. She decided to show no embarrassment at her decision to take an impromptu dip because she knew Nikos would love it if she did, and instead of waiting for him to return, she made her way back to the hotel to meet him.

'Oh, here you are.'

'Thank you.' She took the towel from him, ignoring the smirk on his lips, dried her hair and scooped it behind her ears out of the way. 'Want a coffee?'

'Does that entail lighting the stove?'

'No, it does not. I can assure you that I've now mastered the coffee machine.'

'Then I'd love one, but, as this is your last day of freedom before your guests arrive, I came over here to invite you on an expedition.'

'What kind of expedition?'

Abbie removed a couple of mugs from the kitchen cupboard and fixed them a coffee each, closing her eyes briefly to inhale the freshly ground coffee beans, an aroma that never failed to lift her spirits no matter what life had thrown at her. She handed Nikos his coffee, surprised at the spasm of electricity that shot through her veins when their hands touched, and led him outside to the veranda where they could enjoy their drinks in the shade.

'So, I've just been speaking to Sofia and she told me that you'd shown an interest in spending a few hours hiking in the mountains.'

'Hiking in the mountains?' she laughed. 'No, I definitely did *not* say that, but I'd love a stroll through the countryside and the woodlands around here.'

'Great, I know a place over on the west coast, well away from the tourist trail, with the most spectacular view out to sea. So, come on – and you might want to grab your camera.'

'Now?'

'No time like the present. Why? Are you busy?'

'No, well, not until later.' Nikos raised his eyebrows in enquiry, and she really wished she didn't have to say her next sentence. 'I have an appointment at six o'clock with Alex Stephanopoulos in Corfu Town.'

She saw his lips twitch at the corners, and she braced herself for another of his snippy comments about her decision to sell the hotel to the highest bidder, but, thankfully, for once he decided to keep his own counsel.

'Sofia also asked me to give you a message.'

'What message?'

'Unfortunately, Panos' brother can't find anyone to help with the catering for your guests, so she's offered to come over to the hotel and cook their dinner on their first night here, then you could perhaps ask them to make reservations of their own at a local taverna of their choosing.'

'Oh, that's so kind of her.'

Her conversation with Felix and Sofia the previous day came flooding back, about Nikos himself being a Cordon Bleu trained chef, but so far, for whatever reason, he'd chosen not to disclose that piece of information, so she decided not to mention it either. She couldn't work him out; one minute he was grouchy and irritable with her, the next he was going out of his way to help her – and not just with the hotel, he seemed to have taken on the task of personal tour guide, too.

'Okay, so, grab your things. We need to make the most of your last day a freedom before you step into the role of the new chatelaine of the Hummingbird Hotel!'

'Do you have the car or the motorbike?'

'The motorbike.'

'Oh I—'

'Don't worry, I'll drive slowly, *yiayia*.'

Abbie sighed and, against her better judgement, decided to go with it. She collected a bottle of water, slipped it into her satchel, and followed Nikos down the hotel's front steps to where he'd left his motorbike, thanking the Greek god of modesty that she had chosen a pair of shorts that morning. This time she knew what to expect and, after clambering onto the back seat, she hooked her arms around Nikos' waist and they set off, grandma-style as promised, down the driveway.

Once on the open road, Abbie began to relax and take

in the scenery; a tapestry of greenness as far as the eye could see, embroidered with pretty white-washed villages, lemon groves and the jewel-blue of the occasional swimming pool. Everywhere she looked there was a profusion of flowers sprouting from a myriad of containers, from the usual ceramic pots and decorative planters to old-fashioned watering cans, hollowed out logs, and even kitchen colanders that had been painted in vibrant colours.

After ten minutes she came to the conclusion that she loved being on a motorbike; there was something so liberating, so joyously exhilarating about feeling the breeze rush across her body, and, as they neared their destination, delivering the gentle scent of the salty sea air to her nostrils. Nikos parked in the shade of a palm tree and pointed her towards a hidden pathway that snaked through an olive grove. After a mere fifty metres of hiking, they emerged from the foliage to face one of the most spectacular views Abbie had ever seen.

'Wow!'

She stared at the expanse of deep azure ocean stretched out in front of her, the horizon merging almost imperceptibly with the translucent sky with merely the occasional wispy white cloud scudding towards the east coast of Italy. Below her, down a narrow, dusty path was a picture postcard perfect cove with a pristine crescent of golden sand lapped gently by turquoise waves, and best of all it was completely deserted – no tourists, no tavernas, no bars, just the beauty of what nature had created.

'Come on.'

Nikos reached for her hand as though it was the most natural thing in the world, and together they zig-zagged their way down the hill to the beach and, still holding hands, strolled to the far side of the bay where Nikos pointed to a rock jutting from the cliff face, a place he had clearly lingered before. She sat next to him, staring out to sea where a luxury yacht had anchored, its passengers taking turns to dive or jump feet-first into the water, kitted out with snorkels and flippers.

'I come here when life gets complicated and I need a place to think,' said Nikos. 'There's something about watching the rhythmic undulations of the waves that calms the soul and reminds us that our problems are transitory.'

Abbie was surprised by the intensity of his statement and by the dark spectre of sadness that stalked across his eyes. Time seemed to stand still, a snapshot of paradise, and once again she felt that undeniable pull towards him, a sensation that they were kindred spirits who understood each other without having to say the words, that perhaps they had been soulmates in a previous life.

But then the spell was broken and Nikos' mood seemed to change, as though he suddenly regretted bringing her to his special place and admitting the fact that there were times when he needed to escape there. She wanted to reach out to him, to offer him her support, a listening ear so that he could confide in her about what had caused his sorrow.

'Do you miss working in Paris?'

Nikos gave her a puzzled look.

'Dimitris told me.'

He held her gaze for a long moment, and Abbie thought he was going to brush her enquiry away, but instead he averted his eyes to contemplate the antics of the yacht's owners who had now moved on to some kind of swimming race.

'I loved my time there, if that's what you're asking. The restaurant I worked at had two Michelin stars; it was a frenetic lifestyle, high-octane, high pressure, high stakes, high stress, but every day was different, and every minute was filled with an insatiable passion to create the most exquisite food for our discerning diners. It was theatre at its most immediate. But however much I enjoyed being a supporting actor in the culinary show, Paris can never compete with Corfu. How can I not want to be back here; there's beauty everywhere you look, don't you agree?'

His dark eyes bore into hers with the question.

'I can't stay here, Nikos. I understand that this is your home, where your family and friends are, but it isn't *my* home. Don't get me wrong, I would love to have what you have here, especially a garden as amazing as you have at the winery – even if it does need a bit of attention – but my home is Devon, the place where I grew up.'

'In a cottage with roses round the door?'

'Yes, I—'

'But you have it already – well, you have a hotel with pink bougainvillea around the door. Home is more than just somewhere we grew up, it's a place where people love us, and that can be anywhere in the world, and it could be here for you.'

Abbie stared at him, her emotions starting to churn. How could she explain to someone who knew nothing about her or what she had been through over the last five years – the grief of losing her mum, the pain of realising that she was now alone, cast adrift into the big scary world, with no one to steer her to safety when a storm hits, and how that fact had gnawed away at her confidence, resulting in an overreliance on her now ex-boyfriend which had sent him running for the hills? Even if she wanted to explain all that to Nikos, she didn't think she would be able to find the words without crumbling into tears, so instead she jumped to her feet.

'I think we should be getting back to the hotel.'

'Of course, don't want to be late for Alex, do you?'

The mention of her aunt's lawyer put a further dampener on things and conversation was minimal as they made their way back up the hill to where the motorbike was parked. The return journey was completed in silence and when Nikos dropped her at the steps of the hotel, he barely said goodbye before shooting off back down the driveway, scattering pebbles in his wake.

Chapter Ten

The Offices of Stephanopoulos & Florakis, Corfu Town.
Flower: Rat Tail Cactus

Abbie changed out of her dusty clothes, hopped in the shower, then stepped into the only dress she had brought with her – a lemon and white sundress with shoestring straps which she'd borrowed from Emily. She had just grabbed her white cotton cardigan when she heard a toot from the taxi that she'd booked to take her to Corfu Town and her meeting with Alex Stephanopoulos.

The journey didn't take long and as soon as the hustle and bustle of the island's main town came into view, the taxi screeched to an abrupt stop, so abrupt that she lurched forward in her seat with a cry of alarm. Did everyone in Corfu drive like a rally driver? The taxi driver grinned at her as she handed over the fare and offered her one of his business cards for the return journey.

'*Efharisto*,' she muttered, wishing she'd allocated some time to learn a few more Greek words and phrases.

She was a little early for her appointment so she took the opportunity to saunter through the labyrinthine streets, marvelling at the elegant architecture of the arched colonnades, the balconied buildings with burnt orange and ochre facades, the canopied corner cafés with spindly bistro tables and chairs drawing in holidaymakers in search of a coffee or a frappé, the shady courtyards resplendent with palm trees and colourful hanging baskets.

Scooters flew past her, just inches away, twisting and turning through the grid-locked traffic, their riders dicing with serious injury or death for want of a helmet, shopkeepers lingered at their doors to welcome in potential browsers, restaurants pumped out delicious aromas of garlic and freshly baked bread to entice early diners into their establishments, and stray cats and pigeons sought a tasty morsel for supper.

She would have loved to have been there with Nikos, listening to his insider comments about which restaurants were good, which to avoid, where to get the best coffee, and regretted the coolness between them as they'd parted earlier. When she'd left London, she had thought her visit to Corfu would be straightforward, that she would spend a couple of days sorting out her aunt's belongings, pay a visit to her lawyer, and then spend the rest of her time relaxing by the pool with a book or exploring the surrounding countryside, maybe heading to the taverna to enjoy a cocktail or two.

But that hadn't happened, and, if she was honest, the sun-bleached island had started to get under her skin. No, one of its *inhabitants* had started to get under her skin. Okay, so Nikos was handsome, attractive and had proved, several times, to be a lifesaver, but there was something different about him, something he was hiding from her. She gave a joyless laugh; Nikos was harbouring secrets and she was *desperate* to uncover hers.

Was she about to find answers?

Would her aunt's lawyer have a letter that would explain why she had left Abbie the Hummingbird Hotel? Or some other kind of document – like a will or a codicil – or even just some information about her past? Her heart hammered out a concerto of trepidation, along with a flutter of excitement.

At last, after asking two random strangers for directions, she managed to find the offices of Stephanopoulos & Florakis, which from the modern glass frontage looked as though it was doing very well. She climbed the flight of stone steps, smooth from years of visitors, and was greeted by a cheerful receptionist in sky-scrapper heels, and immediately offered a coffee which, to her surprise, arrived in a dainty Royal Doulton cup and saucer and was delicious.

As she sat in the waiting room, her nerves churned and she began to feel lightheaded. Even the impressive collection of pink-flowering rat tail cactus plants in shiny silver plant pots couldn't distract her, so she was relieved when a tall, broad-shouldered man with thick dark hair greying attractively at the temples, strode into the room bringing with him a waft of Aramis – which she recognised because it had been Dan's favourite cologne. His sharply cut business suit was clearly designer, as were his polished Italian leather loafers, and he oozed charisma, charm and confidence.

'Alex Stephanopoulos,' he announced in a deep gravelly voice, his strong Greek accent only adding to his attractiveness, his palm outstretched to welcome her. 'It's good to meet you in person at last, Abbie. Please, come through to my office.'

Abbie followed him down a narrow corridor lined with original watercolours of the island, which opened into a huge room that was as far removed from a lawyer's office as she could have anticipated, with floor-to-ceiling windows providing a view that would have travel journalists and bloggers drooling.

'It's a magnificent view, isn't it?'

'Breath-taking.'

She took in the higgledy-piggledy terracotta roofs, interspersed by the occasional splash of greenery, and then the glossy white boats and yachts bobbing in the marina beyond, set against the backdrop of shady mountains in the distance.

'Did you know that's Albania over there?'

'Really?'

She couldn't think of any words that would do the scene justice so she didn't try. 'You're so lucky to have all this to look at every day; it's inspirational.'

'I am, I am. Please, take a seat.'

Abbie wasn't in the least bit surprised to see her aunt's Greek lawyer had chosen to decorate his office in modern furnishings; his sleek glass desk held only a laptop and mobile phone, the walls displayed neat pen-and-ink illustrations, and there was a faint scent of wax polish mingled with coconut. There was none of the yellowing documents tied up with pink "lawyer's ribbon" or the ancient mahogany bookcases crammed with leather-bound tomes that the solicitor who had handled her mother's estate in Devon had surrounded himself with in his freezing-cold office.

'Permit me to start by saying how sorry I am for your loss. Your aunt was a well-respected and popular member of her community. She had a great many friends here who also mourn her passing.'

'Thank you.'

Alex reached into a drawer and removed a buff-coloured file from which he extracted a sheaf of papers and placed them on the desk in front of her.

'These documents pertain to the administration and distribution of your aunt's estate. I take it you've spoken to your aunt's lawyer in the UK and he's explained the process to you?'

'Yes, yes, I have, thank you.'

'So, if you are happy, I require your signature here, and here, and here, please.'

Alex handed her a heavy silver fountain pen that she suspected cost more than she earned in a month, and she scribbled her name on each of the documents, hoping that Mr Thompson himself had read them through on her behalf and not his not-quite-on-the-ball assistant.

'Do you have any questions?'

'Erm, yes, actually I do.' Abbie's heart gave a nip of trepidation. This was it. Could she be about to learn the secrets that had been plaguing her all of her life? 'Did she… did my aunt leave anything for me? I mean, like a letter or something?'

'I'm sorry, no she didn't. Elizabeth visited me only once to record her wishes and to ask that I inform her solicitors in

London when the time came.'

'So you don't have any information on why she left me the hotel, none at all?'

'All I know is that your aunt purchased the Hummingbird Hotel ten years ago using the funds from the sale of the vineyard and winery she and her late husband, Greg Harris, had owned in California.'

'Do you know why she sold the winery? Why she decided to come to Corfu?'

'Sadly, her husband passed away from cancer, and she couldn't face running the business on her own. It had been his dream to produce wine and, as I understand it, he was very successful. They had a good life there, I can assure you.'

'But no children.'

'No, I was led to believe it was something that saddened them both. You and your mother, Jennifer, were her only living relatives.'

'Who she had no contact with for the last twenty-eight years.'

'Yes, she mentioned there had been a family estrangement, but I'm afraid she didn't confide in me about the reasons.'

'And do you know why she chose to come here?'

Abbie saw Alex smile, his sharp eyes filled with sympathy, and she realised she was starting to sound desperate for even the tiniest morsel of information he was able to impart.

'I don't know the answer to your question, but what I *do* know is that she found a community here in Corfu that loved and supported her – a surrogate family, if you will – and she was very happy.' Alex shuffled the papers with her signature on, replaced them in their file, and then extracted another file from his drawer, this one a moss-green colour, removing another set of incomprehensible documents for her to look at. 'Okay, this is the paperwork relating to the sale of the Hummingbird Hotel. I've taken the liberty of speaking to a friend of mine who owns the real estate business next door, and he's not only happy to market the hotel on your behalf, but advised me that he could potentially already have an interested buyer lined up.'

Abbie's stomach performed a somersault of surprise.

'Really? Already? I thought it would take a while to sell. I mean, it's inland; there's no view of the sea and no beach within walking distance. It's not really a touristy place, more a place people can come if they want to escape from the stresses and strains of their normal, day-to-day life, a place of peace and tranquillity where guests can relax with a book and slow down, take a few moments to smell the roses…'

Oh God, what was she doing? She sounded like she was making a sales pitch!

'Which is exactly what makes the hotel appeal to certain buyers. I can assure you that Andreas will negotiate a fair price for you and you'll be able to leave Corfu next week, safe in the knowledge that everything is in hand, and you should have your inheritance within the next few months.'

Alex smiled and handed her his silver pen for a second time so she could confirm she was happy for the hotel to be placed on the market for sale, the reason she had come to Corfu in the first place.

She paused, the nib of the pen hovering over the dotted line with her name printed underneath. Why was she hesitating? Hadn't Alex just told her that she could return home, as planned, get on with sorting out her grenade-strewn life, and, hopefully, move forward sooner than she had thought?

'Do you have any details on who the interested buyer is or what he or she intends to do with the hotel?'

Alex stared at her in surprise, clearly confused at her question and her obvious hesitation over signing the documents. 'No, I'm afraid I don't.'

Abbie swallowed down hard on her swirling emotions, her heart now hammering so hard against her ribcage that she was finding it difficult to breath. She placed the expensive silver pen down on the desk next to the paperwork and met Alex's gaze.

'Actually, there are a couple of questions I'd like to talk to Mr Thompson about, and I think I might have a chat with the estate agent you've recommended before I sign anything, just to make absolutely sure I've got everything covered.' She knew she was prevaricating and she had no idea why, but it felt right so she continued. 'I didn't know my aunt, but I do know she loved the Hummingbird Hotel; it was more than just a collection of buildings and a tiny vineyard to her, it was the people, the community, and the visitors who stayed there who came back year after year. I've only been here for a few days but I already feel more relaxed than I ever have; the Hummingbird Hotel is like a little oasis of serenity.'

She realised that Alex was staring at her as though she was crazy and she suddenly felt the need to get out of the elegant office with the view to die for as quickly as possible.

'Anyway, thanks for all your help and advice. If it's okay with you, I'll give you a call when I've spoken to Andreas.'

She jumped up from her chair and all but dashed from the room, through the reception area and out into the street beyond where she immediately spotted the offices of the Corfu Town estate agent that Alex had referred to. It was obviously just as successful as Alex's legal practise because the storefront was also stylish and classy, the huge window showcasing the properties for sale on hi-tec screens instead of the more usual A4 laminated posters. She crossed the street, only just avoiding a run-in with a speeding Vespa, and was about to push open the door when she paused.

What was she going to say?

Despite her reaction in the lawyer's office, she still wanted to sell the hotel… didn't she? She couldn't see that there was any other option – there was no way she was going to move to Corfu and become a hotelier and occasional retreat host. But what about employing someone to run the hotel on her behalf? Could that be an option? But she knew that wouldn't really work – she would be forever worrying about the business and the admin side of things like dealing with all the licenses, the insurances, the accounts, and the difficulties of doing something like that from a distance.

No, whichever way she looked at it, selling the hotel was the most sensible solution.

She stepped inside the office and was greeted warmly by a man who could have been Alex's brother, wearing a pair of smart navy-blue shorts, a white Ralph Lauren polo shirt and the biggest, heaviest gold Rolex she had ever seen. For some reason, she imagined him on one of the sleek, white yachts in the marina, drinking a cocktail with an umbrella in it, flashing his business card and talking up the real estate opportunities on offer on Corfu and the adjacent islands.

'Andreas Savas. Can I help you?'

'Hello, I'm Abbie Coleman. I've just come from a

meeting with Alex Stephanopoulos and he recommended I engage your services to market my aunt's hotel.'

'Ah, yes, of course, the Hummingbird Hotel over in Ropa Valley. I'd be delighted to help you in any way I can. In fact, I don't know if Alex mentioned this to you, but I do already have someone who's expressed very serious interest in the property.'

A wriggle of irritation wound its way through Abbie's stomach. She knew she was being unreasonable, but for some reason it annoyed her that Alex and Andreas had immediately assumed she would sell the hotel without bothering to check with her first, and that Andreas had even gone on to locate a potential buyer. She watched Andreas reach for his brand-new top-of-the-range mobile phone and start scrolling through his emails, before fixing her with his best customer-service smile.

'Mr Konstantinou has indicated that he would be prepared to pay market value for the building and the land attached.'

'What does that mean?'

'That he's not interested in the business side of things, so I'm afraid that wouldn't be taken into consideration in the valuation, or the price negotiated.'

'Why not?'

'I assume it's because he doesn't want to run it as a hotel, at least in its current form.'

Abbie took a moment to assimilate exactly what Andreas was telling her.

'Then what does he want to do with it?'

'I don't know; perhaps use it as a home for his family.'

The estate agent smiled at her, but Abbie knew he was

fudging the issue, telling her what he thought she wanted to hear in order to achieve a quick sale and collect his no-doubt hefty commission for minimal effort.

'A second home?'

'Again, I don't know, but rest assured, I will negotiate a really good deal for you.'

'It's not about the…'

She had been about to say that it wasn't about the money, that that side of things hadn't even entered her mind, but now that the estate agent had mentioned it, she realised that had been what everyone else she'd met since arriving in Corfu had been thinking; that all she was interested in was sorting things out as quickly as possible so that she could take her inheritance and run. She suddenly felt lightheaded, embarrassed that was what people thought of her. However, she had to admit, when she looked at things objectively, that was exactly what her actions had suggested and heat suffused her cheeks.

'I'm sorry, I just need some time to…'

'Of course, I understand. Here's my business card. In the meantime, I'll contact Mr Konstantinou and pin down a ballpark figure so you know what you're dealing with, and then I'll give you a call, okay?'

'Okay.'

Abbie experienced an overwhelming urge to leave the neon-bright office and inhale some fresh air. She mumbled her thanks and stumbled out to the street, oblivious to the swarm of tourists, her thoughts colliding until she was well and truly lost in the maze of narrow shady alleyways strung with telephone and electricity wires, as well as washing lines. She spotted a tiny café, sandwiched between a gift shop and a newsagent's, and sank down into a chair and ordered a drink, waiting for her heartrate to return to normal so she could calmly, and as dispassionately as possible, re-examine everything that had happened in the last hour.

She had never felt more confused.

On the one hand, surely she should be delighted that all the formalities had been dealt with so professionally and efficiently. It meant that after the weekend guests had left, she could pack up her suitcase and head for home.

But when she thought of someone else living in her aunt's beloved hotel, either as a second home or something else, she found she baulked at the thought. And then something else occurred to her. What if the new buyer wanted to change the hotel? To rip up the vines her aunt had lovingly tended, or build an ugly extension, or knock the whole place down to build a luxury resort?

With a sudden rush of clarity, she realised that these were the things that Nikos and Sofia were worried about; that any expansion to the hotel and its guest annex would have an adverse impact on the area, especially on Nikos and his vineyard. No wonder he had been unable to keep his feelings to himself over the last few days whenever the conversation strayed into the territory of her selling up and high-tailing it back to the UK as quickly as she could.

But none of this was her fault. She couldn't be held responsible for what a future owner did to the hotel; that wasn't fair.

Abbie finished her coffee and ordered another, and then, as dusk descended, transforming the ancient buildings' facades from butter-yellow to rich gold, the streets filled with a throng of residents and holidaymakers alike, every one of them in search of sustenance. She decided to treat herself to dinner. She studied the menu, all the dishes tantalisingly exotic, and finally settled on moussaka and a Greek salad with a side order of minty tzatziki and a glass of white wine.

As she ate, her emotions settled and she realised that unless she wanted to view her sanity in the review mirror, she had to concentrate on one thing at a time. She had four guests arriving the next day in search of an escape from their hectic lives, and she intended to ensure they experienced the same delicious home-cooked food, fantastic choice of locally produced wine, and haven of tranquillity her aunt would have provided had she been around to do so.

Chapter Eleven

The Lobby at the Hummingbird Hotel
Flower: Scarlet Hibiscus

'Hello everyone, welcome to the Hummingbird Hotel!'

Abbie smiled at the four surprisingly immaculate holidaymakers standing in front of her on the driveway, clutching their suitcases – also pristine and obviously expensive – as they took in the place that would be their home for the next three nights. She thought back to when she'd arrived only a few days earlier, heartbroken, dishevelled and exhausted, wearing crumpled jeans and a past-its-best grey hoodie, her hair – as always – like candy floss on steroids. Her guests, on the other hand, looked like they were on their way to a royal garden party, or a film première in Cannes, sporting designer sunglasses and brightly coloured summer attire with immaculately styled hair – although, the latter wasn't a surprise as three out of the four of them worked at a prestigious hair and beauty salon in Knightsbridge that catered for VIPs and celebrities.

'I'm Abbie Coleman, and I'm the… I'm the owner of the hotel.'

Wow, did those words sound weird!

'Pleased to meet you Abbie, I'm Savannah Cooper, the bride-to-be, and before we go any further, can I just say how sorry I am that Liz is no longer with us. She was an amazing person, and you must miss her dreadfully. We're very grateful that you have decided to continue her legacy.'

'You knew my aunt?'

A whoosh of surprise rushed through Abbie's veins as she gaped at Savannah, taking in her expertly applied makeup and her straight, white-blonde bob, superbly cut and styled with not a single strand of hair out of place. She automatically reached up to smooth down her own curls in a pointless attempt to look less unkempt.

'Yes, I was here eighteen months ago for a week of rest and relaxation after one of the most stressful catwalk shows I've ever had to deal with. What was supposed to be a fairy-tale grand finale of the most exquisite wedding gown and floral headpiece, turned into a nightmare after someone switched a bucket of confetti for a bucket of ice-cold water. The model's hair was completed ruined, and of course those were the photographs that appeared in the press the next day, attributed to Jazz Salon. Lots of our clients cancelled their appointments; it was a very difficult time, so I came over here and your aunt helped me to put the whole thing into perspective. There's a peacefulness here, an oasis of calm where real life and all its challenges feel like a million miles away. I wish I could have come back earlier, but life gets in the way of the best laid plans.'

Abbie's chest tightened with anxiety; she now felt even more pressure to deliver a faultlessly choreographed stay for the group who were all now staring at her expectantly. She shoved her apprehension into the dark recesses of her mind and inhaled a deep breath. She could do this!

'Okay, if you'd like to follow me, I'll get you checked in before I show you to your rooms so you can freshen up, or maybe take a swim in the pool before dinner.'

She led them into the lobby, smiling at the noisy clickety-clack of heels on the marble floor, and scooted behind the glass reception desk so she could process the paperwork that she'd found on the hotel's computer system. She experienced another jab of trepidation – she hoped she was doing everything correctly, the thought of incurring the wrath of the Greek hotel authorities made her feel quite queasy.

'Loving the cute passport cover, Liam!' Savannah laughed.

Abbie stared at the pink floral wallet – designer, of course – which, to her surprise and a twist of envy, matched Liam's suitcase. She glanced at the photograph in the passport, then at the guy standing in front of her, his skin flawless, his toffee-coloured quiff streaked with golden highlights, his eyes hidden behind a pair of trendy Ray-Bans. She wasn't sure whether he was wearing them to guard against the sun or to protect his eyes from the glare of his psychedelic Hawaiian shirt which he wore open almost to the navel to reveal a thick gold chain and smooth tanned chest.

He was clearly a man who took his appearance very seriously, but not as seriously as his choice of cologne, which was so eye-wateringly pungent it masked the delicate fragrance of the jasmine in the vase on the reception desk.

'Thank you, sweetie. It was a gift from Carlos, who, I might add, was *so* disappointed he couldn't join us.'

'Only because he's at a gallery opening in New York!'

Abbie smiled at the woman with the musical Scottish accent who had given Liam a friendly shove out of the way so she could hand Abbie her own passport. She glanced at the name on the back page to see that this was Savannah's best friend and chief bridesmaid, Bree Farrier, who, unlike Liam who looked like he'd stumbled into a rainbow, was dressed head-to-toe in white – white ankle-length sundress, white high-heeled sandals, multiple white bracelets jangling at her wrists, even a chunky white ring on one of her fingers – her copper-coloured curls completely under control.

'Thanks, Bree.'

Abbie handed back her passport and turned to the last, and clearly the youngest, member of the hen party; a petite willowy woman who clearly preferred a more natural, less highly polished look to the others, her long, wavy blonde hair loose and flowing, her face devoid of cosmetics apart from a slick of brown mascara and lip gloss. She wore a pretty chiffon top, short denim hotpants that displayed naturally tanned legs, and a pair of bejewelled flip-flops.

'Hi, Abbie, I'm Paige. I'm Savannah's receptionist, and this is my first trip abroad. I'm *so* excited to be here.'

'Well, I hope you enjoy your stay.'

'Paige, darling, you are so much more than a receptionist!' Savannah chastised, rolling her eyes with impatience, clearly having stated that fact many times before. 'Not only are you a superb gatekeeper, protecting us daily from the outrageous demands of some of our more challenging clients who insist on out-of-hours consultations and last-minute appointments, you are a cherished friend. Without you presiding over our diaries, I think Liam and I would dissolve into a twitching, trembling mess!'

'Totally!' Liam agreed, pulling Paige into a hug.

Over Liam's shoulder, Abbie saw Paige twist her lips slightly, but before she could dissect the meaning, Bree was calling to them from the French doors that led outside to the courtyard.

'Wow, guys, come and take a look at the view!'

'Oh my God, this place is absolutely darling! I definitely think I'm going to like it here!' Liam gushed before pointing to the colonnade on the left of the fountain. 'Are those our rooms?'

'Yes.' Abbie smiled, grabbing the suitcase Savannah had left abandoned at the entrance to the lobby and joining them in the courtyard.

'Oh my God, they're *soo* cute. I bagsie this one, sweeties!'

'Liam! Don't you think Savvie should get first choice? She paid for the trip and it is *her* hen weekend, after all!' said Bree, giving him a stern stare, which only served to make his smile brighter, delighted that he'd riled her.

'Bree, I don't mind which room I have,' said Savannah. 'I just want everyone to have *the* best time!'

'It's okay, all the rooms are exactly the same and they all

have amazing views over the Ropa Valley and the hills beyond.' Abbie laughed, especially when she saw the look of triumph Liam bestowed on Bree. 'And the swimming pool is through this stone archway over here.'

She guided the group through the pergola and a surge of gratification rushed through her veins when she saw the expressions of delight on their faces when they arrived at the pool, a mesmerising rectangle of aquamarine glistening in the late Friday afternoon sunshine, the blue and white upholstered sunloungers adding a sophisticated touch to the scene.

'It's stunning.'

'Feel free to take a dip whenever you like.'

'What time is dinner tonight, Abbie?'

'Eight o'clock, on the veranda at the rear of the hotel.'

'I can't wait to try some authentic Greek food,' said Liam, dropping down onto one of the sunloungers and stretching his arms above his head, his eyes closed, his face turned towards the sun. 'Hey, Savvie, remember when we were at that Tuscan cookery weekend in Florence last summer?'

'How can I forget? You fell in love with the Italian chef, what was his name?'

'Luca. He said I created the most exquisite *ricciarelli* he'd ever tasted.'

'Aren't they just biscuits?' Bree smirked as she perched on the sunlounger next to Liam.

'They're melt-in-the-mouth Italian delicacies, just like our tutor.'

'You have to agree with Liam, Bree, he *was* gorgeous.' Savannah smiled.

'Not as gorgeous as the Spanish guy who taught us how to make paella, and then gave us a free flamenco lesson afterwards. I can still feel the throb of his muscular body when he held me close to his chest and spun me around the room.' Bree wafted her hand at her cheeks.

'Well, if I had to pick my favourite, it would be the Parisian pâtisserie course we did last Christmas,' said Savannah, dropping down on the sunlounger next to Bree. 'Abbie, will you be preparing our dinner this evening?'

'Oh God, no way!' She laughed. 'No, I'm the world's worst cook, I'm afraid, so I've arranged for Sofia, a friend of my aunt's who owns the taverna at the end of the driveway, to provide the food for you this evening. She's making a selection of Greek meze dishes – tzatziki, *dolmades*, calamari, *keftedes* – which are meatballs – *spanakopita* – these gorgeous little triangles of flaky pastry filled with spinach and feta – so that you can try a little of everything and decide which you like the best.'

'I'm a useless cook, too,' said Paige, tossing her hair over her shoulder, the light penetrating through her flimsy blouse and making her look like a forest nymph who'd been given a weekend pass from the woodland kingdom for a visit to the Greek countryside.

'I have to admit, I'm better at mixing cocktails.' Bree laughed. 'And drinking them.'

'Oh, I'm so looking forward to spending the next few days just relaxing by the pool, in the sunshine, with a few glasses of ouzo, gossiping with my best friends in the whole world,' Savannah declared, reaching up to tuck her hair behind her ears and revealing a pair of daisy-shaped diamond studs that matched her necklace. 'We've got so much to catch up on; all the wedding stuff, *lots* of gossip from the salon, as well as checking out the local Greek guys.'

'Hey, don't let Enrique hear you say that!' said Liam, wagging his finger.

'Oh, he knows my heart totally belongs to him.' Savannah flashed her large emerald-and-diamond engagement ring, a broad grin on her face, her eyes filled with adoration for the man she was marrying at the end of the month. 'I can't wait to be his wife. I'm so disappointed he didn't organise his stag party here in Corfu. The guys could have hired a yacht and sailed around the islands; all this gorgeous scenery would have been so inspiring for his photography.'

Abbie thought she caught a glint of something strange in Bree's green eyes, but she couldn't put her finger on precisely what it was. She knew Liam and Paige worked with Savannah at her hair and beauty salon in Knightsbridge, but she wasn't sure what her best friend did.

'Do you work at the salon, too, Bree?'

'Oh, God, no, I—'

'Bree owns her own hair and beauty salon, too.' Savannah giggled, glancing at her best friend with affection. 'Her appointment book is even more jam-packed than mine and Liam's. You have to wait weeks and weeks to get an appointment with Bree herself, but believe me, it's worth waiting for – she's an absolute maestro at the new colouring techniques. But there's one advantage I have over her.'

'What's that?' asked Abbie.

'At least my clients don't bite me!'

'Bite you?'

The shadow that had stalked across Bree's eyes a few seconds earlier had now completely vanished and she laughed at the look of horror on Abbie's face.

'I run PoshPaws; it's a doggy beauty salon.'

'Ah, okay.' Abbie laughed.

'Bree's won lots of awards, too, just like Savvie and Liam,' Paige gushed, from where she was sitting on the edge of the pool, her feet dangling in the water. 'You should have seen the Labradoodle she did last week. Show Abbie the photographs, Bree.'

Delighted to be the focus of attention, Bree scrabbled around in her over-sized white leather handbag and produced her phone, scrolling through the images until she found the one that she was looking for, and then turned the screen towards Abbie.

Abbie just about managed not to do a double-take. She couldn't believe her eyes. She stared at the fluffy, snow-white Labradoodle with bright, cerise-pink ears wearing a matching collar of sparkling gemstones. She wasn't sure what to say.

'Wow.'

'Show her the starry sky one!' said Savannah, scooting onto the sun lounger next to Bree.

Abbie stared at the Bichon Frise, whose coat had been dyed a dark midnight-blue colour, liberally dotted with white star shapes and sporting a large round white circle which Abbie assumed was supposed to be the moon. She must have looked horrified because Bree was quick to explain.

'Don't worry, it's absolutely safe; the dye is specially manufactured for dogs. It's non-toxic, with no accelerants, no bleaches or peroxides, and it usually washes out after eight or so washes. I think this one is my favourite, though – this is Marlowe, he won best in class!'

'Oh my God, I loved Marlowe!' announced Liam, pushing himself from his sunbed so he could take a look, too. 'That photo has *the* most likes on my Instagram page.'

Abbie took in the poodle, its fur dyed pale blue, with a white cloud and a rainbow across his back. It was the weirdest thing she'd ever seen and she made a note to ask Emily – a passionate dog-lover – what she thought about it.

'Okay, I'll leave you to settle in. If there's anything I can get you – extra towels or pillows, or toiletries, then please don't hesitate to come and find me. See you on the veranda at eight.'

She left the group chattering by the pool and made her way back to the courtyard, wheeled the four suitcases to the doors of the guest rooms, and then went to the kitchen to fix herself a coffee, smiling when she heard cries of delight half an hour later as the group checked out their rooms.

When six o'clock arrived, she decided to make a start on preparing the veranda for dinner, setting the long scrubbed wooden table in the shade of an ancient olive tree with the Hummingbird Hotel's logo'ed china, silver cutlery and glassware, and making sure the white wine was chilling in the fridge, and the red wine was opened so it could breathe.

As she arranged a few sprigs of scarlet hibiscus in a blue ceramic vase for the table's centrepiece, there remained a hard nugget of stress lodged in her stomach. Even though this weekend was a one-off, she still wanted to deliver the calm, serene retreat that Savannah was hoping for. The group – with the exception of Paige – were clearly veterans of European jaunts and she didn't want to let them, or the Hummingbird Hotel, down. She also wanted to make sure they enjoyed the best cuisine that Corfu food had to offer.

She wasn't sure exactly what Sofia had planned for the buffet-style evening meal, but she knew everything would be delicious and, obviously, authentically Greek. Nikos had helped Abbie select decent wine from their supermarket trip, and had even donated a few bottles from the Angelopoulos estate, and she had bought a selection of soft drinks, fruit juices, and plenty of sparkling water.

With less than an hour to go until dinner, she dashed up to her room and hopped into the shower, revelling in the luxury of the Hummingbird Hotel's branded beauty products, hoping that the gorgeous, rose-fragranced conditioner would help to tame her hair into something bordering manageable. She then dusted a little bronzer on her cheeks, added a squirt of her favourite perfume, and stepped into Emily's lemon and white sundress, praying she wouldn't be letting the side down when it came to her appearance.

When she eventually returned to the kitchen and checked her mobile phone, her stomach began to churn when she saw she had several missed calls from Nikos. Before she had chance to listen to the voicemails he'd left, the phone started to buzz in her hand.

'Hi, Nikos, I—'

'Abbie, at last!'

She heard the panic in his voice and her heart sank.

'What's wrong?'

'I've been trying to call you for the last hour!'

'I'm sorry, I was just—'

'Listen, Sofia's had an accident, she—'

'Oh my God, is she okay? What happened?'

'She's fine, she's fine. She tripped over a kerb when she was shopping in Corfu Town and she's broken her ankle. She's in the hospital, in good spirits, but devastated that she can't help you out at the hotel tonight.'

'Oh, yes, of course, I…'

Abbie was torn. She was upset about Sofia's accident, and that she was probably in pain, but what was she going to do with four ravenous guests expecting food to rival that which they'd enjoyed on previous trips to Tuscany, Andalusia and Paris?

Oh God, why on earth had she thought she could do this?

Chapter Twelve

The Kitchen at the Hummingbird Hotel
Flower: Blue Delphiniums

'Abbie? Abbie? Are you still there?'

'Yes, I'm still here, but I've no idea what I'm going to do about dinner tonight.'

'That's why I'm calling.'

'What do you mean?'

'I'm on my way over.'

'You're—'

'I've just picked up the food from the taverna and I'll be with you in five minutes.'

'But what… Nikos, there's no way I can…'

But the line had gone dead and before she had the chance to fully process the conversation, she heard the crunch of tyres on the driveway, and rushed out to help Nikos carry plates, trays, platters, and Tupperware boxes of food into the kitchen. When everything was set out on the marble island unit, she paused to meet his eyes.

'Thank you, Nikos.'

'It's okay, but…'

'What?'

'Well, Sofia hasn't prepared any of the dishes.'

'What do you mean?

'These are just the ingredients.'

'Just… just the ingredients?'

'Yes, she planned to make the *dolmades*, the *spanakopita*, and the tzatziki this afternoon so that everything was fresh when she brought it over here for your guests.'

Abbie's stomach contracted painfully.

'But… it's ten minutes to eight. I don't know the first thing about Greek cookery – or any type of cookery, to be honest. There's absolutely no way I can have a meal ready for everyone by eight o'clock, or even midnight, for that matter!'

'And that's where I come in.'

She stared at him, taking in the upward curl of his lips as he held her gaze, the sparkle of mischief playing around his eyes, the delicious scent of his cologne that always seemed to set her senses alight, and she didn't know what to say.

'Nikos, that is so generous of you, but I'm sure, even with your training, you'll struggle to get a whole array of Greek meze prepared in ten minutes.'

'I agree.'

'So, I…'

'And I've had an idea.'

'You have?'

'Yes, and it's brilliant, even if I do say so myself.'

She smiled at the excitement on his face, despite her distress that she was about to be forced to admit to her guests that she was a totally incompetent hotelier who had been arrogant enough to think she could simply step into her aunt's shoes and pull off a relaxing weekend for a group of stressed-out professionals keen to spend a few days in the sun recharging their batteries.

'What's your idea?'

'That we turn the evening into an impromptu cookery class!'

Abbie gaped at him. The enthusiasm zinged from his body as he peeled off the lids of the boxes, tore the coverings from the platters, and lifted up a ceramic pot to sniff the contents – which clearly met with his approval.

'But, Nikos, this is a hen weekend, not a cookery school.'

'Do you have an alternative suggestion?'

'No, but I—'

'Okay, so we go with this, and anyway, it looks like the decision is out of your hands because your guests have just arrived.' Nikos pointed to the veranda where Savannah – dressed in a gorgeous crimson jumpsuit, her pale blonde hair so shiny it almost glowed – was busy regaling her friends with what was clearly a hilarious story. 'Why don't you take this dish of mixed olives and a bottle of white wine from the fridge, and go and welcome your guests to the most amazing experience of their lives? Go on, shoo!'

Abbie hesitated, anxiety whipping through her veins and every fibre in her body screaming at her to spin on her heels and run for the hills, to escape the calamity that had befallen her very first attempt to do something out of her comfort zone. But then, wasn't this misfortune of her own making? Why hadn't she just cancelled the booking? She could have asked for a loan from her bank and paid the money back when the small legacy her aunt had left her was released or the hotel was sold, leaving Savannah free to book somewhere more appropriate for her hen party celebrations.

She glanced at Nikos who was busy decanting myriad aromatic ingredients onto the counter top and her stomach growled in anticipation. She collected the bottle of white wine, dropped it in a silver ice bucket, then paused on the threshold between the kitchen and the veranda, taking in the glamorous group who had chosen to celebrate one of Savannah's last weekends of singlehood, not in the vibrant clubs and bars of Kavos, but at a quiet hotel in the middle of the Greek countryside. It was an unusual choice, but Savannah was a unique person who clearly worked extremely hard styling the wealthy of west London and had craved a few days of solitude before the full-on pandemonium that would be her wedding.

'Hey, Abbie darling, you look super-cute in that dress. Is it Stella McCartney?'

'Erm, no, I don't think so.'

Abbie's spirits lifted. She couldn't help but smile at Liam who had swapped his Hawaiian shirt for an even more outrageously colourful formal shirt with long pointed collars and turned-back cuffs, and a pair of stunningly cut black dress pants. His quiff had been restyled into a neat side parting and slicked back with plenty of product, and that evening's cologne was industrial-strength oriental spice.

However, her heart beat painfully in her chest as she prepared to deliver the news about their evening meal. She poured everyone a drink and waited for a pause in the animated conversation about the time Savannah had been asked to style a reality TV star.

'Erm, I hope you don't mind, but there's been a change of plan.'

'What kind of change of plan?' asked Bree, who'd chosen a stunning pair of wide-legged palazzo trousers and a figure-hugging tee-shirt, both in white to match her stilettos and chunky beaded necklace, and a hairband which enhanced her vivacious amber waves.

'Well…'

Abbie had been about to launch into a detailed explanation about Sofia and her unfortunate accident, and the fact that all they had for dinner was a bunch of raw ingredients, but to her surprise she experienced a burst of unexpected confidence. Maybe she could turn this disaster to her advantage.

'Okay, so I really wanted you to experience the taste and textures of authentic Greek food in a more… hands-on way, and at the same time have a little fun.'

'What do you mean?' asked Paige, a look of uncertainty appearing in her eyes as she sipped on her glass of white wine. Abbie had noticed she'd added a generous splash of sparkling water to her wine; she clearly wasn't as big a drinker as the rest of the group and with her long wavy hair and pale skin, in a pale-blue sundress with spaghetti straps, there was an ethereal quality about her that made her look a lot younger than her friends.

'I—'

'Okay everyone, ready to be entertained?'

Abbie glanced at the French doors where Nikos had appeared, so handsome with his carefully spiked chocolate-brown hair, sexy swathe of stubble across his jawline, and muscular biceps testing the fabric of his white collared shirt. If she hadn't known better, he could have been a movie star joining them for aperitifs on the veranda.

'Wow, who's that?' whispered Liam, running the tip of his tongue along his lower lip.

'Everyone, I'd like you to meet Nikos Angelopoulos; he owns the vineyard and winery next door and he's very kindly come to help with the activity we have planned for you tonight.'

'Oooo, what kind of activity?' She saw Liam's eyebrows rise and his lips twist into a mischievous smile. 'Whatever it is, you can count me in straightaway. Come on girls, let's not keep Nikos waiting!'

Liam grabbed a bottle of red wine from the table and all but sprinted towards the French doors, the three women following in his wake rolling their eyes and giggling at his reaction.

'Okay, if you'd like to take a place here…' Nikos pointed to where he'd set out six separate sets of ingredients on the kitchen's central island unit. 'I'll guide you through our impromptu Greek cookery class, and then you can eat what you've prepared.'

'Oh, how wonderful! What a fantastic idea!' Savannah smiled. 'Oh, oh, I've got to take lots a photographs for

Enrique – he's going to be *so* jealous that we get to immerse ourselves in everything Greek and delicious while he's spending his stag weekend in the rainy Cornish countryside riding quad bikes and launching himself down zip wires. Ergh, give me sunshine, a pool and a Mai Tai any day!'

'I love cookery classes!' declared Bree, taking her place next to Savannah at the bench top.

Liam, on the other hand, requisitioned the place nearest to Nikos – which caused Nikos to grin at his enthusiasm – whilst Paige hesitated, her eyes wide with trepidation. Abbie totally understood her reticence. She, too, was a little anxious at having to showcase her dire cooking talents in front of other people; she'd already proven she couldn't even make coffee without setting the place on fire.

'Paige, why don't you stand next to me? We can encourage each other.' When Paige took her place at the island, Abbie lowered her voice. 'Don't worry, you can't be as bad as me. I've been known to burn water!'

Paige laughed and Abbie was relieved to see her relax.

'Okay, so tonight you will experience the very best meze Corfu has to offer.'

'What's meze?' asked Liam.

'It's a selection of individual dishes, kind of like Spanish tapas. So, we will start with a particular favourite of mine, *dolmades* – which my grandmother used to call "little bites of heaven". This evening we will be making the vegetarian version. First, we take a vine leaf—'

'A *vine* leaf?'

'Yes, these have been pre-prepared, and so has the filling, which is comprised of rice, onions sautéed in olive oil, dill, parsley and the juice of two lemons. Okay, take a teaspoonful of the mixture and place it on your leaf like so, then fold the stem edge up over the filling, then both sides, and finally roll it up like a cigar, like this. Be careful not to roll too tightly or the rice will escape during cooking. Now it's your turn.'

Liam grimaced as he selected a vine leaf and placed it on the bench in front of him.

'It looks disgusting!'

'But you will soon discover that it is delicious!'

Nikos spent the next ten minutes walking around the group, offering advice on their *dolmades*-folding techniques which varied from proficient – Savannah and Bree – and passable – Liam and Paige – to inept – Abbie, who managed to drop her filling on the floor and spent the whole time wiping the tiles, her cheeks burning in embarrassment that she couldn't even handle a simple culinary task without making a mess, a fact that didn't go unnoticed by Nikos.

'Okay, great job everyone. Now we layer them in this pot and bake them in the oven while we turn to an easier recipe, one which I'm sure you will all be familiar with, but which I know you won't have made yourselves. Tzatziki.'

'Mmm, I love tzatziki!' Paige announced, at last exhibiting a spark of enthusiasm.

'Okay, so everyone has a dish and we will fill it with our own recipe. Perhaps you will prefer more chunky cucumber, or a little less garlic, or maybe a splash more lemon juice, it's your choice. We will eat it with our *dolmades*, some warm pitta bread and also Sofia's home-made hummus, chunks of grilled halloumi, *tiropita* and *spanakopita.*'

'What's spanky pita?'

Nikos laughed. '*Spanakopita* is spinach and feta pie made with filo pastry, and I promise you'll love it.'

While everyone created their own individual versions of tzatziki, Nikos rustled up a huge Greek salad with cubes of crumbly feta cheese and drizzled over a generous helping of extra virgin olive oil, then whizzed up a batch of rich creamy hummus. Conversation flowed, laughter burst forth regularly, and Greek music played in the background as the kitchen filled with delicious aromas from the baking *dolmades* and the *spanakopita*. Everyone was happy and relaxed, enjoying the camaraderie that sharing a cooking class engendered, as well as the opportunity to learn about a different country's national dishes.

'Okay, shall we eat?' Nikos finally asked.

A chorus of approval reverberated around the kitchen and everything was carried outside and placed in the middle of the table so everyone could share. As well as the recipes the group had prepared themselves, there was calamari marinated in ouzo and then fried, *taramosalata*, and *skordalia* dips, with Sofia's home-made meatballs and Panos' bread to soak up the fragrant juices, to which Nikos added an over-laden cheese board draped in a bunch of grapes. The sun had long since dipped below the horizon and the veranda was now washed in a golden glow from a collection of storm lanterns and garlands of solar fairy lights twisted around the branches of the olive tree. It was the perfect setting for Savannah and her friends' first meal in Corfu.

'*Kalí óreksi! Bon appétit!*'

The group fell on the food as though they hadn't eaten

for days.

'Wow, this is delicious, especially as we made it ourselves!' said Savannah, scooping up a generous portion of hummus with a slice of pita. 'And it all looks amazing, too. I've already had eight hundred Likes on my Instagram post – loads more than I got after spending over six hours creating that gem-encrusted beehive for Vanessa Carrington-Smythe last week.'

'You mean the VIP client you nabbed from me?' Liam asked.

'I didn't "nab" her from you, Liam. I just thought she deserved a little extra-special attention – she *was* on her way to the première of her most recent film. It was also the perfect opportunity to promote the salon to a wider audience.'

'And it had nothing to do with the fact that she's our best tipper?' Liam mumbled, his eyes darkening.

'So, Abbie, what did you do before coming over here to run your aunt's hotel?' asked Bree, clearly keen to divert the conversation from Savannah and Liam's professional bickering, even though her razor-sharp eyes were filled with curiosity.

'I worked as a florist at a small boutique called *FlowerEssence*.'

'Oh my God, really?' said Savannah, twisting round to face Abbie. 'Did you supply the flowers for Pierre Fontaine's catwalk show last month?'

'Yes, we did.'

'They were absolutely stunning, especially the floral chandelier you created with the bright blue delphiniums and yellow sunflowers. You are *so* talented.'

'Thanks.'

A squirm of discomfort wriggled through Abbie's abdomen. She had been about to go on to explain that it had been a team effort, *and* that she no longer worked at the boutique, but Savannah was still talking.

'I've already got my flowers sorted for my wedding, but would you be up for supplying Jazz with a few of your floral sculptures for our tenth anniversary celebrations in September? I'm always on the look-out for new ways to enhance our clients' experience, and fresh floral artwork is the perfect way to introduce more colour and fragrance to the salon. What do you think, Liam?'

Upon hearing his name, Liam reluctantly wrenched his gaze from where Nikos was in the process of pouring everyone a glass of ouzo to look at Savannah.

'Mmm?'

'Never mind.' Savannah laughed, shaking her head at her head stylist and the guy she had picked as her man-of-honour. 'Abbie, Nikos, on behalf of us all, I'd like to thank you for doing this for us this evening. You're right, the best way to learn about any local cuisine is by making it yourself, and I for one have had lots of fun. Would it be too much to ask if we could take another class, maybe on Sunday afternoon? Perhaps this time concentrating on sweet treats? Baclava is one of my all-time favourites.'

'Oh, yes please!' said Bree, rising her glass of ouzo to toast Savannah's idea and then downing it in one, gasping as the alcohol hit the back of her throat, then grimacing, before replenishing her glass with a second shot and repeating the process.

Abbie cast a glance at Nikos who was relaxing in his chair

at the head of the table with his ankle hooked over his thigh as he nursed a glass of red wine and watched the various interactions between the group. There was no way she could expect him to drop everything and become a freelance Greek culinary guru for the benefit of the Hummingbird Hotel's guests; he had his own business to run, and he'd done enough for her already.

'Oh, Savannah, no, I'm not sure we can—'

'Sounds like a great idea,' Nikos interrupted. 'How about I do *samsades*, *melopita*, and *melomakarona*, as well as baklava?'

'Mmm, they sound fantastic, thank you. Okay, Bree, I think we'd better call it a night before you slide under the table. Liam, will you take her other arm? Thank you, again, Abbie, this evening has been so much more than I expected. You've done your aunt proud. Come on, Paige, time for bed.'

Paige woke from her slumber in one of the upholstered rattan chairs, and scuttled off after Savannah, more like a lost puppy than a member of the group, and Abbie wondered why she had decided to tag along with the others, although as it *was* an all-expenses-paid trip she couldn't blame her. She watched them disappear towards the colonnade, their chatter growing ever more indistinct until the only sound floating on the midnight air was the indefectible cicadas chirping their eternal symphony.

'Fancy a coffee, Nikos?' Abbie met his gaze as she asked the question and saw amusement there.

'Shall I prime the fire extinguisher?'

'Very funny.'

She grabbed a pile of empty plates and made her way

to the kitchen, kicking off her shoes at the doorway and relishing the feel of the cool marble tiles beneath her feet. She'd only had one glass of wine with her meal and yet she felt more relaxed than she had for years, as though a blanket of calm had wrapped itself around her shoulders, insulating her from the trials and tribulations of running a hotel in Greece.

'Why don't you make the coffee, then, while I finish clearing up?'

After she'd collected the plates, loaded the dishwasher, wiped down the surfaces, and returned the kitchen to some semblance of normality, ready for breakfast the following morning, she found Nikos on the veranda, sitting in one of the rattan chairs, staring out at the panoramic landscape, now bathed in silvery moonlight. High above their heads, the sky twinkled with stars, and in that moment, as she inhaled the scent of baked earth and Nikos's lemony cologne, Abbie thought she had never experienced anywhere so beautiful.

'Magnificent, isn't it?' said Nikos.

'It is.'

They sat in contemplative silence, enjoying their coffee, until Nikos jumped up from his seat and held out his hand.

'Come on.'

She smiled and took his hand, surprised when he pulled her upwards, tucked her arm through his, and guided her down the steps of the veranda and into her aunt's vineyard.

'These grapes make great wine – your aunt certainly knew what she was doing.'

'I think she planted them as a reminder of her home in California.'

'Well, unlike your aunt, I'm not really an expert in the care of vines. Cookery has always been my passion, and my family were horrified when I told them I wanted to pursue a career as a chef and not a vintner.'

Abbie saw a complicated expression flash across Nikos's face, so she decided to steer their conversation in a different direction.

'Well, I for one am very grateful you did. I don't know what I would have done if you hadn't stepped into the breach this evening. I can't thank you enough, Nikos. Are you absolutely sure you want to give up your Sunday afternoon to deliver a masterclass in Greek desserts though?'

'I'm actually looking forward to promoting our wonderful pastries, although… Can I tell you a secret?'

Abbie paused at the end of a row of vines to meet Nikos's gaze, seeing his lips twitch mischievously as he waiting for her confirmation that he could confide in her. For a few magical moments, she felt as though time stood still, that there was no one else in the world apart from the two of them, standing in the moonlight amongst the vines.

'What sort of secret?'

'Promise not to repeat it to anyone?'

'Okay, I promise.'

'I prefer French pâtisserie.'

She laughed. 'Really?'

'It's sacrilegious, I know. After graduating from Le Cordon Bleu, I spent five years at a variety of hotels and restaurants in Paris learning how to create the most exquisite pâtisserie from some the best pâtissiers in the world, and I loved every single minute of it. It was a dream come true, and, if I'm honest, I miss it every single day.'

'So why did you come back to Corfu?'

A flash of raw agony shot across Nikos's face. Abbie realised in an instant that she'd inadvertently hit on a nerve and wished she could have taken back the question as soon as it left her lips. She saw him struggle to swallow down on the upsurge of emotion and her heart gave a squeeze of sympathy. She knew only too well how difficult it was to reply to certain questions without having a well-rehearsed response ready to trot out when the need arose.

'Sorry, Nikos, I shouldn't have asked you that.'

'No, it's okay, I—'

When he turned towards her, an unexpected sizzle of electricity coursed through her veins and radiated out to her extremities. She realised that if she leaned forward just a few centimetres, their lips would meet. The shock of the realisation forced her to take a quick step backwards and the moment was broken. However, when she met his eyes, she knew Nikos had experienced the same undeniable attraction and she saw the confusion dart across his face before his smile returned.

'Come on, it's late. We should call it a night.'

They meandered back to the marble steps at the front of the hotel where Nikos had parked his rust-blistered Peugeot, and Abbie smiled, wanting to make sure he knew how much she appreciated his help that evening.

'Nikos, again, I don't know how to thank—'

'No thanks are needed, Abbie. This is what we do for our friends in Corfu.'

'Okay, well, even so, I really appreciate it.'

So, she was his friend now? She hoped so. As he held her gaze for a few seconds longer than necessary, her stomach gave another lurch of attraction but she shoved it away. She'd only split from Dan a few weeks ago and had no intention of allowing romance to enter her life, particularly not of the Greek variety; that way heartbreak lay and she'd had enough of that to last her a lifetime.

She waved him off with a promise to meet him for a coffee at the taverna the following day, and meandered upstairs to her room, exhausted but filled with relief that she had, against the odds, performed the role of competent hotel owner. She had settled four guests into their spotlessly clean rooms in the courtyard, and, as far as she knew, with the help of Nikos, had served them a delicious smorgasbord of Greek delicacies without poisoning them.

She called that a win!

However, when she slipped beneath the cool cotton sheets and lay watching the flimsy voile curtains ripple in the breeze at the open window, the successful accomplishment of her first foray into the hotel business was not what was uppermost in her mind. Despite her determination to banish romance from her life, she couldn't help replaying that moment in the vineyard over and over in her mind, contemplating the scenario from all angles, trying to work out if she had been mistaken.

Had Nikos really been about to kiss her?

Chapter Thirteen

The Veranda at the Hummingbird Hotel
Flower: Morning Glory

When Abbie woke the next morning, the birds were already well into the second verse of their dawn chorus. She climbed out of bed, padded over to the window, and pushed back the shutters to take in the view of the sun rising above the hills to her left, drenching the whole valley in a shimmering, golden glow. It was early, just after seven; a low mist hung amongst the olive groves and vineyards like spun sugar, and the air held a fresh, crisp tang of a new day.

She jumped into the shower, took a few extra moments to smooth a generous dollop of the Hummingbird Hotel's rose-fragranced leave-in conditioner through her frizzy hair, then pulled it into a high pony tail. From her meagre wardrobe, she selected her white capri trousers, a red-and-white striped tee-shirt, and a pair of sand shoes with leather laces, then skipped down the stairs to sort out breakfast for her guests, humming a random tune as she gathered the china cups and saucers for the coffee, and set out two silver platters – one with fresh, sliced fruit, the other with a selection of pastries she'd bought from the supermarket the previous day.

When everything was done – all the worktops wiped and the washing up complete – she made herself a cappuccino and went to sit outside on the veranda to enjoy listening to the animals and the insects that called this part of the world home preparing for the day ahead. This was what she missed the most about living in London, amidst the urban sprawl – nature, not only the trees and the plants and the flowers and the shrubs, but also the birds, the squirrels, the hedgehogs, the bees, even the wasps, all of whom had visited the garden of her childhood on frequent occasions.

She also missed the snatched moments of solitude when she could slow down and reflect on the good, and not so good, things that were going on in her life, gain some perspective. She contemplated everything that had happened over the last month, and, to her surprise, a surge of accomplishment washed over her. If Emily had told her when she was on her way to meet Dan at the Sky Garden that in a few weeks' time she would be sitting on the veranda of a hotel in the Greek countryside, sipping coffee and marvelling at the view having scrubbed four guest rooms, sorted out the swimming pool area, and got to grips with a complicated computer system, she would have thought she was crazy. Add to that the fact that she had actually prepared a recipe – a Greek recipe at that! –

from scratch, and served it to a bunch of guests, albeit with the help of a Cordon Bleu-trained chef, she would have had serious doubts about Emily's sanity.

She suddenly experienced an overwhelming desire to hear her best friend's voice, so she took a few photographs of the spectacular sunrise over the Angelopoulos vineyard, texted them to Emily, and then dialled her number, smiling when a rather muffled voice answered her call – until she remembered the time difference between Greece and the UK was two hours.

'Hi Em!'

'Oh, hi Abbie. How are things with you over there in sunny Corfu? How's life as a luxury boutique hotel owner? Have you met any gorgeous guys yet?'

Abbie laughed; trust Emily to cut straight to the chase.

'Maybe.'

'What?!'

That got her attention; she was certainly wide awake now.

'Okay, Miss Coleman, dish the gossip to Auntie Em. I'm all ears!'

Abbie's spirits soared, just as they always did whenever she spent time with Emily, whether in person or chatting to her on the phone. No matter what life threw at her, she faced every challenge with a smile, a positive outlook, and faith in the future. The only fly in the ointment was the fact that she couldn't be honest with her parents about the change in direction of her dreams.

'Well, to answer your first two questions, life as a hotel owner is actually going really well, if you don't count the small matter of setting fire to the kitchen.'

'You set fire to the kitchen?'

'Well, I inadvertently filled it with smoke, but more importantly I've checked in four, yes *four*, new guests!'

'You have people staying?'

'Yes.'

'Real people?'

'Yes!' She laughed at the incredulous tone in her friend's voice. 'But that's not the most impressive part. Guess what I did last night?'

'What?'

'I helped to prepare dinner for them.'

'Was it Pot Noodles?'

'No.'

'Olive sandwiches?'

'No, we made a Greek meze, which is a variety of—'

'I know what a Greek meze is, Abs, what I *don't* understand is how on earth you managed to do that for a group of paying customers. Did they know what kind of risk they were taking? Did they sign the appropriate disclaimers? And are they still alive?'

'Well, I haven't actually seen them yet this morning…'

'Oh my God, don't you think you'd better go and check?' Emily giggled, the cheerful sound sending Abbie's mood even higher. 'Seriously, Abbie, what's going on? You can't cook, you *never* cook! How are you even… Ah, I get it.'

'What?'

'There's a guy involved, isn't there? What's his name?'

Abbie briefly thought of denying it, but she knew she'd never get away with it; Emily knew her too well.

'Nikos, his name is Nikos. He owns the vineyard and winery next door to the hotel.'

'Well, you didn't waste much time, did you?'

'He's just a friend, Em. Actually, I don't know what I would have done without him, to be honest. Not only did he sort out the kitchen when I thought I'd burnt the whole place down, he also came to the rescue last night when the chef I had organised to feed the guests unfortunately had an accident and broke her ankle. We only had the raw ingredients, which was why we decided to put on an impromptu cookery class featuring a whole load of Greek recipes. And do you know what? It was great fun.'

'So, what are your guests like?'

'It's actually a hen party.'

'A hen party? In the wilderness of Corfu?'

'We're not in the wilderness.' Abbie laughed, glancing at the white-washed houses scattered along the hillside, their pretty terracotta roofs peeking out from the vegetation. 'There's a taverna at the end of the driveway, a village with a supermarket and a couple more cafés two kilometres away, and a beach just a few kilometres after that.'

'It's not Kavos or Sidari though, is it?'

'No, it's definitely not a tourist hotspot, but that's not what Savannah wanted. She owns and runs a very busy, upmarket hair and beauty salon in Knightsbridge with lots of demanding clients, and she just wanted a relaxing break with a few friends before all the madness of her wedding activities started.'

'Well, it sounds amazing, I'm so jealous. So…'

Emily paused and Abbie knew immediately what she was going to say next and she braced herself for the effect the turn in their conversation would have on her. She knew they had to talk about it – how could they not – but already her stomach had started to churn, and her throat felt dry.

'… has Dan called you?'

'No, he hasn't.'

'Have you tried to call him?'

'To be honest it's been good to have some distance from him after what happened, take some time out to put everything into perspective—'

'And allow a gorgeous handsome Greek guy to act as a diversion?'

'No, I told you, we're just friends.'

'Send me a photo and I'll be the judge of that. What about the sale of the hotel? Have you had your appointment with the lawyer yet? Have you signed all the legal documentation to sort out your aunt's affairs?'

'I have, and apparently there's already a potential buyer. Andreas, that's the estate agent, told me he would send me the details as soon as he's spoken to the buyer and finalised a figure.'

'Does that mean you'll be coming home soon?'

'I hope so.'

'You can definitely count me in when you go searching for that little country cottage with the roses around the door. I'm so happy for you, that your dream is about to come true. Did you ask the lawyer whether your Aunt Liz left you a letter or anything?'

'I did, and she didn't, not with him anyway.'

'And have you made any progress in finding out why she and your mum fell out? Did Liz have any friends over there that you could ask?'

'Actually, she did. I've met a good friend of hers, Sofia Diakos.'

'And?'

'Well…'

'You haven't asked her?'

'No, it didn't feel like the right time.'

'It's never the right time, darling, but you need to do it anyway. It might be the one chance you have to find some answers. What about her personal belongings? Was there anything in there that might give you a clue?'

'I… I haven't actually been in her room yet.'

'You haven't? Oh, Abs, why not?'

She hesitated; she didn't have an answer to give Emily. Why *hadn't* she made a start on sorting out her aunt's things? Because it felt like an invasion of privacy? Because she'd been too busy with tasks around the hotel? Because she was scared of what she might find? Or because she was scared she wouldn't actually find anything, and all hope of finding out about her past would be extinguished forever? She didn't think she could bear that.

'Abbie, look, you need to do this. It's what you went over there for in the first place, isn't it? You can be respectful and considerate, but you do have to go through her belongings. You might find a letter in her desk, or in her dressing table drawer, or even better, a diary or a journal. You need to do a thorough search under the bed, on top of the wardrobe, behind the picture frames, and you'll find something, I know you will. I know you, Abs, if you don't do this, you'll regret it.'

'I know, I know, you're right.'

'Ever since I met you you've been agonising over what happened between your mum and her sister all those years ago, and why your Aunt Liz went off to California. This is your chance to understand, to uncover the secrets from almost thirty years ago, to find your place in the world. Don't lose it. Oh, I wish I could come over there and help you look.'

'Then why don't you?'

An uptick of excitement shot through Abbie's veins, and not only because she saw an opportunity to change the subject.

'How are things with you, anyway?'

'Ergh, I had a really late night last night. I met a couple of friends – Zack and Jocelyn, remember them? They're in the chorus line of Mamma Mia and they spent the whole time plying me with drink and trying to persuade me to accept the offer of a role as one of the village women.'

'Sounds fab.'

'That's what Mum said when I told her. She's already planning a trip down to London with a bit of shopping in Knightsbridge, afternoon tea at the Ritz, and a front row seat in the Grand Circle to watch their soon-to-be Oscar-nominated daughter in a West End show.'

'But you don't agree?'

'Abbie, you know I only take the parts I'm offered to make money for the rent. I feel really guilty after Mum and Dad indulged me in my desire to tread the boards instead of the court room, like they do, but that was before I discovered the amazing world of pastry. This is what I love… actually, not just love, I'm completely and utterly passionate about it. How will I ever be able to make them understand that? That my dream now is to go over to Paris and take a course in pâtisserie with a real

French pâtissier? They would have a coronary!'

'Oh my God, Emily, I've just had the most amazing idea.'

'You have?'

'Yes, yes, I have. Nikos trained as a chef in Paris – at Le Cordon Bleu – and then he worked for quite a few years with some of the best pâtissiers in Paris. Would you believe that he's actually agreed to run a Greek pâtisserie course for our guests tomorrow afternoon, here at the Hummingbird Hotel? Now, I know it's too short notice for tomorrow, but if you could wangle a few days off work in the next week, I'm sure he'd love to teach you a few techniques. He even confided in me that he preferred macarons and madeleines to baclava and *spanakopita*.'

'When you put it like that, it sounds amazing. I'll see what I can do. Okay, darling, I've got to go get ready for my shift. Say hi to Nikos for me… Hey, how do you say "I love you" in Greek?'

'I have no idea.'

'Perhaps you should start taking a few lessons, just in case.'

'There's no chance of that. Anyway, I'll be back in London at the end of next week.'

'Maybe, maybe not. *Yassou*, darling.'

'Bye, Em.'

Abbie always felt energised and elated after speaking to Emily and that morning was no exception. She knew how fortunate she was to have such a wonderful best friend, and she also knew she needed to take her advice.

So, she scribbled a quick note to her guests telling them to help themselves to breakfast, spent a few minutes raiding the flower pots in the courtyard and arranging a pretty posy of flowers, then grabbed her satchel and made her way down the driveway to the taverna to find out how Sofia was, and to, maybe, start what would be one of the most difficult conversations of her life.

Chapter Fourteen

Taverna Sofia, Ropa Valley
Flower: Orange Blossom

'Hey, Abbie, good to see you. Coffee?'

'I'd love one, thanks, Rachel. How's Sofia?'

'I haven't seen her yet this morning, but when she got home from the hospital last night, she was complaining loudly about Panos insisting that she took a break from the taverna. Apparently, if she did that they'd be out of business before the end of the month. It looks like he's managed to talk some sense into her, though, as she's usually down here ordering us around by eight o'clock and it's almost nine now. Take a seat, I'll bring your coffee over to the balcony.'

Abbie sauntered over to her favourite table and settled into her seat, her lips twisting into a smile when she glanced into the garden. Despite her aversion to real-life exercise classes, she couldn't seem to drag her eyes away from where Felix was performing a complicated yoga pose that involved his firm-as-steel buttocks jutting into the air. That morning's choice of attire was another pair of skin-tight psychedelic cycling shorts – green this time – and nothing else, giving her a gasp-inducing view of his muscular torso, bulging biceps, and firm thighs.

She was about to call over a cheery "hello" but decided it was probably best not to disturb him whilst he was "in the zone", especially as he was currently balancing only on his palms with his knees tucked into his armpits in what she knew was the "crane" pose. She barely noticed Rachel delivering her coffee whilst she focussed on Felix moving on to the next seemingly impossible pose, which involved a complicated handstand on his forearms with his feet dangling over his head. Even though she wasn't the one doing all the hard work, she felt a whoosh of relaxation waft over her.

'Oh, hi Abbie. I didn't see you there. Are you here for your yoga lesson?' Felix asked.

'No, I—'

'Great, pull up a mat and I'll talk you through a few of the easier poses.'

'It's okay, Felix, I'm…'

But within seconds he was standing next to her, his sun-kissed skin glistening with perspiration from his intense workout, running his fingers through his tousled curls so he could fix his piercing blue eyes on hers.

'Come on! Live in the moment.'

'I…'

Oh God! Why had she thought it was a good idea to

come to the taverna for a quiet coffee? Okay, so she had watched hundreds of exercise videos on YouTube – including yoga – with Emily whilst sitting on the sofa eating ice cream out of a tub, ogling the buff instructors and marvelling at the crazy positions they managed to twist their bodies into. She had even, after a few glasses of wine, joined Emily on the floor of their living room to make a half-hearted – and frankly hilarious – attempt at getting into one of the poses, always without success. But she'd *never* felt the urge to join a class alongside the body-beautiful devotees, and the thought of standing, sitting or lying next to Felix with her derrière in the air, filled her with dread.

However, it was clear that Felix was not going to take no for an answer. He dragged her out of her seat and led her from the balcony into the garden where there were four colourful yoga mats set out in the shade of the taverna's leafy orange tree. It looked like she was the only one who had turned up for the class that morning, which caused a nip of sympathy, so, against her better judgement, she decided the least she could do was give it a go.

'Felix, I have to warn you that I've never—'

'We must press restart every morning; it's only what we do today that truly matters.'

'Oh, I—'

'Okay, so, I brought the yellow mat for you, Abbie. I thought it matched your vibe, which I'm pleased to say is much more positive this morning than it was when I first met you.'

'You brought this mat for me? But how did you know that I—'

'I read your horoscope, of course.'

'Of course.'

'It said that you were going to enjoy a zen-filled start to the day with an Aussie Adonis, which would then morph into a dazzlingly vibrant afternoon.'

'A dazzlingly vibrant afternoon?'

'Yes, and something about being in the pink, too.'

'What does that mean?'

'Maybe you'll get to swim naked in the pool?'

Abbie spluttered with surprise and Felix grinned, knowing his comment had hit to spot.

'I really don't think—'

'Or maybe it's got something to do with that bunch of flowers you left on the table over there?'

'Oh, yes, right, yes, that's what it probably means. They're for Sofia.'

'That's a beautiful gesture, Abbie. We must always give freely with a gentle heart. Okay, first I want you to let go of all your worries and all your recent pain-filled experiences that can affect your equilibrium, and just—'

'Pain-filled experiences?'

Felix met her eyes, his smile sympathetic.

'The breakdown of your relationship.'

She stared at him. 'How did you know?'

'It's your vibe, man. I told you, it's off-kilter and that usually only means one thing – heartbreak. But, Abbie, allowing our thoughts to linger on a wrong is a burden to the mind; we have to toss our hurt into the wind and watch it fly away with the clouds, leaving us free to be at one with the universe.'

'Right.'

'So, first we'll start with a few easy warm-up exercises.

Watch me, and then follow when you feel ready.'

She watched Felix with increasing trepidation as he demonstrated the mountain pose, then the forward fold pose, followed by the plank. She knew all the names, knew *technically* how they should be performed, but the thought of actually *doing* them filled her with anxiety – which she was sure wasn't the response Felix was aiming for. Fighting the urge to grab her shoes and run, she inhaled a deep, invigorating breath and tried to copy his downward-facing dog.

'Push into your hands, and lift your hips up and back on the inhale. Like this.'

To her absolute horror, Felix stepped from his mat to hers, placed his hands on her waist and gently lifted her hips a little higher and straighter, his taut thighs straining against the Lycra as he guided her to the correct pose. She suddenly, inexplicably, felt the urge to giggle. How on earth had she got herself into this situation? What would Emily say when she told her she'd spent the morning taking a one-to-one yoga class with an Aussie enthusiast who looked like he'd just jumped from his surfboard, with an eloquent line in spiritual quotes, and an obsession with astrology?

She held the downward-facing dog pose for as long as she possibly could, until her muscles started to scream their objection, then she collapsed onto the mat breathing heavily and praying for the ground to open up and swallow her. She craned her neck over towards the taverna's balcony, relieved to see that it was still devoid of customers, grateful that at least she didn't have an audience to witness her humiliation. She had only done a few poses and already she was perspiring profusely, and she wondered how she could bring this fiasco to a conclusion quickly without hurting Felix's feelings.

'Felix, I don't think I'm cut out for this.'

But he was already helping her into the next pose, telling her to exhale and then release her knees to the floor, pull back her hips to her ankles, and rest her forehead on the mat, her arms stretched above her head.

'Remember what I said.'

Abbie closed her eyes and held the pose, sweat trickling down her temples and between her breasts. There was no way she could even contemplate answering Felix with anything other than a squeak.

'Which bit?'

'Acceptance of imperfection is the route to joy.'

'Well, I can do the first part, but I can't agree about the second. This is definitely not bringing me any joy. In fact, it's the opposite, it's bringing me pain.'

'Yoga is a lifelong pursuit, not a quick fix.'

She crumpled out of her pose and lay on her back, staring up at the translucent sky, gasping for air and a drink of ice-cold water, feeling as though she had just trekked across a desert, before catching sight of Rachel standing on the balcony, her face wreathed in a smile.

'Felix, give Abbie a break. Come on, I've got some home-made lemonade here.'

'Fab!'

Abbie scrambled up from the floor and made her way back to the balcony while Felix pulled on a jazzy aquamarine and yellow tee-shirt, tucked his curls behind his ears and sprinted past her to the table where he downed a glass of lemonade in one gulp, then dropped into a chair, stretching his arms above his head in a satisfied gesture. Abbie followed in his wake, her muscles sulking at the unscheduled early morning exercise.

Concerned that Felix might continue with his surprisingly accurate observations on her personal life, Abbie decided to switch the focus of their conversation over to him for a change, although she had no predictions for the way his day might turn out.

'So, Felix, tell me, how did you end up living above a taverna in the Corfu countryside, teaching yoga to exercise-phobes?'

'Things were crazy in Oz so I decided to opt for a simpler life.'

'What do you mean?'

'I worked as a hedge fund manager for an international bank in Sydney; the pressure was full-on, the hours were brutal, the stress levels were off-the-scale, relationships suffered.'

Abbie gaped in surprise. Felix was as far away from her idea of an investment banker as it was possible to get. For God's sake, the man was wearing *bright green Lycra*! 'You used to be a *banker*?'

'Yeah.'

'And you just decided to give it up? Walk away?'

'Tell Abbie what really happened,' Rachel interjected, dropping into the chair next to Felix and fixing him with a defiant glare.

'Rach…'

Rachel rolled her eyes. 'Tell her.'

'I don't think Abbie's interested in hearing about ancient history.'

'Oh, I am, I definitely am.'

'Felix!'

'Okay, okay.' It was the first time since Abbie had met Felix that he looked uncomfortable, and definitely not as zen-like as he probably would have liked. 'Like you, Abbie, I had a few… relationship difficulties before I came over here.'

'His fiancée left him standing at the altar,' Rachel added, evidently keen to get straight to the revelation. 'Must have been crazy, if you ask me, or blind, or both, maybe!'

'You know,' Felix mused, now reclining in his seat, his ankle resting on his thigh, his composure restored. 'I should have known that would happen. Neptune was in the house of Pisces on the morning of my wedding, which did not bode well, so I—'

'She ran off with your best friend, Felix. Surely the universe didn't engineer that!'

'Relax, Rach, it's all good.' Abbie could tell from the slight twist of his lips that it clearly wasn't and her heart ached with sympathy. 'I'm cool with it now. Anger poisons the soul so I've moved on, and I wish Carlie and Scott well in all of their endeavours together.'

Rachel took pity on him and reached out to give his hand a squeeze before jumping out of her chair when she saw Sofia had appeared on the balcony.

'Oh my God, Sofia, what are you doing here? The doctor told you to rest!'

'Rest? I don't rest.'

Abbie watched Sofia hobble towards them on her crutches, then slowly drop down onto a chair between Abbie and Felix, carefully raising her broken ankle –

bound in a huge black boot – onto a footstool before reclining with a soft groan of relief. Abbie knew straightaway that she had no intention of relinquishing her position as the chatelaine of her eponymous taverna and would probably continue to issue orders from her chair until she was mobile again.

Rachel began to fuss over Sofia until Sofia chastised her, and sent her off to fetch her a frappé and to check on Panos who apparently couldn't be trusted to prepare a couple of breakfast omelettes for the recently arrived customers sitting at the table nearest the bar – a task he had performed almost every day for the last twenty years.

'I brought you these, I thought they might cheer you up.' Abbie handed Sofia the posy of flowers she'd arranged that morning and was thrilled to see the delight on her new friend's face as she raised them to her nose to inhale the delicate fragrance of hibiscus and lavender.

'Thank you, Abbie.'

'How's your ankle?'

'It's fine. I just wish people would stop treating me like an invalid. I've broken my ankle before, and my arm, and my collar bone. What I want to say, however, is how sorry I am that I let you down last night.'

'Oh gosh, no, Sofia, you didn't let me down at all. In fact, things went really well. We had a sort of impromptu Greek cookery class; everyone had lots of fun, and the food was delicious. Well, apart from what I made – I'm the world's worst cook.'

'And I hear the evening did not end there.'

'What do you mean?'

'A moonlit walk amongst the grapevines?'

Heat flooded Abbie's cheeks as she met Sofia's gaze and saw the laughter in her eyes, along with smidgeon of triumph at her reaction.

'Really?' asked Felix, wrinkling his forehead at Abbie to check that it was true. 'Did you kiss?'

'No, we did not kiss!'

'Thought not; that was not written in your stars, not yesterday's at least.'

'Felix—' began Sofia.

'However, if I remember rightly, Sofia, your horoscope *did* predict your accident.'

'No it didn't. Felix, I don't know why you persist in reading that rubbish.'

'How can it be rubbish when it said that Scorpios would be taking an unexpected trip.'

'Because it's just not possible that one twelfth of the population tripped over a kerb and broke their ankle, is it?'

'How do you know?'

'My guru told me.'

'Did you know that gurus—'

'Felix, would you mind asking Rachel to bring my frappé over, please?'

'Sure.'

Felix unfolded his six-foot-four frame from the chair and glided across the balcony to where Rachel was chatting to Kostas at the bar, completely unflustered by Sofia's gentle dismissal of his beloved astrological predictions.

'Did Felix tell you that he used to help Liz out at the hotel with any odd jobs that needed doing?'

'Yes, he did.'

An image of Felix climbing out of the swimming pool on the day she had arrived at the Hummingbird Hotel floated across Abbie's vision, causing her to smile.

'Well, if you can think of anything that needs attending to, anything at all, the more time-consuming the better, then please, *please*, ask him to help, would you?'

'Of course.'

Abbie glanced over to the bar where Felix was now regaling Rachel and Kostas with one of his spiritual anecdotes causing a great deal of laughter. She then looked back at Sofia, suddenly remembering her conversation with Emily earlier that morning. She inhaled a breath, gathered her courage and met Sofia's eyes, but Sofia got there first.

'Did you talk to Nikos?'

'Talk to him? Yes, of course—'

'I mean about his… past?'

'What about his past?'

'Sorry, I just thought he might have… perhaps when the opportunity next arises, you could ask him to tell you about why he came back to Corfu, after so many years in Paris. I know it will be good for him to talk to someone who knows nothing of what happened, someone whom I know will listen with empathy and compassion.'

'What do you mean?'

But she could see that Sofia wouldn't be budged any further, so, now that the issue of the past had been broached, she decided to press her on a subject closer to home.

'Sofia, do you mind if I ask you about Aunt Liz?'

'What would you like to know?'

'Well, why she ended up here in Corfu, for a start.'

Sofia hesitated, clearly considering the question and how much she could, or should, reveal to Abbie, and her hazel eyes softened.

'Liz came here a couple of months after her husband Greg passed away. As you already know, she didn't have any children, or any other family apart from you and your mum. She loved Greg so very much; his loss affected her greatly, and she couldn't continue running the vineyard and winery in California without him. Everywhere reminded her of him. She didn't want to go back to the UK so, when the place was sold, she used the money to buy the hotel, which she named the Hummingbird Hotel because that's what the business over in California was called – Hummingbird Valley Wines.

'Did she…' Abbie swallowed down hard. 'Did she say why she didn't want to go back home to Devon?'

Once again, Sofia hesitated and this time she looked a little uncomfortable.

'Yes, she—'

'Your coffees!' announced Felix, to Sofia's evident relief.

The moment had passed, but at least Abbie knew there was a great deal more to tell, and she was determined – after her guests had left – to invite Sofia over to the hotel and to spend as much time as it took to find out the whole story. She took a sip of the frothy cappuccino, then she glanced at her watch.

'Oh my God, it's ten o'clock! I'd better get back to the hotel.'

She hugged Sofia, waved goodbye to Felix, and Rachel – who was still sitting on a stool at the end of the bar, her chin resting in her palm as she watched Kostas prepare his bar for the day, and completely ignoring the table of newly arrived customers trying in vain to catch her attention – and meandered down the driveway towards the hotel, her heart skipping a beat when the building, so pretty adorned in the flounce of pink bougainvillea, came into view.

She couldn't believe that so far, against all of her expectations, everything was going according to plan; she had met with her aunt's lawyer, spoken to an estate agent, and made a little progress in unravelling the secrets her aunt had been keeping, and she had barely thought of Dan and their devastating break-up. However, the best thing of all was that she had successfully welcomed four visitors to the Hummingbird Hotel, who were happy and settled in their guest rooms, enjoying a relaxing break from the treadmill of life.

Chapter Fifteen

The Swimming Pool at the Hummingbird Hotel.
Flower: Tickled Pink Dianthus

Surprised to find that no one had ventured into the kitchen for breakfast, Abbie decided to go and see if any of her guests had surfaced from their beds. She'd only got as far as the courtyard when she heard squeals of laughter coming from the direction of the swimming pool so she made her way through the stone archway, pausing briefly to break off a stalk of lavender and tuck it behind her ear, its woody aroma boosting her mood instantly.

Everywhere she looked nature showcased its finest flora and fauna, and once again she felt the familiar urge to don her gardening gloves and get her hands dirty. She sighed; her mum would have loved it there. She had adored her own garden in Devon, spending every spare moment she had, when she wasn't teaching primary school children how to read and write, tending to the flowers and plants she had nurtured from seed.

What would she have thought of this tropical paradise? The pink bougainvillea, the fragrant jasmine, the fluffy lemon hollyhocks, the spiky palm trees, the exotic herbs in the terracotta pots? She likely would have loved to have spent time here at the Hummingbird Hotel pottering amongst the colourful geraniums, marvelling at the mini-vineyard. A rush of sadness washed over Abbie as she wondered, yet again, what had happened between the two sisters that had caused them to be estranged for so long. Her mum had still been alive when her aunt bought the hotel ten years ago, and they could have spent a whole five years getting to know each other, supporting each other first through the loss of Liz's husband, and then her mum's diagnosis.

'Hey, Abbie, are you going to join us?' called Bree from where she perched on her tiptoes at the edge of the swimming pool – modelling a miniscule white bikini – her arms raised high in the air as she dove into the water with the minimum of splash. 'Whoa, it's gorgeous in here! Come on, Paige!' she said after surfacing.

'Coming!'

Paige abandoned the glossy fashion magazine she had been reading, tossed her sunhat – more like an over-sized sombrero – onto the table, and pushed herself up from her sunlounger. She took a moment to adjust her pretty pink swimsuit with frills around the hips and waist, twist her hair into a high ponytail and secure it with a band. Then, with a shriek of joyous exhilaration, she launched herself into the pool feet-first and swam over to join Bree where they engaged in a brief water fight before wading to the shallow end and relaxing on the pool steps, their toes floating in the surface of the water, their heads tipped towards the sun.

'Liam! What are you doing? Come on!' Bree called.

'I'm not really a swimming-pool-sort-of-guy, sweetie, you know that. You have no idea what the chlorine does to someone with sensitive skin like mine, not to mention their freshly tinted butterscotch hair.'

'Then just come and dangle your feet over the side,' Paige suggested.

Liam rolled his eyes and reluctantly left his sunbed, gifting Abbie with a front row view of eye-scorchingly satsuma swim-shorts that made her grateful she was wearing her sunglasses. That morning Liam had chosen to showcase yet another hairstyle – this one more like something from the closet of Madam Pompadour. Trying not to giggle, she kicked off her sandals and went to sit with him on the side of the pool next to the girls who clearly didn't have the same objection to pool chemicals.

'So, what do you guys have planned for the day?'

'We're taking a trip over to Corfu Town for a bit of retail therapy,' said Bree, her Scottish accent not as pronounced as it had been the previous evening after she had consumed an excess of white wine and ouzo. 'Want to come?'

'Oh, I—'

'Oh, yes, please come with us, Abbie,' urged Paige, flipping over onto her stomach so she could face Abbie. 'You can be our tour guide!'

Abbie laughed. 'I wouldn't make a very good tour guide, I'm afraid. I've only been in Corfu for a week and I've not had chance to explore the area, or visit any of the tourist sites.'

'All the more reason to come with us. We can explore together,' Bree said.

'Oh, oh, I've had a fabulous idea,' Liam declared, his eyes flashing with sudden excitement. 'Why don't you give your boyfriend a call? Nikos would make the *perfect* tour guide, and I, for one, would follow him anywhere.'

'Liam, Nikos is *not* my boyfriend.'

'Ignore him, Abbie, he's just teasing you,' said Bree, giving Liam a friendly slap on his leg. 'But I have to admit it *is* a great idea. What better way to learn about the culture and the history of the island than from someone who was born and raised here? Although, if I'm being completely honest, I'm only really interested in which bars serve the best cocktails. Will you give him a ring?'

'I don't think—'

'Pleeeeease?' Liam placed his palms together and turned his pleading eyes on Abbie.

Abbie sighed. She didn't want to claim any more of Nikos' time. She was sure he had lots of other things he would rather be doing than act as the Hummingbird Hotel's unofficial tour guide – as well as emergency chef and fire warden – but she also didn't want to disappoint her guests either. She wanted them to have the full Corfiot experience, and explaining the island's rich and varied heritage – from Venetian, to French, to British – did not form part of her skill set.

'Okay, I'll ask him.'

'Great, the taxi's due in an hour,' Bree said.

'By the way, where's Savannah?'

Abbie was surprised the bride-to-be hadn't joined the rest of the group for their mid-morning swim, but she assumed Savannah must be taking advantage of a well-earned lie-in – she was on holiday, after all.

'I'll go and see if she's okay,' said Bree. She scrambled out of the water, wrapped a pristine white beach towel around her waist, and was about to go off in search of her best friend when she glanced over to the stone archway and gasped out loud. 'Oh my God, Savvie!'

All eyes shot to the entrance to the terrace where Savannah stood, dressed in a gorgeous ankle-length sundress that Abbie was sure she'd seen on the Pierre Fontaine spring/summer catwalk. But it wasn't the peppermint dress that caused the air to be whipped from her lungs and her jaw to drop in horror.

'Savvie, sweetie, what on earth have you done?' cried Liam, also jumping up from the side of the pool and dashing forward to take hold of a rather dazed looking Savannah's arm and guide her to a chair in the shade before she collapsed in a heap in front of them. For a few long moments, she sat there motionless, clearly in shock. Then, to Abbie's surprise, she burst into tears.

'I… I don't know what happened, I really don't.'

'You mean you didn't do *this* on purpose?'

Liam waved his hand theatrically at Savannah's previously almost-white-blonde hair which was now a pale candy pink colour, his lips turning upside down in a grimace of dislike.

'What do *you* think, Liam!'

'Well, it *is* a little…'

'Awful?'

'Well, I was going to go with Pink Lady, but awful would

do.'

Bree shot Liam a warning look and took the seat next to her best friend, placing her hand gently on her arm as she wiped away her tears with a scrap of tissue.

'Savvie, don't listen to him, he clearly has no taste. I think it's fine; it's just a bit of a shock, that's all. I had no idea you were planning to change your hair colour while you were over here.'

'But I didn't do this.'

'What do you mean?'

'I didn't dye my hair.'

'But… you must have done.'

'I didn't!'

'Sweetie, your hair doesn't just change colour overnight. I mean, I know you drank a lot of Nikos' amazingly delicious rosé last night, but that doesn't turn a person's hair the same colour – if it did, I'd have showcased a rather fetching grasshopper green last Saturday night after downing the best part of a bottle of crème de Menthe Carlos brought back from Monaco.'

'Liam, not helping!' Bree hissed.

Abbie tried to swallow down on the lump that had formed in her throat as she had stood listening to the increasingly worrying conversation that was taking place between her guests. She had no idea what was going on, but she could see that Savannah was clearly distressed and panic began to swirl. She took a step forward and met Savannah's gaze.

'Savannah, what exactly happened?'

'I got up this morning, jumped in the shower and washed my hair. I smothered on a generous dollop of conditioner, then wrapped a towel round my head and spent the next hour relaxing on the balcony, chatting to Enrique about our cookery class last night, asking him about his stag night and checking a few emails. When I went back to the bathroom to wash off the conditioner, I nearly had a coronary when I saw my hair in the mirror. Oh my God, what am I going to do?'

'But I don't understand,' said Paige, her eyes wide with confusion and distress as she stared at Savannah's new hair colour, which was as far away from the glamorous white-blonde she had supported the previous day as you could get.

'Darling, you must have mixed up your bottles and used hair dye instead of conditioner.'

'I… I didn't mix up my bottles, Liam, because…'

'Because what?'

'I used the hotel's conditioner.'

The bottom fell out of Abbie's stomach. She gasped, her hand flying to her lips as she was ambushed by a sudden wave of nausea and her mind went into freefall. She opened her mouth to speak but no words ensued.

Oh God, what had she done?

Heat rushed into her cheeks and mortification burgeoned through her whole body as her heart hammered out a concerto of panic against her ribcage. Silence expanded through the air as all eyes fixed on her in accusation until Bree broke the spell.

'Are you sure, Savvie?' she asked gently.

'Absolutely sure. If you don't believe me, I'll show you.'

Savannah jumped up from her seat and strode off through the stone archway. Everyone followed in her wake, with Abbie bringing up the rear, her legs like jelly as she crossed the courtyard, feeling as though she'd been parachuted into a role in a disaster movie. She waited outside Savannah's guest room with a very uncomfortable Liam and Paige whilst Savannah and Bree went inside to retrieve the offending bottle of conditioner that Abbie had left – along with shampoo, soap, bath gel and body lotion – in each one of the rooms for her guests to enjoy.

'Here.'

Liam took the bottle of conditioner from Savannah – who understandably was steadfastly avoiding meeting Abbie's gaze – unscrewed the top and sniffed the contents.

'Well, it smells okay – gorgeous, actually.'

'Savannah, I'm so sorry, I have no idea how… no idea how—' But Abbie couldn't continue, her mind was blank.

She couldn't for the life of her understand what was happening, but it didn't matter because Savannah wasn't listening; she was too busy staring into the mirror on the wall next to the guestroom's door, tears running down her cheeks again, her distress clear for all to see.

'What am I going to do?'

'Did you bring any products from the salon with you?' asked Bree.

'No, of course not.'

'Well, we could organise a consultation with a hairstylist in Corfu Town—'

'Are you kidding me? I'm not risking another disaster! Anyway, it took me ages to decide on what shade would go best with my wedding gown and I'd rather wait until I get home and I can have it done properly at the salon.'

'You know, I think it'll probably wash out.'

'What do you think I've been doing for the last two hours?'

'Sorry, Sav—'

'I can't go out looking like this.'

'Of course you can, sweetie. No one knows you here, only us, and we love you whether you have green, orange, or sky-blue hair with pink dots on, don't we guys?'

'Absolutely!' Bree said.

'Of course!' Paige added.

'So, I vote that you wrap that Barbie-esque hair of yours into one of Bree's cute bandanas, and we'll go on our jaunt to Corfu Town just as we planned, and I promise that as soon as we get home, I'll spend every waking moment with you in the salon transforming your crowning glory back to its silvery lusciousness. Okay?' Liam asked.

Savannah nodded, dabbed her eyes with a tissue, and forced a smile onto her lips.

'Okay.'

At last, Abbie emerged from the fugue that had engulfed her.

'I'm so, so sorry this has happened, Savannah. I really don't understand it. These are the same products the Hummingbird Hotel always uses; maybe one of them has gone off or something, or…'

She really couldn't think of anything else that could have happened, and as tears pricked at her lashes, she saw Savannah step forward and to her surprise rest a hand on her arm, her eyes filled with understanding and not the anger she had expected.

'It's okay, Abbie.'

'I—'

'Right,' Liam announced, his face flooding with relief. 'Now that's all settled, let's get changed into our glad rags; the taxi will be here any minute!'

Everyone dispersed back to their rooms and Abbie was left to stumble towards the veranda at the rear of the hotel, a cauldron of emotions swirling through her body. Even though Savannah had very generously absolved her from blame, she still felt responsible for what was yet another in a long line of unfortunate occurrences that had befallen the Hummingbird Hotel since she had arrived. She dropped down into a rattan chair, and wondered whether her aunt had had to deal with so many incidents, but she somehow doubted it.

Her thoughts spiralled, then began to ricochet from one possibility to the next until she became disorientated and breathless. What was she going to do? This was her fault; she should have checked those toiletries before she put them out for the guests. If they were past their sell-by dates, then it was no wonder something like this had happened. Abbie was grateful that Savannah hadn't completely flipped, which she would have been completely within her rights to do, but that didn't eradicate the intense feeling of guilt that now threatened to overwhelm her.

She desperately needed to share what had happened with someone.

But she had no one to confide in; no partner, no relatives, no colleagues. With every ounce of her being, she wished her mum was still around, or that Dan hadn't dumped her, or that she had anyone, anyone at all she could call to ask for their advice about what to do.

She had never felt as alone as she did in that moment.

However, as the maelstrom of emotion began to abate and her thoughts calmed, she realised that she had to learn to rely on herself, to have the courage and the confidence to face difficult issues and to deal with them in the best way she could. She might not do everything right, but the more she practised relying on her own abilities instead of relying on others to do things for her, the better she would get at it.

And anyway, she *wasn't* alone.

Just as her Aunt Liz had found, there were people *here* she could talk to. All she had to do was seek them out and ask for their help. What was the worst that could happen? They could refuse, of course, but she suspected they wouldn't.

Chapter Sixteen

The Hummingbird Hotel, Ropa Valley, Corfu
Flower: Purple Heartsease

Abbie hesitated on the front steps of the hotel, watching Savannah and her friends pile into the back of the taxi for their trip to Corfu Town, trying to build up the courage to tell them that she had changed her mind and wouldn't be accompanying them. The thought of spending the day with four people who clearly thought she was a completely incompetent hotelier didn't fill her with joy.

However, the main reason for her reticence was that she needed the space to think about what had just happened, as well as undertake her housekeeping duties, and to remove the Hummingbird Hotel's toiletries from the guest bathrooms and replace them with new ones. She might even try out some of the conditioner on her own hair to answer, one way or the other, the question that was swirling around in her brain. Had this really been her fault?

'Abbie, are you coming?'

'Actually, if you don't mind, I think I'll take a rain-check. It's kind of you to invite me but there's lots I need to do here at the hotel; the kitchen to clean, the rooms to sort out, the towels to wash and dry, new toiletries to buy.'

She gave Savannah a rueful smile, relieved to note that despite her unexpected change in hair colour, she seemed to have recovered from the shock. Instead of taking Bree up on her offer of a bandana she had decided to flaunt her new look by pairing it with a gorgeous dark emerald sundress with gold accessories and the largest pair of sunglasses Abbie had ever seen. She looked like she'd just stepped off a Pierre Fontaine runway.

'Can I just say again how sorry I—'

'Abbie, please, it's fine. As soon as we get home, Liam will work his magic and return my hair to its usual colour, which, as you have probably guessed, is not my natural colour, anyway. Look, I've been in the hairdressing business for almost twenty years, I know that things can occasionally go wrong, although I've never known a hair product to have such a dramatic effect on a client, thank God. I don't want this to spoil our trip, so I've decided to make the best of it, and to be honest, I actually think this shade is kind of cute, don't you?'

'I—'

'Savvie, hurry up! We're wasting valuable drinking time, sweetie!'

'I'm sorry I freaked out earlier; it was just the shock.

Are you okay?'

'Yes, I—'

Abbie saw something in Savannah's eyes she couldn't quite put her finger on.

'Are you sure I can't persuade you to come with us?'

'No, thanks, I'd better not. I need to go to the supermarket to pick up the ingredients for tomorrow's dessert and pastries class with Nikos, that's if you still want to—'

Savannah laughed. 'Of course we do! Liam would never speak to me again if we cancelled it! Okay, well, if you're sure, I'll see you later.'

'Have fun.'

Abbie watched the taxi head to the end of the driveway, then turn left and disappear from sight. She lingered on the steps, staring at the horizon, replaying her conversation with Savannah over and over in her mind, her confusion increasing each time.

Whilst she was relieved, and grateful, that Savannah had been so forgiving over the hair fiasco, she was also puzzled, and if she were honest, a tiny bit suspicious. For a woman who held great store by her appearance, who chose her outfits with infinite care, whose skin was blemish-free and hair immaculately styled, her swift turnaround from shocked, mortified and understandably upset at the unscheduled change of hair colour to accepting, conciliatory, and almost apologetic, surprised Abbie.

It was almost as if she'd realised that it wasn't Abbie's fault after all.

But what else could it be?

Maybe Savannah had realised that she had indeed made a

mistake, that she'd inadvertently used one of her own haircare products and there was nothing wrong with the Hummingbird Hotel's conditioner. But if that was the case, why hadn't she just admitted that? No, it had to be something else.

And then an idea burst into her head from left of field and her breath caught in her throat. Surely not! She tried to push the thought away, to come up with another scenario for Savannah's about-turn in attitude, but that same idea just kept returning even though it caused Abbie even more distress than when she had thought it was her fault.

Could someone have sabotaged the bottle of conditioner?

No, no, that was just plain ridiculous.

Who would do that, and why?

Oh God, she was completely losing it. After everything that had happened to her since the Dan Debacle, she was clearly skirting the realms of fantasy, or paranoia. This wasn't some sort of murder-mystery show where the guests at an isolated hotel targeted each other because of previous misdemeanours, it was a tranquil countryside retreat where visitors could relax and recharge their batteries without fear of inadvertently changing their natural, or chosen, hair colour.

She dropped down onto the steps, her heart racing, tears brimming, unable to line up her thoughts into any semblance of order, let alone make a start on cleaning the guest rooms or making a shopping list. She had no idea how long she sat there – it could have been a few minutes or a few hours – but she was grateful when she was interrupted from her downward spiral of self-reproach by the arrival of Nikos in his clapped-out old Peugeot. Though even the fact that the door slipped from its hinges when he jumped out of the driver's seat wasn't anywhere near enough to raise a smile.

'Abbie? Are you okay?'

'Not really.'

'Why, what's happened now?'

She saw the quirk of amusement in his eyes but she looked away, not even sure whether she wanted to reveal the next exciting episode of Abbie Coleman's Crazy Life at the Hummingbird Hotel.

'Nothing.'

Nikos clearly wasn't going to let her get away with the use of deflection as an avoidance mechanism. He plonked himself down next to her on the step, his expression serious, the waft of his cologne for once not raising her spirits. Her head felt like it has been stuffed with marshmallows; she couldn't think straight and it was making her feel woozy and disorientated.

'Abbie, I—'

'What happened to your motorbike?' she asked, stalling for time in the hope she would have a flash of inspiration on how to deal with the problem.

'My motorbike? Oh, yes, I…'

To her surprise, when she met Nikos' gaze, she saw his cheeks had coloured slightly and his body language became awkwardness and uncomfortable as he searched for an explanation to what she had thought would be a simple, and completely uncontroversial, question.

She groaned inwardly. Oh God, what now? What had she

done to anger the gods of former florists who had spent the last five years purposely living life beneath the excitement radar, allowing others to take credit for her achievements so that she didn't attract any untoward attention and leave herself open to yet another devastatingly painful and catastrophic event? A quiet, unassuming life was all she craved, but it seemed that wasn't what the director of her fate had planned for her.

'I'm sorry, Nikos, I didn't mean to—'

'Actually, I sold it.'

'You sold it? What for?'

'Never mind my motorbike, tell me what's going on here? Where are your guests?'

'They've gone to Corfu Town for a day of sightseeing and retail therapy.'

'Sounds like a great idea. So what's wrong? Don't tell me – you've flooded the bathroom, or accidentally unplugged the fridge, or substituted peanuts for coffee beans in the grinder, or overloaded the washing machine with powder and inundated the kitchen with soap suds?'

Abbie shook her head.

'Worse than that.'

'Really?'

And the whole story came tumbling out about Savannah's inadvertent change of hair colour, about it being her fault because she should have checked the use-by dates on the boxes before filling the guest rooms with the products, and as soon as she had finished, she felt an immediate sense of relief for being able to share her ordeal with Nikos.

'Oh my God, that's hilarious!'

'No, it's not.'

'Sorry, Abbie, you're right, it's not.'

She saw his lips twitching though.

'This is the hotel's reputation at stake.'

'I thought you were selling the hotel?'

'I am, but—'

'So why are you so upset?'

'Wouldn't you be if someone accused you of selling them substandard wine?'

'It's not the same.'

'Of course it is; but what would you say if it wasn't your fault?'

'What do you mean?'

She now had Nikos's attention.

'You'll think I'm crazy.'

'No, I won't, just tell me what you mean.'

'Well, first of all Savannah was really upset, and adamant that it was her use of the Hummingbird Hotel's conditioner that had caused her hair to switch from white-blonde to Barbie pink, but then, just before they all left to go to Corfu Town, she was all relaxed and laid back about it, telling me not to worry, that she loved her new hair colour, that mistakes happened and she's just going to embrace the new-look Savannah – or words to that effect, anyway.'

'So what are you worried about?'

'I don't believe her.'

'You don't… why not?'

'Call it intuition.'

'What are you saying, then?'

'That she thinks someone sabotaged the conditioner.'

Nikos stared at her; his jaw slightly ajar.

'You mean one of her friends did it as some kind of a joke?'

'Yes, it's the sort of thing that happens on hen and stag weekends.'

'But who would do such a thing?'

'Well, there's only three people it can be.'

'But if that's the case, why wouldn't they confess when Savannah was accusing you?'

'I don't know.'

'Don't you think this might be a bit far-fetched?'

'Well, I'm about to find out.'

A surge of indignation spurred Abbie into action. She jumped up from the step, strode through the lobby, out to the courtyard, and along the colonnade to Savannah's guest room where she found the offending bottle of hair conditioner in the wastepaper basket. She grabbed it and then made her way to the other three guest rooms and snatched up their bottles of rose-scented conditioner too, before making her way to the kitchen.

'What are you doing?'

'All the conditioners came from the same box, the same batch, so if there's something wrong with Savannah's, there must be something wrong with the others, too, don't you think?'

'I suppose—'

Abbie selected a strand of her hair, and smoothed on a generous dollop of the conditioner from the bottles she'd taken from Liam's, Bree's and Paige's rooms.

'Abbie! Stop! Are you sure you want to do that?'

But she ignored him.

'I have to know what's going on, Nikos.'

Nikos opened his mouth to contradict her, but he changed his mind, and instead rolled his eyes at her and went to make them both a coffee, bringing the two cups of espresso back to the table where her curls were still the same frizzy blonde as they'd always been.

'Okay, so I think we can safely assume that there's nothing wrong with the Hummingbird Hotel's toiletries.'

She took a quick sip of her coffee for courage, her heart racing as she dipped her finger into the almost empty bottle they'd found in Savannah's room. She scooped out the last drops and dabbed a small amount onto an inch-long tip of her hair. Thirty minutes later, her hair had turned the same colour pink as Savannah's and she snipped the coloured ends off with the scissors.

'Oh my God,' said Nikos. 'What's going on?'

'Like I said – someone has tampered with this bottle; switched the conditioner for hair dye.'

'As a joke?'

'I don't know.'

'But who would do that?'

'Well, if I had to guess, my first choice would be Bree.'

'Why Bree?'

Abbie gave him a brief outline of what Bree did for a living, recalling that the ears of the snow-white Labradoodle she'd seen in one of the photographs were almost the same colour as Savannah's hair had been.

'A doggie beauty salon? Are you serious?'

'I know, I'd never heard of it either.'

'Okay, so what are you going to do next? Call in the sniffer dogs?' Nikos laughed at his own joke and Abbie had to smile at his attempt to lighten the mood.

She finished her coffee and found that her earlier anxiety had abated as a consequence of having someone to talk to, someone who listened to her without denigrating her – like Dan had whenever she'd made suggestions on how they might increase business at *FlowerEssence* – someone who took her seriously and was there to offer his help in whatever way he could. Why had she felt she was alone?

'I don't know what I'm going to do. Savannah clearly wants to move on.'

'Do you?'

'I'm not sure.'

'Well I am. Someone was quite happy for you to take the blame for this, Abbie. Why should they get away with that, whatever Savannah thinks? If you think it's Bree, then you have to talk to her, tell her to come clean to Savannah, and *then*, and only then, we move on and can forget about it, when everything is out in the open.'

Abbie smiled at the indignation on Nikos's face, her heart ballooning with appreciation.

'Thanks, Nikos.'

'What for?'

'For your support. I was devastated, sitting out there on the front step before you arrived, wondering why – when I'd just started to think that everything was going smoothly at last – life decides to toss in another grenade. Now I feel so much better for having someone to share this with.'

Nikos laughed. 'You know, I thought I was coming here to have a relaxing coffee by the pool and to persuade you to have lunch with me over in Nissaki where my friend owns a taverna on the beach. It's quiet there on a lunchtime, with perhaps just a couple of intrepid tourists brave enough to leave the side of the pool for a cool beer or a frappé. Why don't we shelve this conundrum for the time being – there's nothing we can do until Savannah and her friends come back from Corfu Town anyway – and take a well-deserved break from all the turmoil that you seem to attract.'

Nikos rinsed their cups in the sink, then strode towards the door, looking back over his shoulder at Abbie who remained at the table, still trying to come to terms with how she'd managed to land herself in such a complicated situation.

'I won't take no for an answer.'

Chapter Seventeen

Taverna Christos, Nissaki Beach, Corfu
Flower: Garvinea Sweet Summer Surprise

Thirty hair-raising minutes later, Nikos had parked the car in shady spot just off the coast road, and led her down a very steep hill, through an olive grove and along a pebbled beach to a thatched bar where she was surprised to see they were the only customers. Nikos' friend, Christos, greeted them like family, served them drinks, and then left them in peace to marvel at the panoramic scene spread out in from of them.

'Wow, this is paradise.'

Abbie stared at the view; the waves lapping against a sun-scorched jetty with a solitary wooden boat moored at the end, the sea a rich sapphire-blue merging into the translucent, cloudless sky, and, in the distance, the hazy outline of the

Albanian mountains. The soft bouzouki music playing from behind the bar, accompanied by the midday cicada concerto, added to the ambiance, as did the sweet fragrance of the frangipani entwined around the eaves mingled with the tang of the sea air, and Abbie felt the day's tribulations finally start to seep away.

'I agree. This is truly my idea of heaven,' said Nikos. 'Christos is a lucky guy. It's always been my dream to own a restaurant like this, except I would extend the daily menu beyond grilled fish and French fries.'

They sat in companionable silence, the heat rising as the afternoon progressed, watching a large cruiser filled with partying tourists from nearby Ipsos sail sedately across the bay heading for one of the hidden coves along that stretch of the coastline and a couple of hours of sunbathing on the beach and cooling off in the sea. Suddenly, Abbie could think of nothing better than joining them, for a paddle at least, so she kicked off her shoes and turned to Nikos.

'Come on.'

Nikos smiled, took her outstretched hand, and walked with her to the veranda's steps, strolling by her side as she paddled in the deliciously cool shallows while he walked a little higher up on the narrow beach until they came to a halt at the jetty.

'Is that Christos' boat?'

'Yes, it's his pride and joy. He's been working on it for as long as I can remember.'

The conversation Abbie had had with Sofia that morning sprang into her mind and she decided there was no better time to do what Sofia had urged her to do and ask Nikos about his past. She guided him out along the jetty, intending to find the perfect spot on the wooden planks where they could sit, their toes dangling in the sea, and talk. A burst of confidence rushed into her chest – perhaps she would find the courage to share some of her own story with him, too.

They reached the end of the jetty where Christos' little boat bobbed merrily on the waves. She had no idea what made her do it – probably the wonderful scene from Mamma Mia where the whole village launched themselves, *en masse*, into the sea from a similar jetty, or maybe it was the fact that the sun was now at its highest in the sky and she was really, *really* hot. Whatever it was, she surprised herself because she wasn't known for being impetuous.

She inhaled a breath, tightened her grip on Nikos' hand, and took a flying leap into the water, pulling him with her, causing a huge satisfying splash, and receiving an instant, and satisfying, escape from the heat.

'Whoop!' she cried.

Exhilaration flooded her body. She spun round to smile at Nikos and was shocked when she saw the alarm in his eyes as he scrambled back towards the jetty as fast as he could, his jaw clenched tight as he hauled himself onto dry land. A mixture of anger and terror exuding from every pore of his body, his breath exhaled in ragged spurts, and his fists balled tightly as he wrestled to keep his emotions in check.

Abbie had no idea what was going on, and was even more astonished when she saw Christos run from the bar, along the beach, and down the jetty towards them, his face wreathed with panic. When he reached Nikos, he placed a gentle hand on his friend's shoulder to make sure he was okay, before kneeling down to offer Abbie a hand to climb out of the sea.

Well, that didn't go how she had expected.

'Nikos, I…'

But he had already spun on his heels and was striding back down the jetty, his head lowered, his shoulders stiff, his hands shoved deep into the pockets of his shorts. Without looking back, he walked along the beach and disappeared into the bar, leaving Abbie to stare after him, her emotions tumbling in confusion.

'Sorry Abbie, Nikos obviously hasn't told you what happened.'

'What do you mean?'

Christos ran his fingers through his dark hair, scratching at the back of his neck as he strolled by her side to the end of the jetty, clearly struggling with what to say to her.

'I think you should ask Nikos to explain.'

'I'm not sure he's speaking to me after what I've just done.'

'He'll come round. Grab a seat over there,' Christos pointed to the far side of the bar, to a more secluded spot in the shade of a mango tree where there was a canopied and upholstered garden swing. 'I'll go find him, and send some drinks over.'

Abbie did as Christos suggested, guilt and regret swirling through her veins that what she had thought would be a fun activity had inadvertently upset Nikos so much, especially when he'd been doing his best to cheer *her* up after what had happened that morning. The longer she sat there, the more she realised that what was going on had something to do with what Sofia had been talking about, something in his past, and she was keen to offer whatever support she could.

'Sorry, Abbie, I shouldn't have—' Nikos started as he appeared next to her.

'No, Nikos, please, it's completely my fault, I have no idea what came over me. I didn't know you couldn't swim, I—'

'It's not that.'

Nikos placed a tumbler of sparkling water on the table in front of Abbie and took a seat next to her on the swing, his eyes fixed on the shimmering horizon, a tic working overtime at his temple. It was a while before he spoke, and when he did, his voice was strained with the effort of producing the words.

'Two years ago, my father and my brother, Matthias, took the family's yacht over to Paxos to meet up with some friends who own a vineyard over there. It was kind of an annual tradition; they would spend the weekend together eating good food, drinking each other's wine, and putting the world to rights, then one of their friends would sail the boat back for them so they could continue the party, except this time they chose the wrong friend.'

'Oh…' Abbie's stomach turned; she knew from the expression of raw agony on Nikos' face what had happened.

'The weather turned, one of those freak summer storms that can take even the most proficient and experienced sailor unawares, and Leonidas was neither of those things. He struggled with what Mother Nature threw at him that night, and my father and Matthias had consumed a great deal of alcohol so they weren't at their best and… and… the boat… it… it sank and…'

'Oh Nikos, I'm so very sorry.'

Tears rolled down Abbie's cheeks, her heart cracking at the most painful of stories. She reached out to thread her fingers through Nikos', distressed at the eternal sadness she saw etched deep in his soul. They sat there for a while, listening to the waves trickle over the pebbles and the cicadas continue their never-ending song. Nikos seemed to have retreated into a world of his own, delayed in another time, and the sharp anguish she saw in his eyes whipped the breath from her lungs, but a few moments later he swallowed down on his pain and continued.

'My mother and sister were inconsolable. I got the call about the accident whilst I was catering a wedding at the Hôtel Plaza in Paris. I dropped everything and caught the next flight out of there, but, of course, there was nothing I could do. I would give anything – everything – I have for just one more day with them. My father never understood my desire to leave the island to go off chasing my dreams in another country, and I was stubborn. I couldn't understand why he didn't want me to be happy, so we parted on bad terms when I left to study at Le Cordon Bleu, and our subsequent meetings were cordial, polite, like two strangers meeting for the first time, definitely not how father and son should behave. I didn't know I would never see him, or Matthias, again.'

Nikos paused, clearly wrestling with regret.

'Matthias loved the Angelopoulos winery – he especially enjoyed handling the marketing side of things. He had lots of creative and innovative ideas about how to expand the business, bringing in much-needed extra income, while Dad just wanted to be with his vines. I'm no good at either, which is why I sought to pursue a different career, and my mother understood that.'

'Is that why your mum moved to Athens?'

'Yes, she couldn't stay here after the accident, so she went to live with Helena and her husband who's an architect there. She looks after her grandchildren, does some charity work to keep her from dwelling on her loss, and I promised her and my sister that I would take over at the vineyard, that they didn't have to worry about anything, I would sort everything out, and so that's what I did. I gave up my job in Paris and came home, but…'

'But what?'

'I'm useless at it. I don't have the affinity with the vines my father and grandfather had; they loved the vines like they were part of the family. Dimitris does his best, but you've met him; he'd much rather be singing in front of a bunch of people than a bunch of grapes. I'm also struggling with running the winery, and, well, we're losing money every month – which is why I've sold my motorbike.'

Abbie released the breath she didn't know she had been holding, searching for the right words to tell Nikos that she understood, especially about the impact the loss of a parent could have on a person, having been through the same thing herself. Unfortunately, her brain seemed to be a jumble of disconnected thoughts, ricocheting from one statement to the next, none of which felt right, so she simply squeezed his hand and muttered 'I'm sorry, Nikos.'

'No, *I'm* sorry, Abbie. Sorry I reacted like I did. Two years ago I would have been happy to spend the whole afternoon jumping from the jetty, splashing around in the sea, maybe taking you to one of the secret coves in Christos' boat, but now… well, I'm embarrassed to admit that I seem to have developed a water phobia. Mum has suggested I think about getting therapy, but I just can't seem to find the time… or the inclination.'

Nikos released her hand and reached out to take a sip from his glass of lemonade, before resuming his contemplation of the horizon. As Abbie's thoughts began to calm, she understood how brave Nikos had been, sharing such a momentous and life-changing event with her, especially as he'd only met her a few days ago. She didn't underestimate how difficult that must have been.

'I'm sure your father understood why you wanted to go to Paris, Nikos. There's one thing all parents want for their children and that's for them to be happy, to follow their dreams, and that is exactly what you were doing – he would have been proud of everything you've achieved. I…'

She paused, then forced herself to go on; if Nikos could share his story, then so could she.

'I didn't follow my dream. I became a florist, not a botanist. I worked with the plants, shrubs, flowers and foliage that *other* people had nurtured when that was what I really wanted to do. After my mum died, I just didn't have the strength to forge my own path, so I accepted the first job I could get. I even allowed someone else to take the credit for the floral arrangements that I created. Life was easier that way. I've never admitted to that to anyone before but I can see it now.'

She hesitated, not daring to look Nikos in the eye.

'Mum would have been so disappointed. She adored her garden; it was her whole life, watching her flowers travel through the seasons, marvelling at the beauty and endurance of nature, and she was thrilled when I said I wanted to study botany at university. I have no idea what she would think about me living in an upstairs flat in the middle of London without a green shoot in sight. I let her down by *not* following my dreams, but I'm going to put that right, and maybe you should, too.'

'Give up the vineyard? I couldn't do that.'

'Not give it up; get someone who knows what they're doing to run it. Someone whose passion is growing grapes, then turning them into the best wine in the whole world.'

The smile returned to Nikos' face as he nodded slowly, clearly contemplating her suggestion before draining the last inch of his drink and checking his watch. 'Come on, I think we should head back.'

They called their goodbyes to Christos and meandered back along the beach, through the olive grove, and up the hill to where Nikos had left the car, which felt like the inside of a sauna. Abbie wound down the window to let in the breeze whilst Nikos navigated the twists and turns of the coastal road back towards the hotel.

'Have you decided how you're going to handle the shampoo-switching shenanigans?'

So much had happened over the last few hours that Abbie had completely forgotten about Savannah's unfortunate change in hair colour, an event that paled into insignificance when she compared it to what had happened to Nikos' family. However, whilst she would like to, she knew she couldn't ignore it.

'I think I should talk to Bree.'

'I agree.'

'You do?'

'Yes, of course. Whoever did this, even if it was a joke, was clearly happy for you to take the blame, which is not fair. Want me to come with you?'

'I…'

She had been about to refuse – this wasn't Nikos' problem and he obviously had a great deal more to cope with than the trials and tribulations of the Hummingbird Hotel, but then she had never been faced with this scenario before and she could really do with his support to get to the bottom of what was going on. Whilst she knew that she had to learn to be more independent, to face whatever life threw at her without hiding behind someone else like she had with Dan, it also took courage to accept help when it was offered.

'Yes, please.'

'Good answer.' Nikos grinned. 'It seems life in Corfu isn't as dull as I thought.'

Chapter Eighteen

The Veranda at the Hummingbird Hotel
Flower: the 'Magical Mystery Tour' Peony

When they arrived back at the hotel it was after six and there was no sign of the guests, so Abbie offered to make coffee whilst Nikos rustled up a salad from the previous evening's leftovers, then they carried their food out to the veranda, chatting about everything and nothing in particular. Dusk had turned the sky into a magnificent dusky pink, washed with streaks of apricot and salmon, and the still-humid air held a scent of scorched earth and crushed rosemary from the tiny herb garden her aunt had tended.

Moments after consuming her last mouthful of feta cheese, Abbie heard the crunch of a taxi's wheels on the driveway, followed by a cacophony of high-pitched laughter as the group tumbled from its confines and clattered up the hotel's front steps.

'Hey Abbie, hey Nikos!'

'Hi guys, did you enjoy your trip?'

'It was am-az-ing. We had dinner at this little fish restaurant overlooking the sea, with *the* sexiest waiters, and I might just have tried most of the cocktails on the menu!' Savannah giggled, her hair, despite its unusual colour, still as smooth and glossy as it had been when she left the hotel earlier. Abbie reached up to pat down her curls, a gesture that made no difference whatsoever.

'Can I get you all some coffee?'

'Yes please!' said Bree, plonking herself down in one of the chairs next to Nikos, tipping her head back, her arms dangling loosely at her sides, her cheeks pink from spending too much time in the sun.

'I'm afraid we've all consumed rather a lot of alcohol, darling,' said Liam, unnecessarily. 'We ended up in this really cute bar next to what looked like a cricket pitch in the middle of the town. I mean, who knew that the Greeks played cricket?'

'Cricket was brought to Corfu by the British when they occupied the island in the nineteenth century,' said Nikos with a grin. 'And I'm proud to inform you that we're home to eleven out of the fourteen cricket clubs in Greece. We call it *fermaro kai issia*.'

'What does that mean?'

'It means "block and wallop", which I think sums up the game perfectly, don't you?'

'Can I help you with the coffees?' Paige asked Abbie, rolling her eyes in boredom now that the conversation had turned to sport.

'Thanks, that would be great.'

Paige padded behind Abbie as she made her way to the kitchen. 'Look what I bought.' She produced a selection of hand-plaited leather friendship bracelets in different colours and laid each one out onto the countertop.

'They're lovely, but why do you need twenty?'

Paige laughed. 'Oh, I volunteer for a women's refuge in Harringay. Some of the people we help arrive with nothing but the clothes they're wearing, and we try to provide them with all the essentials, but something like this, something personal and pretty, can really help to lift the spirits.'

Abbie saw the kindness in Paige's eyes and her heart softened.

'That's very thoughtful of you, Paige.'

She handed Paige the tray of coffee paraphernalia, collected two large cafetières, and followed her back to the veranda where the group seemed to have settled in for the duration. She plugged her phone into the sound system, chose a random selection of music, and joined Nikos and Liam who were chatting about an engagement party that they realised they had both attended – Liam as a guest of the bride-to-be, Nikos providing the high-end catering – held in a penthouse apartment in a very exclusive arrondissement of Paris.

'I've always said that hair professionals provide more than simply stunning hairstyles; we're agony aunts, counsellors, and well-being advocates. We're an outlet for all the angst our clients keep locked away when they are at home or at work. When they're sitting in the chair, we become their therapist, someone they can trust with their secrets or their troubles, someone who will listen, sympathise and occasionally offer advice. My mum always said that I have a healthy interest in other people's business but I find the human condition intensely interesting. The unexpected cancellation of a luxury holiday in St Tropez might be devastating to one person, but a totally trivial development to another, and for every failed driving test or exam, there's someone else's milestone occasion to celebrate. I have *the* best job in the world. Every day is different; it's like we provide a community service at Jazz.'

'At three hundred and fifty pounds a pop,' Paige muttered so that only Abbie heard. 'One colour, cut and blow-dry can feed a family of four for a month!'

Abbie turned to smile at Paige but instead of the eye-roll she had been expecting, she saw an angry twist of the lips. Liam hadn't noticed though, or he simply chose to ignore her and continued on with his soliloquy.

'The only downside is that there's so little opportunity to meet potential dates. My clients are all VIPs or socialites or celebrity influencers; most have partners or spouses, and by the time I've finished a long day at the salon, my feet are absolutely killing me and I'm fit for nothing but a long soak in the bath and then bed – by myself.'

'What about Josh Bartlett?' asked Paige, her eyebrows raised in innocent enquiry.

'Ah, yes, Joshua. Tall, tanned, toned, and tastefully attired, with absolutely gorgeous caramel curls – all his own, too, darling. I sensed the little zing of electricity between us right from the start, and I'm never wrong about these things.'

'So what happened?' Abbie asked, leaning back in her chair with her coffee, eager for a nugget of celebrity gossip. She'd seen Josh Bartlett in Mamma Mia when Dan had treated her to tickets for her birthday and she had thought he was excellent. However, instead of leaning forward to regale them with his story, Liam's smile slid from his face and was replaced by an expression of annoyance. He shot a glance over his shoulder to where Savannah was giggling at something Bree was showing her on her phone and his mood seemed to deflate like a pricked balloon.

'I can't talk about it, I'm so upset.'

'Savvie pulled rank, that's what happened,' said Paige, helpfully.

'What do you mean?' Abbie asked.

'The next time Josh rang for an appointment, she insisted I put him in with her.' Paige sipped her coffee, her face showing her disdain for what had happened.

'But why?'

'Why do you think, sweetie?' Liam asked.

Abbie genuinely had no idea.

'For the kudos?' she tried.

'Well, maybe, but she has a whole stable of much more important and famous clients of her own. No, if you want to know what I think…' Liam paused again to check Savannah wasn't listening to their conversation, then lowered his voice and leaned towards them as if about to confide a state secret. 'It's because he's one of our best tippers.'

'Oh…'

'You know, I really think we could have had something.' Clearly upset, Liam shoved back his chair and strode from the veranda into the kitchen. Abbie exchanged a glance with

Nikos, then with Paige who simply shrugged her shoulders, probably having heard the complaint many times before.

'Leave him; he's always like this when he's had too many cocktails. He'll be okay once he's cooled off.'

But Abbie couldn't leave him when he was so obviously distressed, so she followed in his wake. When she couldn't find him in the kitchen, she went to the courtyard and found him sitting on the wall surrounding the fountain, fingering his mobile phone, his face creased in misery.

'Liam? Are you okay?'

'I will be.'

'I'm sorry you're upset.'

'Thanks, Abbie. It's just… well, I thought me and Josh really connected on a deeper level, you know, more than just client and stylist. Of course, Savvie frowns on relationships between staff and customers, but if you want my opinion, it's a much better way to meet a future partner than to steal him from your best friend.'

Abbie stared at Liam who gave her a defiant look back.

'You mean Enrique?'

'Yes, sweetie, I mean Enrique. He used to date Bree; that's how he and Savvie met.

'Oh, I…'

'Don't worry, Bree's completely fine about it. They'd only been dating for a few months and she's moved on. I think since then she's had at least a dozen other "he's the one" boyfriends; she's all about variety, our Bree. However, I do admit to being shocked when Paige told me what Savvie had done with Josh. Okay, so he might be our best tipper, but she doesn't need the money, she's the salon owner for God's sake, she has plenty of money sloshing around in her bank account; I don't.'

'I'm sorry, Liam.'

Then something occurred to Abbie with the force of a runaway express train. What if Liam was responsible for switching the hair products? It seemed from what he was saying that he had a grudge against Savannah for what he clearly thought was her stealing his client *and* potential date, someone he'd made a personal connection with. Whether she'd done it because she didn't want her head stylist fraternising with the salon's esteemed and wealthy clients, or because, as Liam suggested, she wanted to keep his generous tip for herself, he was clearly upset about it. Maybe he wanted to teach her some kind of lesson, or simply to embarrass her and have a bit of fun at her expense on the hen weekend.

Abbie sighed. She would have loved to have put the subject on the shelf marked "none of my business". However, if it *was* Liam, he'd been happy enough to allow her, as the Hummingbird Hotel's naive new proprietor, to take the blame for what had happened to Savannah. She didn't think it was fair for him to do that and indignation swirled through her veins.

'Liam, can I ask you something?'

'Sure, sweetie.'

'I don't suppose…'

Oh God. She had no experience of how to do this without it sounding like she was accusing him. Where was Nikos when she needed him? With a flash of self-insight, she recognised that she was doing what she always did whenever a problem arose at *FlowerEssence* – deferring to Dan to let him sort things out. This was *her* hotel, these were *her* guests, and this was *her* problem to deal with.

'I don't suppose you can help me understand what happened to Savannah's hair this morning?'

Fortunately, Liam didn't explode over her audacity in raising the question with him. In fact, to her surprise and relief, he smiled.

'Whilst I would love to declare that she looked totally ridiculous, I'm sorry to say that I think she looks fabulous. The colour really suits her, don't you think? I'm rather jealous, to be honest. Did you check your supplies, Abbie? I personally have never known a hair product to degrade to such an extent that it dyes a client's hair pink, but I'm sure it *could* happen, given the right, or wrong, conditions.'

'I've checked all the other conditioners and they're all perfectly fine. It was just the one in Savannah's room that seems to have had this unfortunate effect, which leads me to think…'

She paused and met Liam's eyes, watching as they widened with surprise.

'Oh my God, you think… you think I might have something to do with this? What? That I'm so devastated about the "Joshua incident" that I decided to get my own back on Savvie by sabotage one of her hair products?' Liam gaped at her, shock flittering across his face. 'I would *never* do something like that! I might moan and groan about her pinching all the best clients and pocketing the great tips, but actually I adore her. She's my *best* friend and I'd happily hand over every client she wants. She *is* the boss, after all, and she's been very good to me. She gave me a job when everyone else, even my family… well, let's just say I was floundering, and if it wasn't for her, I wouldn't be where I am today.'

Abbie's heart gave a twist of sympathy for Liam, followed by a sharp spasm of guilt.

'I'm sorry, Liam, I didn't mean to…'

'Darling, it's fine, I'm a big boy, and I've been accused of much worse. Sooo, you're stepping into Jessica Fletcher's stylish brogues, are you? How exciting! I'm thrilled to have been at the top of your list of suspects—'

'Oh, no, Liam, you weren't—'

'But I'm sorry to say that I'll have to be the first name you strike off, too. Who else do you have on there? Oh, wait…'

Abbie smiled. She could almost see the cogs turning in his brain. 'What?'

'Well… I shouldn't really be saying this…' Liam furtively surveyed the courtyard as though he was a licensed-to-kill spy on an undercover mission to flush out an International Shampoo-Switching Scoundrel, and Abbie had to work hard not to giggle. 'When we were in the airport waiting for our flight over here, I heard Savvie and Bree arguing behind the lipstick counter in Boots.'

'What were they arguing about?'

'What else, darling? Enrique.'

'I thought you said Bree was okay with them being together.'

'Maybe the lady doth protest too much? I think you should talk to her, Abbie. Oh my God, yes, I've got it!'

Liam leapt up from the fountain's wall and began pacing backwards and forwards in front of Abbie, stroking his chin with his fingers – all he needed was a deerstalker and his image would be complete.

'What now?' Abbie smirked, happy to see he had cheered up after his earlier upset.

'Isn't it obvious, darling? She used the doggy hair dye! Oh my God, Savvie will absolutely freak if she thinks she's modelling the very best canine haircare products the world has to offer!'

Liam's hand flew to his lips, but seconds later, as he met Abbie's eyes, mischief danced around the corners of his lips and he burst out laughing, which caused Abbie to join in, too.

'Hey, you two! What are you doing here? What are you laughing at?'

The question, coming as it did from Savannah, only made Liam laugh harder, so much in fact that tears started to roll down his cheeks, especially when his gaze landed on her hair that seemed to have taken on an even more effervescent sheen under the glare of the silvery moon.

'Sorry, sweetheart, can't stop. My pillow's calling.'

Chapter Nineteen

Loukas' Bakery, Corfu Town
Flower: Candy Floss Poppy

The next morning, Abbie took her time preparing a platter of fresh fruit – papaya, mango, pineapple, melon, and oranges – along with a bowl of rich creamy Greek yoghurt with local honey, and a selection of pastries for her guests. She then took a coffee for a leisurely saunter through her aunt's beloved vineyard to think through everything Liam had said the previous evening.

When she reached the end of the first row of the vines and paused to take in the view over the Angelopoulos estate, she heard singing, but this time it wasn't Dimitris, it was Nikos with his headphones on, busy tending the vines and completely oblivious to her presence. She took the opportunity to watch him without his knowledge; taking in his muscular physique, his sun-kissed forearms sporting a ripple of dark hairs, his facial features, so handsome in repose, and her heart performed a somersault of attraction.

She couldn't believe how close they had grown over the last few days. She knew about the tragedy that had befallen his family, and why he had returned to Corfu, and he knew about her own issues with her family's estrangement, and how *she* had come to be in Corfu, too. It seemed neither of them actually wanted to be there – which was surprising given that it was as close to her idea of paradise as it was possible to get.

Wasn't she passionate, obsessed almost, with all-things botanical? She only had to take a look around; everywhere she looked there was a tree, a plant, a shrub, a flower, a collection of grasses to appreciate. Why couldn't this be where she made her life, instead of a little cottage in the Devonshire countryside with roses around the door? Why couldn't she have a little white-washed hotel in the *Greek* countryside with bougainvillea over the door, a few pots crammed to bursting with tropical plants, and her own vineyard with some of the best vines known to the grape-growing world?

What if she made her own wine from them?

Or maybe she could persuade Nikos to collaborate with her?

She continued her covert surveillance of him until he grabbed a spade and started to dig up a patch of artichokes.'

'No! Nikos! Stop!'

With his headphones on he couldn't hear her, so she vaulted over the fence and sprinted down the avenue between the vines towards him, flapping her arms in the air like an out-of-control human windmill – it was the most exercise she'd done in months.

'Stop!'

'Oh, hi, Abbie.'

'Stop digging!'

'Why? I have no idea why these are here.'

'They're artichokes.'

'I know they're artichokes. I *am* a chef.' Nikos laughed, his eyes sparkling with amusement.

'They've been planted there for a reason.'

Nikos looked sceptical. 'I struggle to grow the grapes, Abbie. I have no intention of taking on the additional role of market gardener, too.'

'I think they might have been planted there as some kind of pest control. Why don't you leave them there until I've had chance to do a little research?'

'Okay. You see, I told you I'm a useless vineyard owner.'

'Don't worry,' Abbie laughed, 'I'll keep you on the right track.'

'How can you? I thought you were leaving next week?'

She saw his eyes narrow, his jaw clench, and awkwardness descended as the silence between them stretched whilst she tried to come up with a suitable reply to his question, but all she could think of was changing the subject.

'Are you still okay about delivering the pâtisserie session this afternoon?'

'Of course. I'm actually really looking forward to it.'

'Great. I need to try and get Bree on her own at some

point to ask her about an argument she had with Savannah about Enrique.'

'Who told you about that?'

'Liam did, last night.'

Abbie went on to fill Nikos in on everything Liam had told her in the courtyard, not only about his own frustrations with Savannah but also about Bree's previous relationship with Enrique.

'And you definitely don't think it's him?'

'No I don't. I know he was telling me the truth.'

'Okay, I'll try and orchestrate an opportunity for you to chat to Bree on your own. From what Liam told you it does sound like she's still the most likely culprit – she had the means and the motive. Oh God…' Nikos laughed, a rich uplifting sound that made Abbie smile. 'I feel like we're playing the roles of investigator and her sidekick in a crazy Corfiot detective show. Did you bring your trusty magnifying glass with you from the UK?'

Despite her anxiety over what had happened to Savannah, Abbie had to admit she was enjoying the opportunity to share the unravelling of the mystery with Nikos. Out of something so outrageous, it seemed that something good had happened, and their friendship had certainly developed much faster than it might have otherwise.

'Right, I'm off to Corfu Town to collect the ingredients for the cookery class. Want to come with me?' asked Nikos, his dark eyes scorching into hers and sending her senses into overdrive. There was nothing she would like more than to spend the morning with him, mooching around the shops and bars, experiencing the town from the perspective of someone who had grown up there.

'I'd love to, thanks.'

'Great. I'll pick you up in fifteen minutes.'

Abbie dashed back to the hotel to collect her satchel, her spirits soaring, especially when she found her guests chatting away in the courtyard – having devoured every last morsel of the breakfast she had left for them – happily planning their own morning's activities without anyone sporting an unexpected change to their hair colour.

'Hey, Abbie, thanks for a scrumptious breakfast,' said Bree, as usual wearing an all-white outfit, this time a pair of capri pants, a hippy blouse, and a pair of white, sequined Vans with rope laces. 'We're going to spend the day on the beach over in Paleokastritsa, soaking up the rays, swimming in the sea, checking out the talent. Want to join us?'

'Sorry guys, I'm going on a shopping expedition to Corfu Town to collect everything we need for your pâtisserie course this afternoon.'

'Remind me what time we need to be back?' asked Savannah, resplendent in a pale aquamarine sun dress with pearl-encrusted shoulder straps that accentuated her slender figure and her new hair colour to its best advantage. A cloud of Chanel No. 5 floated in the air around her, and Abbie noticed that she had even painted her nails to match her new shade of hair, as well as co-ordinated her lipstick. Abbie wished she had even half Savannah's sartorial style.

'Whatever time is best for you. I'm happy to fall in with your own arrangements.'

'Shall we say four o'clock, then?' Savannah suggested. 'I think we'll have had enough of the beach by then.'

'Perfect.'

Abbie waved the group off back to their rooms, checked the kitchen to make sure she'd switched off all the plugs and had minimised the risk of any catastrophes happening whilst she was away, and skipped down the hotel's front steps at exactly the same time as Nikos arrived to collect her.

'Jump in!'

She hopped into the passenger seat, gasping as the hot air inside the Peugeot slapped her in the face, causing her pores to tingle and her hair to expand into a bouffant of fairground candy floss. She briefly wondered whether Savannah or Liam had anything in their valises of magic tricks that could tame her curls, and filed that possibility away for later exploration.

'Okay, so I've spoken to my friend Loukas who owns a bakery in Corfu Town and he's gathered everything I need for a session of Extreme Pâtisserie. I have to confess that he was a little put out that I intend to include a selection of "those pretty Parisian delicacies that Barbie might feed to her unicorn" in my repertoire, but he still agreed to let me have what I need.'

'Do you know everyone here?' Abbie laughed, thinking of the village she grew up in in Devon where, just like here in Corfu, people helped each other out whenever they could, knowing that if they ever needed a favour themselves, their kindness would be reciprocated. Her mum had often handed out pots and hanging baskets she had planted, as well as wonderful bouquets of garden flowers, to friends and neighbours who were having a party, or a celebration, or going through a difficult time, to cheer them up or brighten up their homes, and in return she had received home-made jams and chutneys, and fruit and vegetables from their allotments.

When the worst had happened, Abbie had been inundated with offers of help and support, from cakes to casseroles, pies to plumbing; one neighbour had mowed the lawn for her, another had fixed a leaking pipe, and another had even offered to help her with the legal issues that she had wrestled with as she navigated the fraught and painful process of sorting through her mum's paperwork and selling the house. Fortunately, the purchaser had also been an avid gardener who had assured her that he would continue her mum's horticultural legacy, which had given her some solace.

'I don't know everyone, but I might know their brother, or their uncle, or their cousin. Hey!' Nikos slammed on the car's brakes to allow a Jeep, filled with laughing tourists, to pass by at speed, shaking his head at their recklessness before continuing. 'Corfu is a small island, especially during the winter months, which is the time when the residents get together to reconnect after the busy summer season. As you know, most businesses here rely on tourism and we have to… what's that saying, ah, yes, we have to "make hay while the sun shines."'

Moments later they arrived on the outskirts of Corfu Town, and after a few fruitless minutes searching for a parking space, Nikos managed to squeeze the Peugeot into a narrow spot between a sleek black Mercedes and a rather ostentatious yellow Porsche, which Abbie thought would make the perfect vehicle for Liam to zip around town in.

'Come on, I want to show you something.'

Nikos hooked his arm through Abbie's as though it was

the most natural thing in the world, and after navigating a few of the winding alleyways, he pointed to a rectangle of grass, surrounded by trees and a collection of handsome stone buildings that looked like they'd been transported straight from the Champs-Élysée.

'This is the cricket pitch Liam was talking about yesterday.'

'The architecture looks more like a suburb of Paris than the typical English village.'

'That's because Corfu was not only colonised by the British, and the Venetians, but also by the French, who built these magnificent buildings to remind them of home. Fancy a coffee?'

'Love one.'

Nikos guided her to a table in the shade outside a tiny café on the impressive Liston, and ordered them a frappé each, and they spent several minutes just sitting and watching the world go by; the tourists taking never-ending photographs, the scooters zooming past like over-sized bluebottles, the birds trying to have their song heard above the cacophony of sound, the waiters weaving expertly between the tables, serving everything from pastries to omelettes, toasted sandwiches to ouzo. The aroma of freshly ground coffee, warm baked bread, and Nikos' lemony aftershave added yet another dimension to the medley.

As Abbie sipped on her iced coffee, staring at the deserted cricket pitch, she was visited by the clearest of visions of her aunt sitting in the same place, indulging in a spot of people-watching, enjoying a well-deserved break from her duties at the hotel, and a question formed in her mind. She tried to push it away, not wanting to start that conversation, but it continued to push its nose above the parapet, demanding attention. She wasn't sure why she hadn't thought of it before now.

'Nikos, you've been back here for two years.'

'I have,' he smiled.

'So you must have known my aunt.'

'I did, although not very well.'

'And she never mentioned my mum, or me, to you?'

Nikos looked uncomfortable. 'I'm sorry Abbie, she didn't, but I'm hardly her ideal confidante, am I?' He laughed. 'Why do you ask?'

'Because, while I'm here, I need to find out as much as I can about her life, and the only way I'm going to do that is by asking questions of the people who knew her.'

'And who have you talked to so far?'

'Only Sofia. She told me about how, and why, Aunt Liz ended up here in Corfu, and how devastated she was when she lost her husband, but…'

'But what?'

'I think she knows a lot more than she's telling me.'

Nikos held her gaze. 'I'm sure she does.'

'Do you think she knows the reason they fell out? Why they never stayed in touch? Why she didn't come to my mum's funeral? I thought she might come, you know. I mean, *I* hadn't done anything to upset her, had I?'

To Abbie's surprise, tears pricked at the corners of her eyes and she inhaled several breaths to calm the cauldron of emotions this subject always whipped up. It was so important to her to understand what had happened, and the closer she got to finding out, the more anxious she felt.

On the one hand, she wished she could just forget it; it was in the past after all, she couldn't change it. However, she also knew that if she didn't find out the truth, the "not knowing" would continue to agitate just below the surface, ready to rear its ugly head at the most inopportune moment, wreaking havoc with her confidence and affecting her future relationships, just as it had with Dan. She didn't want that, but she also couldn't do this by herself. If Sofia did know more than she had told her so far, she needed someone to help persuade her to reveal what it was.

'Nikos, would you… would you be able to talk to her for me? Find out what it is, or at least find out why she's so reluctant to tell me about it?'

Nikos remained silent as he mulled over her request, then he drained the final drops of coffee from his glass and reach out to grasp her hand, his eyes softening as they met hers.

'I understand how you feel, Abbie, I really do. There are so many questions I wish I'd asked my father about his life, about his childhood growing up here, about his love of his vineyard, about his thoughts when he took over the winery from my grandfather. If we think about these unanswerable questions for too long though it can drive us crazy. It's too late now, and it's no use dwelling on what could have been. But nor should we forget our pasts and how they impact on our futures. I will speak to Sofia, but I suspect that she *does* intend to tell you what she knows. She's just waiting for the right time; when you're ready to hear what she has to say.'

'But I'm only here until the end of the week.'

She saw the familiar flash of irritation in Nikos' eyes but he chose not to reintroduce his feelings on the sale of the Hummingbird Hotel into the conversation, which only made her feel more guilty and appreciative of his friendship.

'I'm sure you'll get the answers you need, Abbie. Okay, shall we go and meet Loukas?'

Nikos tossed a few coins onto the table and held out his hand. She took it and they sauntered along the narrow streets until they arrived at the bakery, its frontage hidden in a shady cobbled courtyard filled with terracotta pots of white and red geraniums, a silver bowl on the doorstep for thirsty feline friends. A tall, slender man with film star-esque good looks stood in the doorway, a long baker's apron tied around his waist, clearly waiting for them to arrive. His lips stretched into a broad grin when he saw Nikos, greeting him in a torrent of high-speed Greek as he pulled him in for a man-hug before turning to smile at Abbie.

'Loukas, this is Abbie Coleman; she's Liz's niece.'

'Ah, yes, I can see that,' said Loukas, switching effortlessly to English.

'You can?'

'The cotton candy hair!'

Loukas laughed, reaching up with his large hands to indicate the tousled mess and Abbie rolled her eyes at him, but she couldn't help laughing. She had spent her whole life feeling self-conscious about her hair. Wouldn't it just be easier if she embraced it?

'I'm sorry for your loss, Abbie.'

'Thank you, Loukas.'

'Okay, Nikos, I have everything you need for your Parisian ladies' tea party,' said Loukas with a twinkle of mischief in his chocolate-brown eyes. 'Tell me, have you invited the local platoon of pixies to share in the occasion with you? I mean, macarons and pastry horns, really?'

Loukas' deep belly laugh was infectious as he slapped Nikos jovially on his back, which made Abbie warm to him even more. He stepped back into his tiny bakery, collected a stack of large white confectionery boxes, and handed them over to Nikos.

'Thanks, Loukas, I owe you one. See you later.'

Unable to shake his hand, or repeat the affectionate man-hug of earlier, Nikos bumped forearms with Loukas, and then spun on his heels and made his way out of the courtyard, leaving Abbie to be engulfed in a bear hug instead, her senses enlivened by the delicious waft of warm buttery pastry and sweet honey that came with Loukas' embrace. If this was what all bakers in Corfu looked like, then maybe her aversion to culinary activities could be overcome.

'Thanks, Loukas.'

'You're welcome, just promise me one thing.'

'What's that?'

'That you and Nikos will have dinner with me and Julianna when your guests have left.'

Abbie struggled to conceal her surprise. Did Loukas think they were a couple?

'Oh, no, Nikos and I… we're not…'

She was grateful that Nikos was out of earshot, otherwise she would have been even more embarrassed at Loukas' mistake, but when she met his gaze, she saw the twist of a challenge in his eyes and she laughed. Baker and village matchmaker!

'I'd love to join you both for dinner.'

'Great, I'll look forward to it. *Yassou*, Abbie.'

'*Yassou*, Loukas.'

Loukas disappeared back inside his bakery and as Abbie jogged to catch up with Nikos, she realised again that she knew nothing about his relationship status. Did he have a girlfriend? Or a fiancée? Had he been married, perhaps? He hadn't mentioned anyone, but why would someone as handsome, and generous, and thoughtful, as Nikos not have a romantic partner in his life?

She knew it was a subject she would have to broach at some point, except, if she did, surely that would mean she would have to talk about her own grenade-strewn love life – a place she would rather not stray if she could help it.

Chapter Twenty

The Kitchen at the Hummingbird Hotel
Flower: Cupid's Dart

Abbie spent the next two hours in a role she never thought she would ever inhabit. The tasks Nikos delegated to her as his assistant pastry chef were so alien to her that she felt like she had temporarily stepped into someone else's body; chopping nuts, grating chocolate, weighing out ingredients, and slicing oranges, lemons and fresh figs. To her astonishment, as they worked side by side in choreographed synchronicity, she actually began to enjoy herself – there was something so calming to the rhythmic chores of preparing for an international cookery class. She was so proud of herself that she even took a few selfies to send to Emily, receiving a gobsmacked emoji back.

Of course, she was nowhere near as proficient as Nikos who moved from one task to the next with practised efficiency, never spilling a sprinkle of flour, or a dribble of honey, or a splodge of yoghurt, unlike Abbie who – no matter how much she concentrated – just couldn't seem to master the techniques required to maintain a clutter-free counter top. It was a picture of two halves; Nikos' work area was pristine with not a crumb or smudge in sight, whilst her side resembled a scene from the Corfu Culinary Catastrophe. She reached for a cloth to surreptitiously wipe away some of the evidence of her untidiness, but Nikos realised what she was doing and burst out laughing.

'Here, let me help you.'

To her surprise he did not relieve her of the cloth to wipe down the marble bench top, instead he scooped up a handful of the flour she had spilled and tossed it in her direction. She was so shocked by his action that she remained frozen in her position, her arms outstretched at her sides, her mouth ajar.

'What the…'

The shock abated swiftly, replaced with amusement when she glanced down at the splash of white on the front of her sunflower-yellow tee-shirt. She smiled, her spirits rising as she saw the mischief glittering in Nikos' eyes.

'Ok… ay.'

She picked up a few of the pistachios he was preparing for the baclava, and tossed them straight at him, laughing with delight when one of them bounced off his forehead in a direct hit. Now it was Nikos' turn to laugh as he dipped his finger into a pot of yoghurt and daubed it onto the end of her nose before licking the remainder from its tip.

'Mmm, delicious.'

So many different emotions tumbled through Abbie's body that she was hard-pressed to understand what was happening. Not being the world's most enthusiastic cook, she had never shared the kitchen with anyone, let alone someone like Nikos, and had certainly never taken part in a food fight. If this was how pulling ingredients together usually ended, she had been missing out on *so* much fun, and she now understood why Emily preferred whipping up recipes in the pâtisserie to whipping up emotions in the theatres of the West End.

Having paused to reflect on their crazy culinary caper, she had inadvertently handed Nikos the advantage, and before she knew what was happening, he was snaking his hand around her waist, his chin resting gently on her shoulder as he reached for a silver spoon laden with honey and raised it to her lips.

'Taste this,' he murmured, his breath tickling her earlobe and sending ripples of desire out to her extremities. She could smell his familiar cologne, feel his heart beating through her flimsy tee-shirt, and the surge of heat she felt had nothing to do with the temperature in the kitchen. When she sampled the honey, her tastebuds burst into a kaleidoscope of flavours.

'Wow, that's delicious.'

She allowed the teaspoon of sweet bliss to linger in her mouth for as long as possible, enjoying the rich, thick consistency, savouring the various floral notes; thyme, heather, orange blossom. With Nikos' arms around her, every sense she possessed zinged with pleasure, and she had never in her whole life felt so alive. She turned slightly and saw that Nikos was staring intently at her, his eyes dark and unreadable, his lips parted slightly, his hand resting on her shoulder. Then, holding her gaze, he pulled her towards him, slowly, gently, until they were mere inches apart, the electricity between them sparking wildly, and suddenly nothing else mattered except the feel of his soft lips on hers, and the exquisite joy she knew that would deliver.

The moment seemed to go on forever, suspended in time until, to her intense disappointment, the spell was broken; their mutual hesitation having afforded them both the time to reflect on how taking that final step would change their relationship from friends to something much more complicated. However, Abbie couldn't fail to notice the shadow of regret that floated across Nikos' expression. She felt it too, but after the disappointment had passed, she found she was actually relieved that things hadn't gone any further.

Kissing Nikos would have been amazing, and her body had certainly been screaming "do it, do it, do it!" at the top of its voice, but her head had cautioned her against it. A brief fling with a gorgeous Greek guy might be just what she needed to put what had happened with Dan behind her and move on, but Nikos was not some random guy she had met whilst on holiday. He was so much more than that. Anyway, she had never been a summer-holiday-romance kind of a girl. She smiled awkwardly at Nikos, grateful to see that he smiled back.

'Why don't you go and freshen up whilst I finish up

here?'

'Great, yes, great.'

Abbie could feel her cheeks glowing as she almost sprinted from the room. She dashed up the stairs to her bedroom, stripped off her flour-bedecked clothes, and jumped into the shower, relishing the coolness of the water splashing over her body and calming her raging emotions. Afterwards, she pulled on her favourite powder-blue tee-shirt, a pair of cream linen trousers, and slid her feet into her silver flip-flops.

When she got to the foyer, she paused, not quite ready to return to the kitchen, so she diverted her route to the courtyard and made her way through the stone archway and the pergola to the swimming pool terrace where she came to an abrupt halt, her hand flying to her lips.

'Oh, I…'

It wasn't Nikos who was carving his way through the gentle ripple of the turquoise water, nevertheless, her heart still slammed against her ribcage in a mixture of trepidation and anticipation when she recalled the last time she had seen Felix swimming in the pool – or *exiting* it, to be more precise. Surely he wasn't…

'Oh, hey Abbie, I thought you and Nikos were over in Corfu Town this afternoon.'

'We were, but we…'

Felix swam over to the side of the pool where she was standing and, try as she might to avert her eyes, she couldn't help but glance down into the water, the most intense feeling of relief spreading through her veins when she caught a flash of red fabric beneath the surface. Unfortunately, Felix knew exactly what she had been doing and grinned enthusiastically.

'Being at one with nature delivers such intense freedom. You should try it.'

Abbie laughed, kicked off her flip-flops, and sat on the edge of the pool, dangling her feet into the water as Felix floated on his back in front of her, the warm rays of the late afternoon sun enhancing his tanned and toned chest, his wayward curls spread around his face like a golden halo. She'd never been more grateful that he'd chosen to wear swimming shorts.

'So, where *is* Nikos?'

'He's just finishing up in the kitchen.'

'Really? He's cooking you dinner?'

Felix's blue eyes sparkled, clearly hoping for an invitation, and Abbie's heart ballooned with affection for the guy whose life had changed so dramatically after what must have been one of the most heart-breaking events he'd ever experience. Thankfully, he had clearly found peace in this little corner of the world and she was happy for him.

'No, he's preparing a cookery class for our guests.'

'A cookery class?'

'Yes, well, a baking class, pâtisserie, to be precise – two Greek recipes, two French recipes.'

'Wow, that sounds like fun.'

Abbie laughed. 'Want to join us?'

'I'd love to, thanks, Abbie.'

Felix hauled himself out of the pool in one graceful manoeuvre, wrapped a towel around his waist, and reclined on one of the Hummingbird Hotel's blue and white striped sunloungers, his hands clasped behind his head as he considered Abbie.

'So, you and Nikos seem to be getting close.'

'Oh, we… No, we're just friends, that's all.'

'He likes you, Abbie.'

'Well, I…'

'And you like him – there's no point denying that which is written in our stars.'

Abbie couldn't help but roll her eyes.

'So, what did my horoscope say about today?'

Felix sat up, delighted to be asked to provide his daily dose of astrological predictions. She wondered what Rachel and Sofia thought of having their own on-site oracle.

'Oh, I'm so pleased you asked that, because your horoscope was particularly special. That's why I came over to the hotel, actually, not just to swim in the pool but also to tell you that from sunrise to sunset your day will be filled with a helter-skelter of flavours, textures, aromas, and emotions, but one sensation above all others will take you completely unawares.'

'And what's that?'

'Love.'

'Love?' For some reason, Abbie couldn't meet Felix's eyes.

'Yes, I'm sure you've heard of it. It's where two people —'

'I know what love is, Felix!' She laughed. 'But I think this might be the first time your beloved horoscope source is slightly off-kilter, though.'

'We can't avoid Cupid's arrows, Abbie.'

'I really don't think—'

'Hey guys, here you are, I've been looking all over for you.'

Abbie was inordinately relieved that Nikos was too busy bumping fists with Felix to notice the flush seeping across her cheeks, and she sent up a request to the Greek gods in charge of avoiding embarrassing situations that he hadn't overheard what Felix had been saying before he arrived. When she caught Felix's eye, she saw the triumphant look of glee on his face – he even waggled his eyebrows suggestively – and she smiled, shaking her head at him.

'Come on, Savannah and her friends have just arrived back from the beach and are busy getting changed – the class starts in ten minutes,' Nikos said, urging them towards the kitchen.

Chapter Twenty One

The Kitchen at the Hummingbird Hotel
Flower: Tear Drop Rose

Abbie quickly redistributed the six sets of ingredients to accommodate Felix's request to join in with the bakery session, and then went out to the veranda to join the rest of the group who were filled with animated chatter about their day out at the beach. Nikos introduced everyone to Felix and Abbie smiled when he responded with a cheery "Namaste".

'Abbie, guess what Liam did this afternoon,' said Paige, almost pogoing on the spot next to Liam who was clearly bursting to tell them.

'What did you do, Liam?'

'I went paragliding! I was absolutely terrified, but once I was up in the air, I got this rush of absolute and total freedom, like I was a bird floating on the breeze, looking down on the beaches, the coves, the rocky outcrops, the olive groves. It was amazing, and definitely one of the highlights of my entire life.'

'I think Bree had one of those experiences, too.' Savannah giggled, chinking glasses with her best friend who had changed out of her beachwear into a crisp white cotton blouse with cute turn-back cuffs and a pair of flared white shorts, her hair held back from her freckled face with a white bandana.

'I—'

'Oh my God!' Felix burst out, staring straight at Bree. 'You're an Aquarius, aren't you?'

Bree gaped at Felix. 'Actually I am. How did you know?'

'Well, that's easy; intelligent, quirky, highly creative.'

This description of her characteristics, astrologically speaking at least, clearly met with Bree's approval and she swapped places with a very disgruntled Liam – who until then had been standing next to Felix so he could appraise his attributes from close range.

'What was your highlight of the day?' asked Abbie.

'It was a rendezvous with a very handsome stranger,' Felix supplied, his eyes crinkling at the corners.

'That's right!' Savannah laughed again. 'She had a drink with one of the guys from the water sports company while Liam was doing his impression of a constipated eagle.'

'Hey, I did not—'

'But your aura tells me that far from the romantic dalliance you'd hoped for, your meeting stirred up memories of the past you thought you'd left behind. Ca give you a little advice?'

'Erm, I…' Bree floundered.

'Tall, dark, and handsome, is not where your future happiness lies.'

'Okay…'

Abbie knew she wasn't the only one to see Bree's eyes flash with unease, and suddenly, out of nowhere, tension crackled through the air. She decided to grasp the conversation baton and steer the subject onto safer ground.

'Okay, everyone, shall we get started on the cookery course? Nikos?'

'Yes, if you'd like to follow me.'

As Nikos led the group into the kitchen, Abbie saw Liam reach out to squeeze Bree's hand to show his support and she wondered what had just happened. However, she shoved that mystery aside for the time being as she took her place at the marble-topped island in between Felix and Savannah.

'Today I will be teaching you how to make two Greek and two French recipes; all delicious.'

'Just like the guys,' quipped Liam, which produced a smile from Bree.

'Okay, we shall start with my favourite, and probably the most well-known of all Greek pastries, baklava. Sticky and sweet, filled with chopped pistachios and walnuts, and wrapped in layers of filo pastry – hand-made by my friend Loukas – then drenched with honey and finished with a sprinkle of cinnamon. *Nóstimo*!'

As the taste-bud-tingling aroma of warm caramelised sugar and cinnamon infiltrated the kitchen, Abbie's mouth watered in anticipation. The group listened carefully to

Nikos' instructions, following them to the letter until everyone had produced a passable version of the Greek dessert staple – even Abbie. Once the trays had been slotted in the oven to bake, they moved on to their next sugar-laden Greek treat.

'Okay, let me tell you that no Greek celebration is complete without our next pastry – *kourabiethes*. These are very rich, melt-in-the-mouth, shortbread-style cookies, made with ground almonds and a dash of ouzo, and finished off with a generous dusting of icing sugar and a single clove.'

'Wow, they sound amazing!' said Bree.

Abbie was delighted to see how seriously Savannah and her friends, along with Felix, were taking the baking class, asking pertinent questions about the ingredients, what drink the *kourabiethes* biscuits were usually served with, and how well they stored. When they, too, had been baked in the oven and all the Greek pastries were cooling on a wire rack, Nikos switched to what she could tell was the part of the demonstration he had been looking forward to the most – the Parisian pâtisserie section.

'So, I thought we could make a *tarte tatin* together, with caramelised figs grown in my own garden and braised in butter and a decent splash of Metaxa, then I have a special treat for you all.'

'Yum!' Liam declared.

'My friend Loukas has very kindly baked a selection of puff pastry horns that we will dip in melted chocolate and load up with our own choice of filling – mascarpone flavoured with cinnamon, Chantilly cream, or tangy lemon confectioner's custard – and finish off with a sprinkle of crushed pistachios, or curls of bitter chocolate, or grated zest of an orange. *Allons-y*!'

The next thirty minutes passed by in a whirl of culinary excitement as everyone helped to place the sliced figs in the large frying pan in an attractive star shape, then watched Nikos as he drizzled over Greek honey, then covered everything with puff pastry and popped the pan into the oven. He then handed round the pastry horns Loukas had made for them, removed five separate bowls from the fridge, and placed them in the middle of the island for the students to help themselves, roaming around the group to offer suggestions wherever needed.

'This is fabulous,' said Paige, licking cream from a teaspoon and rolling her eyes in exaggerated ecstasy, then giggling as Liam dunked a large serving spoon in the bowl and shovelled a great dollop of Chantilly cream into his mouth.

'Enrique is the cook in our house,' said Savannah, her eyes filling with adoration for her husband-to-be. 'You know, he can rustle up an authentic Valencian paella that would challenge the most accomplished of chefs, but he always adds an extra-special ingredient for me.'

'What's that?' asked Paige.

'Don't tell me,' Liam scoffed. 'Love?'

'Of course!' Savannah placed her hand over her heart and swooned.

'And I bet his talents don't end at cooking, do they, darling?' Liam shot a quick glance to the other side of the kitchen where Bree was helping herself to a slice of the sticky baklava she had made, wrapping her tongue around her fingers to catch the dribbles of honey.

'I have no idea what you mean.'

'Well, didn't he just land that role as one of the Jets in West Side Story?'

Savannah laughed. 'He did.'

The conversation continued to swirl with Liam asking Felix how he came to be in Corfu, which to Abbie's surprise he side-stepped by suggesting that as it was their last night on the island, maybe they should treat themselves to dinner at Sofia's taverna as it made the best moussaka in the whole of Greece.

'Sounds like a plan.' Savannah smiled, turning round to see if Paige approved.

'I agree,' said Paige, before looking around the room. 'Hey, where's Bree?'

Abbie's heart gave a jolt of sympathy that Bree's friends hadn't noticed her absence. She'd seen her slip out of the kitchen when the conversation had turned to Enrique, but she had expected her to have returned by now.

'Why don't you all grab a selection of cakes and a coffee and take them out to the veranda? I'll go and see if I can find her,' said Abbie, removing her apron and exchanging a glance with Nikos, receiving a nod in return. She headed off towards the courtyard, determined to use the opportunity to talk to Bree about the hair dye incident. The more she thought about it, the more she knew it had to be the chief bridesmaid, not only because of the colour – which in her opinion at least would be the last choice of any discerning client at the prestigious Knightsbridge salon – but because of her history with Enrique. Was she really, as Liam had suggested, over him?

It was after seven and the cicadas were in full voice. The sun had left for the day, and the solar lights and lanterns were aglow, washing the scene in a soft amber light, but there was no sign of Bree. Abbie made her way through the stone archway towards the swimming pool where she spotted her sitting on one of the sunloungers, her head down, her shoulders stiff, staring at the sparkling surface of the water.

'Hi, Bree, everyone's adjourned to the veranda to taste-test their pastries if you want to— Hey, are you okay?'

'Yes, yes, of course, I'm fine.'

But Abbie knew she wasn't. She dropped down on the sunlounger opposite Bree and waited for her to look up from studying her manicure, her heart giving a twist of sympathy when she saw her eyes were ringed in red.

'I'm sorry, Bree, I really am.'

'I don't…'

But Bree clearly knew there was no point denying how she felt to Abbie; the carefully crafted mask she had worn since arriving in Corfu had slipped, and her face revealed the pain etched deep in her soul at the loss of someone she had obviously cared a great deal about, made even more difficult to bear because her best friend was about to marry him – and she was performing the role of chief bridesmaid.

'I've tried, Abbie, I really have, but it's just so hard seeing them together. I know how happy they are, and what makes it worse is that I always knew in my heart that Enrique and I would never have made it. But I did love him, and it was a huge shock when he told me it was over because he'd fallen in love with someone else.'

'Had he been seeing Savannah?'

'Oh no, no, Savvie wouldn't do that, but of course they'd

met through me. I'd be lying if I said I didn't notice the way they connected, that instant spark that ignited between them, almost like love at first sight. I knew it was only a matter of time, and I was right. Enrique broke things off with me and two weeks later he invited Savvie out for dinner and the rest, as they say, is history. I pretended I was fine with it, and I should have been – these things happen, don't they? – but my heart kept telling me otherwise. I still loved him, so I…'

'What?'

'I thought that the best way to get over him would be to start dating again. And boy, did I date! A different guy every week, but no one made me feel like Enrique had. Then…' Bree swallowed down hard and Abbie could see her gathering the courage to say her next words. 'Then they announced their engagement. It was like a physical blow, but I pinned on a smile and told them how happy I was for them. And I truly *am* happy for them; they are both amazing people and they make a fabulous couple, and it's clear to everyone that they adore each other, so I pushed my pain aside and threw myself into helping Savvie organise her wedding. I thought I could do it, I thought I could be the best friend and the best bridesmaid ever, but it's just been *so* hard.'

'I'm sorry, Bree, I…'

Could she do it? Could she really talk about what had happened with Dan? Wouldn't she sound like a complete idiot? But what if, in some small way, what she had been through helped Bree to know she wasn't the only one struggling with heartbreak?

'Abbie?'

'I know exactly how you feel.'

'You do?'

'My situation is different, and, well, much more embarrassing.'

That did the trick. Bree's interest was piqued; she pushed herself up from the sunlounger, her eyes widened, shoulders straightened, as she waited for Abbie to elaborate, and when she didn't, she nudged her.

'What happened, Abbie?'

'I… I thought my boyfriend was going to propose. I'd seen him in Tiffany's, and then he booked a table at my favourite restaurant in the whole of London, so, of course, I jumped to the totally unjustifiable conclusion that—'

'It's not totally unjustifiable, I would have, too.'

'That's not the worst part.'

'It's not?'

'Oh my God, it's just so mortifying, even now.'

'More mortifying than inadvertently losing your boyfriend to your best friend?'

'Much.'

'Tell me.'

Abbie exhaled a long breath. 'I arranged for all our friends, colleagues – we worked together, you see – and even a few clients, *everyone*, to be at the restaurant, hiding behind a screen, so that when Dan proposed they could leap out with whistles and party poppers, shouting "Congratulations". I thought it would be a fabulous surprise for him, but… well, he didn't propose, and when he reached down to pick up the napkin I had dropped, everyone we knew burst out and made a huge fuss, other diners joined in, as well as all the staff and even the chef came out of the kitchen with a special cake. I was so embarrassed, but that was nothing compared to seeing the look of pure horror on Dan's face. It was clear he had never even entertained the possibility of a forever with me.'

'Oh, Abbie, I'm so sorry that happened to you.' Bree reached over to place her hand gently on Abbie's arm, her eyes filled with compassion. 'Thank you for sharing your experience with me, I know how hard it must have been, and it really helps to know I am not the only one to have made a complete fool of myself in the name of love.'

Abbie smiled; she had to admit that she felt better having shared her story with Bree, someone who was basically a stranger who knew nothing about her or her background, and who hadn't judged her for misinterpreting her boyfriend's intentions so erroneously. She knew now that each time she was honest about what had happened it would get easier, feel less immediate, less raw, less painful.

'Thanks for listening, Bree.'

'You too, Abbie, I feel so much better about things now. Okay, I think we should get back to the party, don't you? Otherwise, Liam will have scoffed all the delicious pastries.'

As the conversation with Bree had taken such a diversion, Abbie had almost forgotten the reason she had sought her out in the first place. After such an intense heart-to-heart in which she'd divulged the most shame-filled incident of her life, how could she now proceed to cross-examine Bree on the circumstances surrounding Savannah's abrupt change in hair colour? But if she didn't do it now, she probably wouldn't get another chance, so she corralled every scrap of her courage.

'Erm, before you go, Bree, do you mind if ask you something?'

'Sure, anything.'

'Savannah's hair?'

'Oh, gosh, yes, it was a shock, I agree, but trust her to make it look fantastic. I'm almost tempted to do something similar myself, not pink, though. I'm not sure that shade would suit a red-head, but maybe a light shade of mermaid green.'

'No, actually, I meant…'

Abbie's nerve failed her. Bree was a guest at the Hummingbird Hotel; she didn't want to upset her, or worse, make completely unfounded accusations. How would that look in a review? Unfortunately, when she met Bree's gaze, it was too late to extricate herself from the awkward conversation and heat flooded her face.

'You think… you think I had something to do with that? Really?'

'No, I just wanted to—'

'It's okay, Abbie, after what we've just been talking about, I can see how you might think that, but I promise you that I had nothing, absolutely nothing to do with it. I would never, *ever* do anything to hurt Savvie. I love her, she's my best friend, and she's done nothing wrong apart from fall in love with someone whom I thought – hoped – loved me but didn't. I'll get over it, in time, but I'm afraid you need to look elsewhere for answers.'

'I'm sorry, Bree, I didn't mean to—'

'Actually, if you want my opinion, my money's on Liam. He's really annoyed about Savvie pinching all of his VIP and celebrity clients – she does it all the time. I don't know why though. She obviously doesn't need the money, although she does have a very expensive wedding to pay for. So, does this mean that you think somebody sabotaged Savvie's hair products? Hey, maybe you should talk to Paige.' Bree was on a roll now.

'Why?'

'Because there's definitely something going on between them.'

'What do you mean?'

'A few days before we flew out here, Savvie told me that she was going to cancel Paige's ticket. I don't know the details, but I do know they had a huge argument about something at the salon, and when I asked her what she was planning to do she told me she would mull things over whilst we were in Corfu, then decide. If you want, I can ask her about it for you.'

'No, no, please don't. I think we should just leave it. I really don't want to spoil your last night here. It's fine.'

'If you're sure?'

'I'm sure. Thanks, Bree.'

'Come on then, let's join the party.'

With her brain spinning, Abbie followed Bree back to the veranda where the group were already on their fourth bottle of wine and talking about making a move to the taverna for the final dinner of their trip.

'Is everything okay?' asked Nikos, his eyes filled with concern at her longer-than-expected absence as he handed her a glass of wine and watched her down it in one. 'Did you talk to Bree?'

'Yes, I did.'

'And?'

'She says it wasn't her.'

'So it's Paige?'

'Only person it can be.'

Chapter Twenty Two

Sofia's Taverna, Ropa Valley
Flower: Olea Europaea

After taking a lot longer than Abbie had hoped to get ready for their last night out in Corfu, the group made their way down the driveway towards Sofia's taverna, and if Abbie hadn't known better, she would have thought her guests were on their way to the Oscars. She'd never seen so much glitz and sparkle outside one of Pierre Fontaine's fashion shows.

The reminder of her old life caused a sharp stab of pain to shoot through her chest, so she forced herself to think about something else, a task that proved difficult because her head was filled to bursting with a jumble of disconnected thoughts. Even the beauty of the surroundings – the final rays of the sun sending ribbons of apricot light floating across the darkening sky, the rustle of nocturnal creatures making a start on their nightly chores punctuated by the whine of a lone scooter, the rich scent of jasmine lingering in the air – wasn't enough to banish the mounting anxiety from her mind.

She sighed; the sooner she confronted Paige, the sooner she could relax – although she had no idea what she was going to do if Paige denied her involvement in the shampoo saga just as Liam and Bree had done. So many different scenarios whirled through her mind that she felt disorientated and disconnected from reality, so that when they arrived at the taverna she had continued walking on past it, in a world of her own, until she was brought back down to earth by the sound of laughter.

'Abbie!' Nikos called.

'Oh, yes, sorry.'

She spun on her heels and re-joined the group as they made their way through the gate at the side of the taverna and round to the rear terrace with the mesmerising view, only to find that every table was occupied by sun-kissed tourists and local families alike. Conversation, punctuated by cries of delight in a multitude of languages, swirled through the air, easily masking the soft bouzouki music that emanated from the speakers on either side of the bar. The delicious aroma of warm red wine, rosemary and garlic caused her stomach to growl in expectation.

'*Kalispera*!' Sofia beamed her welcome before being engulfed by an over-enthusiastic Felix who then strode off to his studio to "change into something a little more comfortable". 'I'm sorry, as you can see, we're very busy tonight, but if you like I can ask Rachel to set up a table for you over there in the olive grove.'

'Wow, really? I'd love that,' said Savannah, skipping down the steps to a grassy area beneath an ancient tree, its gnarled branches strung with garland upon garland of fairy lights. 'It's perfect; it'll be like we're dining in a real-life fairy glade!'

'Absolutely adorable,' Liam declared, as he followed Savannah into the clearing, looking extra-handsome in a pair of white chinos and a loose-fitting saffron-yellow silk shirt, his Ray-Bans lodged in his super-gelled quiff. 'And *so* Instagram-friendly, too!'

Nikos helped Panos to manoeuvre a long trestle table into place, along with a set of mismatched chairs, and Rachel brought a collection of cutlery and crockery and a huge storm lantern to add even more romance to the ambiance. Once everyone was seated, Panos served them with a variety of hors d'oeuvres – green and black olives, tiny deep-fried potato and courgette balls, and triangles of warm pitta with hummus, tzatziki and taramasalata – and Sofia asked Rachel to fetch them a couple of bottles of house wine.

'Sure.'

Rachel floated off towards the bar, her mind clearly on other things because when she returned, she placed two large cafetières of coffee in the middle of their table, along with a jug of cream, a bowl of sugar, and a plate of *kourabiedes* drenched in icing sugar.

'Erm, Rachel, I think we…'

'Mmm? Oh, oops, sorry.'

Rachel whisked the coffee away and deposited it on a table at the other side of the restaurant. Of course, Rachel's confusion meant the wine Sofia had asked her to bring didn't materialise, so Nikos took matters into his own hands and collected a bottle of red and a bottle of white from the bar and poured everyone a drink, much to their relief.

'To our last night on the paradise island of Corfu!' Savannah said, raising her glass in the air. '*Yamas*!'

'*Yamas*!'

'Cheers, sweetie, and a huge thank you for bringing us to this wonderful place,' Liam said.

'Thank you for coming. I know it's not what most people want for their hen party celebrations, but I've had an amazing time here, and I'll definitely be coming back to the Hummingbird Hotel.'

'Me, too!' said Paige, sipping at her white wine.

'Me three,' added Bree, pouring herself a second glass of red wine and draining half of it in one go. 'What do you think the odds are on us getting what we order for dinner tonight? Our waitress seems a little… distracted.'

'Oh, don't mind Rachel, she's always like that,' said Felix, sliding into a chair next to Nikos, his "something more comfortable" a luminous orange shirt, open to the navel, and a pair of what looked to Abbie like pyjama bottoms in a rich raspberry colour, his curls held away from his face by a Kermit-green hairband. 'She's a Pisces; creative, empathetic, generous, but most of all, a dreamer.'

'How did Rachel end up in Corfu?' asked Savannah, wrapping her tongue around the tip of her finger to catch a dribble of tzatziki.

'She came here on a gap year last summer to paint – it's her one true passion – and she loved the island, and its people, so much that she decided to stay, much to her parents' disapproval. But only by walking her own path will she find the true meaning of who she is. Anyway, they should have been grateful.'

'Why?'

'Because I think she did the residents of Bristol a huge favour.'

'Really? How?'

Felix's lips twitched at the corners. 'Rachel trained as a dentist; all of her family are dentists – her mother, her father, her uncle and her brother – and they wanted her to join their string of west country dental practices, to keep up the family tradition.'

'Oh my God, really?' Bree giggled as her eyes found Rachel who had just removed an enormous platter of mixed seafood – which included a whole octopus in tomato sauce, tentacles and all – from a table of horrified diners and replaced it with the steak and chips they'd ordered. 'Wow, I can't imagine Rachel in possession of a dentist's drill – it doesn't bear thinking about! An unsuspecting patient could go in for a scrape and polish and come out with a new set of veneers!'

'Our destiny sends us in mysterious directions, Bree.'

'And I see it wasn't only the *island* she fell in love with,' Savannah observed, causing everyone to swivel in their seats to locate Rachel who was now ignoring a table of diners who clearly wanted their bill in favour of leaning against the bar, her chin in her hand, watching Kostas prepare a tray of his signature cocktails.

'I don't blame her.' Bree laughed. 'He's gorgeous; I'd consider jacking it all in for a guy like that!'

To Abbie's relief, Sofia had anticipated Rachel's tendency towards absentmindedness and had ordered a selection of dishes for their evening meal – from chicken souvlaki to *spanakopita*, from *keftethes* to home-baked moussaka and stuffed peppers, and a huge bowl of Greek salad topped with cubes of feta cheese – all of which worked perfectly as it meant they could sample several different recipes at once.

The group fell silent for the first time that evening as they savoured every mouthful. When there was nothing left except a few stuffed tomatoes, their plates were whisked away and dessert was brought to the table, a myriad of honey-soaked treats that were the perfect way to round off such a sumptuous, and authentically Greek, meal.

'Has Enrique told you where you're going for your honeymoon yet, Savvie?' asked Liam as he stuffed the last of Sofia's *kourabiedes* into his mouth, rolling his eyes in appreciation before licking each one of his fingers in turn to make sure he'd caught every single granule of sugar.

'No, not yet.'

'Ooo, maybe it's the Maldives,' said Paige, who, to Abbie surprise, had only picked at her meal while everyone else had devoured every morsel put before them, and still sipped from the same glass of wine that Nikos had poured for her when they arrived. 'Or the Seychelles?'

'Maybe, I'm not sure.'

As Abbie watched Savannah refill her glass, she got the feeling she was avoiding answering Paige's question, and she knew her intuition was correct when Savannah swiftly changed the subject.

'Bree, darling, I've booked an appointment for our

final dress fitting for next Saturday afternoon, if that's okay with you? I thought we could celebrate afterwards with a few glasses of Champagne at The Dorchester.'

'Sounds fab.'

'Hey, what about me?' said Liam, who was now leaning back in his chair, his hands behind his head, his cheeks glowing from all the food and wine he'd consumed and clashing dreadfully with his bright yellow shirt.

Savannah laughed. 'You can come, too.'

Abbie knew she was the only one to have noticed the flicker of something unidentifiable shoot across Paige's face, and her heart gave a nip of sympathy. Bree's words from their chat that afternoon came rushing back to her, and she wondered what Savannah could have been mulling over, and whether it had something to do with the hair dye incident.

Was it because Paige wasn't included in the wedding of the year? And yet that didn't seem to fit with what Abbie knew about Paige, who, to Abbie's mind at least, seemed to be the most sensible of the group, despite being the youngest.

Bottles of brandy and ouzo arrived, along with cups of rich, dark Greek coffee, and Abbie excused herself to seek out Sofia to thank her for accommodating them in the olive grove, and for serving them such a delicious meal. When she arrived on the terrace, to her surprise she saw they were the only diners left at the restaurant, and she spotted Sofia sitting at a corner table with Panos, her injured leg resting on a chair, enjoying a quiet nightcap.

Rachel, on the other hand, was perched on a bar stool, her expression stony as she watched Kostas who was now deep in conversation with a very attractive dark-haired woman with huge gold-hoop earrings, and judging from the way she continuously touched his arm and giggled at everything he said, they clearly knew each other very well.

'Hey, Abbie,' Felix said, startling her as he appeared at her side.

'Oh, Felix, I…'

'I'm calling it a night – a good night's sleep is a gift from the gods – but I just wanted to thank you for letting me join in with the Hummingbird Hotel's cookery class this afternoon. I had more fun than I thought I would, and I hope you're planning on making it a regular event. If you need anyone to fire up the barbie and showcase a few Aussie dishes, then count me in! And I'm sure Rachel would be up for offering a few painting classes if you want to add a little diversity to the creative mix.'

'Erm, well…'

Abbie didn't have the heart to remind him that she was selling the hotel and that there would soon be no more cookery, or any other kind of classes, at the Hummingbird Hotel, although the thought did make her sad. She watched Felix meander towards the steps that led up to his tiny studio above the restaurant, and then returned to the table in the olive grove to try and persuade the group to call it a night so that Sofia and Panos could close the doors and have some quality time together.

'Hey, where's Paige?'

'Oh, I…' Savannah looked around the table, clearly not having noticed her absence.

'Must have gone to the bathroom,' said Bree, her soft Scottish burr a great deal more pronounced after the amount of wine, brandy and ouzo she had consumed over the time they had been at the restaurant. Like Liam, her cheeks were rosy, but her eyes were glazed and she emitted the occasional giggle for no reason at all, followed by a hiccup that seemed to surprise her every time.

'Come on, sweetie, I think we need to get you back to the hotel before you collapse.' Liam laughed, pulling Bree up to her feet, catching her into his arms when she stumbled. 'Whoah, steady! Savvie? Want to give me a hand?'

'Sure.'

Savannah linked her arm through Bree's and the three friends made their way from the restaurant, singing an Abba song at the top of their voices as they stumbled towards the driveway that led back to the hotel.

'I think we can safely say that a good night has been had by all,' Nikos commented, raising his glass of red wine to Abbie. '*Yamas*, Abbie.'

Abbie smiled and raised her own glass of sparkling water, and it was a few moments before either of them realised that Savannah, Liam and Bree had once again completely forgotten about Paige.

'Hey guys, where is everyone?'

'I'm sorry, Paige, they've had to take Bree back to the hotel. I think she's had a bit too much to drink,' Abbie said.

'Nothing new there,' Paige remarked, sinking down into a chair next to Abbie.

'Okay, it's after midnight, I think we should…' Abbie started but then Nikos caught her eye and gave a sharp nod of the head in Paige's direction. Abbie knew immediately what he meant, but that didn't stop her stomach from dropping to her toes with anxiety. She rolled her eyes at him, wondering whether she could invent an excuse for putting off her conversation with Paige until later, but as the group were leaving the following morning, she knew that this was probably the only chance she would get.

She inhaled a breath and once again wondered whether her aunt had had such difficult situations to contend with. She doubted it.

'Paige, is everything okay with you?'

'Of course, why wouldn't it be?'

'It's just that, well… Bree told me that…'

And that was all it took. Paige's expression changed from relaxed to deer-caught-in-the-headlights. 'What did she say?'

'Only that you and Savannah had a bit of a disagreement before coming out here, and it doesn't take a detective to notice that you're not yourself this evening. You've barely eaten anything, and you've hardly spoken a word, either.'

'I'm fine, really, I'm…'

Then, to Abbie's surprise, Paige burst into tears.

Chapter Twenty Three

The Olive Grove, Taverna Sofia
Flower: Scented Geranium Charity

Abbie exchanged a glance with Nikos who jumped up from his seat, dashed to the bar and brought back a bottle of Metaxa brandy, poured them each a measure and handed one to Paige who took a tentative sip, then curled her lips downwards in disgust.

'Ergh, that's awful!'

But it did the trick; Paige's tears dissipated and she was much calmer.

Abbie placed her hand over Paige's and gave it a gentle squeeze, relieved that the whole sorry saga was now out in the open and she could relax in the knowledge that the Hummingbird Hotel wasn't to blame. However, the distress on Paige's face and her tear-stained cheeks didn't make her feel any better, and she wanted to get to bottom of what was going on.

'Do you want to talk about it, Paige?'

'I… I don't…'

'If you tell us, maybe we can help?' Abbie suggested.

Paige swallowed down hard on her rising emotions, then all the fight seemed to drain from her body, her shoulders slumped, her head dropped, and she released a long, ragged sigh of defeat.

'Oh, Abbie, I'm so, so, sorry, I really am. I shouldn't have done it. I feel terrible, not just for what I did to Savvie, but to you, too. I know how worried you've been, and you absolutely don't deserve it, and if it's any consolation, the guilt has been eating away at me from the moment I switched those bottles.'

'But why, Paige? Why did you do it?' Nikos asked, his voice low and gentle.

'I…'

Once again, Paige paused, clearly gathering her courage to explain her actions, and when she spoke her voice was tight and every word sounded like it was a strain to utter.

'A couple of weeks before we came over here, Savvie… well, she caught me… Oh, this is awful… just so awful.'

'What happened?' urged Nikos.

'Okay, so, we use lots of hair products in the salon; shampoo, conditioner, mousse, wax, hairspray, and then there's the beauty products – creams, gels, lotions, masks – all luxury brands that cost an absolute fortune. It's my job to check the supplies, to make sure we never run out, and I also volunteered to be responsible for recycling the hundreds and hundreds of plastic bottles. The stylists are supposed to throw the empty bottles into a special green basket, I rinse them out and parcel them up, and at the end of the month I bike them over to our supplier.'

'Okay,' muttered Abbie, wondering where on earth Paige's explanation was heading.

She would have happily given Paige as much time as she needed to get to the point but Nikos wasn't as patient; he was perched on the edge of his seat, staring at Paige, clearly desperate to hear the full story, which wasn't happening as quickly as he would have liked.

'Paige?' he encouraged her on.

'After a few weeks, I realised that some of the bottles in the basket were still a third, sometimes *half*, full. The guys had just discarded them because it was easier to open a new one than to take the time to squeeze out every last drop. I get it; they don't want to do that in front of our high-end clients in case it looks like they're being miserly with the products, but I couldn't bear to see all that expensive stuff go to waste. So… well, I started to decant the leftover shampoo and conditioner into washed-out water bottles that our less environmentally-conscious clients leave behind.'

'What's wrong with that?' asked Nikos, clearly becoming more and more bewildered by the direction of their conversation.

'Savvie caught me, and the worst thing was that she didn't go ballistic like I thought she would. She just said she was disappointed that I've done it without asking her first. I was devastated; she thought I was selling the products to make some extra cash. I tried to explain, but she wouldn't let me, she said it wasn't necessary and just walked away. I sat in the salon all night, and the next morning I offered to resign, but Savvie wouldn't hear of it. All she would say is that she wanted to mull a few things over for a while, and would tell me what she was going to do when we got back from our Corfu trip.'

'Paige, I'm so sorry—' Abbie started.

'I know she's going to fire me, and so I just… Oh, God, I really don't know what came over me. It was like someone had taken over my body, like a puppet with someone working the strings and I had no control over my actions. I thought if I could just distract her with a bit of harmless fun, then she wouldn't have the chance to dwell on what she's going to do when we get back home. It's stupid, I know. I didn't think things through. I had no idea she would think it was your fault, Abbie, or how that might impact you and the hotel. I've made such a mess of things. Look, let's go back to the hotel, I'll come clean, tell Savvie what I've done, and this time I'll make sure she accepts my resignation.'

'But I don't understand,' said Nikos. 'Why did you do it?'

Paige exchanged a puzzled glance with Abbie. 'I just told you.'

'No, I mean the shampoo decanting. Why did you do that? *Did* you sell it?'

'No, oh my God, no. I wouldn't do that!'

'So what, then?'

Paige's demeanour changed. She raised her chin, straightened her shoulders, and met Nikos' eyes with a look of defiance, before turning towards Abbie.

'Remember when I told you that I help out at a women's refuge in Harringay?'

'Yes, I do.'

'Well, like I said, some of the people arrive with just the clothes they're wearing; no toothbrush, no hairbrush, nothing, and I really couldn't bear to see all those gorgeous, luxury hair products just washed down the plug hole. What was the point of that? So I did what Savvie wanted me to do in the first place – sort of. I recycled it into bottles and handed it out to the new arrivals at the shelter. If you saw how much of a difference something like that makes to a woman in need, Abbie, you would do it, too.'

'But why didn't you just tell Savvie the truth?'

'Tell Savvie what truth?' came a voice from the edge of the olive grove.

Paige's head shot up in surprise and she turned towards the sound of Savannah's voice.

'Oh, I…'

Abbie watched Savannah walk towards them, her immaculately shaped eyebrows raised in question. 'Hi, Savannah, what are you doing here?'

'Well, Bree and Liam have gone to bed. I helped myself to a coffee and waited for a while in the courtyard and when you and Paige didn't arrive, I came back here to see if you were okay. So, Paige, what didn't you tell me?'

Savannah dropped down in the seat next to Nikos, nodding when he offered her a tot of brandy, then waited for Paige to answer her question. Abbie's heart went out to her – she looked absolutely terrified – but to her credit, she pushed herself up in her chair and inhaled a breath.

'I'm sorry, Savvie, but it was me. I added the colour to your hair conditioner. Don't worry, its non-permanent; it should wash out after a couple more washes.'

'You did that? But why? I don't understand.'

Paige cringed under Savannah's steady gaze.

'I just… I just… well, when you found out about the… about the, you know… and you said you needed time to think about what you were going to do, and you refused to let me explain, and…'

Paige was gabbling, every word coming out at a hundred miles an hour in one long almost incomprehensible sentence. Abbie took pity on her, and decided she needed to take up the explanation baton, determined to make sure Savannah understood the reason behind what Paige had done which was, after all, rooted in kindness and compassion for others.

'Paige donated the hair products she decanted at the salon to a women's refuge she volunteers with.'

'Yes, I thought that might be the case.'

Paige's jaw dropped in surprise. 'You did?'

'Yes.'

'But…'

'Oh God, I'm so sorry, Paige. I've been so busy with everything that's going on at the moment, what with organising the trip here to Corfu, running the salon, meeting up with the lawyers and the accountants, sorting out everything for the wedding… Oh, this is all my fault.'

'Your fault? No, Savvie, it isn't, it's—' Paige started.

'I should have told you.'

'Told me what?'

'Okay, I was going to do this when we got back home,

but…'

'Savannah, why don't we go back to the hotel, and…' Abbie began.

'No, it's fine.'

To Abbie's surprise, Savannah was smiling broadly.

'This has been a long time in the making, and I wanted every detail to be ironed out before I told anyone, but… well, I've got two pieces of news. One relates to something that I've been wanting to do for years, since I trained as a hair stylist, really, and the other – which has just been finalised this morning – is because of you, Paige.'

'Me?'

Savannah nodded, suddenly overcome by emotion. Tears glistened at the corners of her eyes as she reached out to take a gobsmacked Paige's hand in hers.

'I wanted it to be a surprise, but from now on, every Tuesday afternoon, you and I will head over to the women's refuge and donate our services to the people there. We'll offer haircuts, blow-drys, facials, manicures, pedicures, whatever treatments are required.'

Paige's eyes widened and her hand shot to her mouth.

'Oh, I…'

'And I've also set up a special fund to make sure that if, for whatever reason, either of us is unable to make it one week, then another stylist can be booked for the Tuesday afternoon session, and their fee and the products they use will be paid for. I'm also planning to set up a donations box at the salon for any of our clients who want to support the initiative, which is going to be called Project Paige.'

Tears rolled unchecked down Paige's cheeks as she stared at Savannah, clearly struggling to understand what was happening.

'Thank you,' she whispered. 'And I'm so sorry for what I did.'

'Are you kidding me? I would never have had the courage to try something like this. I love it; don't you think it suits me?'

Savannah tossed her head, causing the glossy pale pink bob to fan out around her cheeks, then laughed and reached out to pull Paige into her arms, hugging her tightly. Abbie watched them, her heart bursting with affection for what the two women had done – and were going to do – for the vulnerable and disadvantaged, but when she looked at Nikos, she saw his forehead was wrinkled in expectation.

'So, what's the other piece of news?'

'What… oh, yes.' Savannah pulled out of her hug and met Nikos, then Abbie's, eyes.

'Since I qualified as a hairdresser over fifteen years ago, I've had a dream. It's not the dream you would expect an average eighteen-year-old to have of working at a glamourous hair and beauty salon frequented by celebrities, or owning my own salon, or winning trophies for my innovative techniques or modern twists on the classics, but it was what I wanted to do as soon as I could afford it. I never realised it would take so much planning; visas, vaccinations, legal stuff, anyway…' Savannah paused to inhale a breath. 'Enrique and I aren't going to the Maldives, or the Seychelles, or Hawaii for our honeymoon.'

'You're not?'

'No, we're going to Syria.'

'You're going to Syria for your honeymoon?'

Savannah laughed at the look of horror on Paige's face.

'We're not having a honeymoon, instead we're using the time, and the money it would have cost us, to spend two weeks with a voluntary organisation in a refugee camp on the Turkey/Syria border. I'll be offering hair and beauty treatments to the staff and the refugees, and Enrique will be helping out in the canteen. It's one of the reasons I wanted to come here, to the Hummingbird Hotel, for a few days of rest and relaxation; an oasis of calm before the storm.'

Silence reverberated around the olive grove as Savannah's surprise revelation sunk in.

'Wow, that's an amazing thing to do,' said Abbie, bowled over by the kindness on show this evening.

Paige's tears resumed, and she flung her arms around her friend, causing Savannah to join in, and it was several moments before they pulled apart, laughing, wiping their eyes, and chatting about Savannah's travel plans.

'Okay, guys, I think we should make a move if we don't want to be chased out of the taverna with a broom,' said Nikos, pushing back his chair, standing up and holding out his hand to Abbie. 'Come on.'

She slid her palm into his, and, along with Savannah and Paige, they called *kalinychta* to Sofia and Panos, and made their way from the restaurant. They strolled down the driveway towards the hotel, the night air cool and still, the sky midnight-blue with a whole swathe of stars stretching into eternity, something Abbie never got to see in London. When they reached the steps at the front of the hotel, Savannah and Paige bade them goodnight and, their arms still entwined, disappeared into the lobby and their rooms beyond.

'So, the mystery is solved.' Nikos chuckled. 'The Hummingbird Hotel's reputation is saved, and all future guests can sleep easy in their beds knowing they will not wake up with rainbow-coloured hair!'

Abbie climbed to the top of the marble steps and turned around to face Nikos, seeing the laughter in his eyes. 'Thanks, Nikos, thanks for helping me to sort it all out. I couldn't have done it without you.'

'I have to admit, I thought I led an interesting life until I met you, Abbie, but it turns out managing a vineyard and a winery is child's play compared to the skills required to run a successful hotel business! Although I did have *the* best fun that I've had in years presenting the hotel's cookery classes, so if you need someone to offer a few bread-making, or cake-decorating, or maybe even wine-tasting classes, then I'm your guy.'

'I'll bear that in mind.'

When Abbie met Nikos' dark, brooding gaze, she felt the now-familiar frisson of electricity shoot through her veins, and her heart performed a summersault of undeniable attraction. Everything around her seemed to recede from view, leaving just the two of them, standing on the steps together, each waiting for the other to make the next move. Goosebumps rippled along her forearms, every nerve in her body tingled in anticipation, and, finally, Nikos' lips were on hers, softly, gently at first, tentatively exploring their contours, until emotion took over and he pulled her closer so he could kiss her more deeply, more passionately.

And Abbie responded, relishing each and every one of

the myriad sensations that pulsated through her veins, revelling in the sharp, citrusy cologne she would forever associate with him, relishing the feel of his muscular chest pressing against her, and the way his thumb caressed the nape of her neck, sending her rising passion to a higher level.

When eventually she pulled from his embrace, she felt breathless, wanting nothing more than to spend the rest of the night kissing Nikos again, and again, and again, but to her surprise, he took a step back from her, his eyes bright with an unidentifiable emotion. Then his lips curled into a smile.

'*Kalinychta*, Abbie.'

'*Kalinychta*, Nikos.'

Abbie remained on the steps, watching him saunter down the driveway – his hands thrust in his pockets, relaxed and totally at one with his surroundings – until his silhouette merged into the darkness. She released a long sigh of contentment, then stepped into the lobby, locked the front door, and all but floated up the stairs to her bedroom, the memory of Nikos' kisses imprinted on her lips.

Chapter Twenty Four

The Vineyard at the Hummingbird Hotel
Flower: Dancing Hollyhocks

The moment the sun slid through her bedroom window Abbie leapt out of bed and into the shower feeling lighter, brighter, and happier than she had for a long time, and her spirits soared as she recalled everything that had happened the previous evening. Whilst she was relieved the mystery over the hair dye had been solved and the Hummingbird Hotel's reputation had been maintained, she knew her good mood had more to do with the kisses that had rounded off an eventful day.

She sent Nikos a cheery "good morning" text, and skipped down the stairs to the kitchen to begin what had become her daily routine of preparing breakfast for her guests; setting up the coffee machine – which she was now on first name terms with – gathering cups and saucers and filling a plate with a selection of Greek pastries. She suspected that after the amount of alcohol that had been consumed by everyone the previous evening, she might have to raid the medicine cabinet, too.

A burst of accomplishment flooded her chest, and she was relieved that she could wave goodbye to her guests safe in the knowledge that whilst their stay hadn't been without its issues, everything had been ironed out in the end. She hoped that Savannah and her friends had enjoyed their stay in rural Corfu, because to her surprise, she had enjoyed having them. She had made four new friends, people she would never have met if she hadn't come to Greece and perhaps, when she was back home, she could meet up with them for a coffee or a drink, and maybe she could contribute to Project Paige.

'Hi, Abbie… oh, thank God! Coffee! You are an absolute saviour!'

Bree, dressed in her usual ubiquitous uniform of all-white – including a pair of vertiginous wedges – dashed to the table like a woman dying of thirst, poured herself a double espresso and downed it in one, heaving a sigh of relief.

'Ah, that's better. I almost feel human again.'

'Pleased to hear it!' Abbie smiled, offering Bree the pastries, expecting her to take one but instead she took the whole plate and meandered out to the veranda to enjoy her rather indulgent breakfast outside.

'Hey, sweetie, don't you dare eat them all!' Liam said as he strode into the kitchen. He deposited a pair of noisy kisses on Abbie's cheeks, quickly grabbed himself a latte, then dashed out to the veranda to stop Bree from devouring everything in sight.

'It's okay, Liam,' Abbie called after him, laughing. 'I've got plenty more.'

Minutes later, Savannah and Paige arrived with their suitcases in tow, abandoned them in the lobby, then came into the kitchen, arm-in-arm, their heels click-clacking on the marble floor, chattering away excitedly as though they hadn't paused since the previous night. Abbie wondered whether they intended to share what Paige had done with Bree and Liam, but she knew that really wasn't any of her business, although she was sure Savannah would tell them about Project Paige and her, and Enrique's, impending trip.

Once again, her respect for Savannah blossomed. What a wonderful thing to do and it reaffirmed her intention to do something to support the project in whatever way she could when she returned home. Maybe Emily could get involved, too.

'Abbie, before our taxi arrives, on behalf of all of us, I'd like to say a huge thank you for everything you've done. The Hummingbird Hotel is a real gem of a place, and although our stay here hasn't exactly been serene,' Savannah patted her hair and shot a smile across at Paige, 'I've loved every single minute, and I will take lots of fabulous memories back home with me. Who would have thought I would learn how to cook and bake authentic Greek food, or taste wine that has been made only a stone's throw from where I'm drinking it? I will definitely be coming back.'

'Me too,' declared Bree.

'Me three, sweetie!' added Liam. 'Hey, maybe we can come out here at Christmas? Or for my birthday? Yes, let's come over for my birthday in September, and Nikos can give us a masterclass in sugarcraft. I've *always* wanted a birthday cake in the shape of a hair dryer, maybe in pink or pale blue. Can you book us in for that, Abbie, darling?'

'Of course.'

Abbie smiled at Liam, not having the heart to tell him that she wouldn't be there in September, that she had no idea who the owner of the Hummingbird Hotel would be then, or even if it would still be a hotel. That thought caused a stab of regret deep in her abdomen; she hoped the new owner would keep the place exactly as it was, welcoming guests for a few days of tranquillity far away from the hustle and bustle of their normal lives, somewhere they could relax in the sun, enjoy good food and local wine, and generally recharge their batteries, or perhaps spend their time there learning a new skill, just as Savannah and her friends had done.

'Thanks, guys, it means a lot that you've enjoyed your stay here.'

'Where's Nikos?' asked Savannah. 'I'd like to thank him, too.'

'Oh, well, he's at home, at the winery.'

'Okay.'

Savannah gave her a weird look. Abbie realised she had expected him to have stayed over with her at the hotel, and her cheeks reddened as she searched for a suitable response. Fortunately, she was saved by the honk of a car horn.

'Ah, I think that must be your taxi to the airport.'

'Come on, guys, we don't want to miss the plane.'

While Bree and Liam ran off in search of their luggage,

Savannah drew Abbie into a tight hug, followed by Paige, who whispered her own heartfelt thank you and a promise to stay in touch. A few moments later, Abbie was standing on the front steps, waving goodbye until the taxi disappeared in a cloud of dust at the end of the driveway, and, at long last, she found herself engulfed in a mantle of calm. The birds seemed to share her feelings, tweeting their relief that the cacophony of human activity was over and they could claim back the airwaves.

After another revitalising coffee, she collected the hotel's cleaning paraphernalia and got to work on the guest rooms, finding the sweeping, the scrubbing, the polishing, and the bed-stripping therapeutic, and seeing the rooms with fresh white linen and sparkling fixtures strangely fulfilling, although she had no idea why she had made the beds – she wasn't expecting any more guests.

By the time Abbie had finished her chores, she was perspiring so profusely she decided to treat herself to a quick dip in the pool to cool off, savouring the soft caress of the rippling water over her skin, and then dropping down onto one of the sunbeds to dry off. She checked her phone again, a little miffed that Nikos hadn't responded to her text, and, as the remaining time she had at the hotel was her own to do with as she wished, she knew exactly what she was going to do next.

She collected a pair of gardening gloves and set to work on the flowerpots dotted around the pool area, smiling as she inhaled the exotic perfumes, inspected unusually shaped petals and leaves, and enjoyed the feel of the gritty dry soil between her fingers. As she worked, ideas tumbled into her mind; a cluster of dancing hollyhocks here, a collection of red geraniums over there, maybe a few pots of herbs next to the path so that guests could enjoy the aroma of wild sage, or lavender, or woody rosemary, as they brushed past on their way to the pool. Maybe even a cactus garden…

When the sun was at its highest in the sky, she retreated to the kitchen for a cold drink, then resumed her work, this time heading for the mini-vineyard at the rear of the hotel, pulling up weeds as she went, inspecting the vines for pests, googling information on the vines' care, and feeling the surge of her passion for all-things horticultural. She paused, wiping her forehead with the back of her hand as she looked out over the Angelopoulos estate, picking out the front door of the winery, straining her eyes to see if there was any activity there, becoming more concerned that Nikos hadn't contacted her.

Was he regretting their kiss?

She sent him another light-hearted text, offering to treat him to dinner that night to say thank you for everything he'd done for her guests, and, when she didn't receive a reply, she decided to call it a day in the vineyard and take a shower. Then, feeling refreshed – and, more importantly, clean – she poured herself a glass of lemonade, added a handful of ice cubes, and went to sit on the veranda, marvelling at the hypnotic view, at the way the heat caused the landscape to shimmer in the distance.

As she sat, her feet resting on one of the bamboo chairs, her mind wandered to Savannah and her friends who would have landed back in London by now, and it hit her for the first time that she would be doing exactly the same in three days' time – her return flight was booked for Thursday afternoon. A sharp jolt of anxiety brought her to her senses. She had come to Corfu to find answers and she had done everything but ask questions. She knew Sofia was the person she needed to talk to, and her mum had always taught her that when there were difficult challenges to face, there was no time like the present.

Just as she pushed herself out of her chair, her phone started to buzz and her heart skipped a beat.

Nikos!

'Hi!'

'Miss Coleman?'

'Oh, erm, yes, this is Abigail Coleman.'

'Alex Stephanopoulos here.'

'Oh, hello.' Abbie's heart now pounded to a very different beat.

'Sorry for the delay in getting back to you, but I have some good news. The investor I told you about – Georgios Konstantinou – has just confirmed his offer for the Hummingbird Hotel via his lawyers. I think you will agree with me that it is very generous.'

When Abbie heard the figure that he was offering, she couldn't help but gasp.

'Are you sure?'

'Absolutely, and the best thing is that he wants to complete on the purchase right away. The cash is available, I've checked that out on your behalf, and his lawyer has power of attorney so there's no need to wait for Georgios to come over to Corfu.'

'No need to… doesn't he live here?'

'No, he lives in Athens.'

'Oh, okay.'

Abbie's thoughts ricocheted around her head, but there was one question she needed answered.

'Can I ask what Mr Konstantinou's plans are for the hotel?'

She detected a slight hesitation from Alex which immediately put her on her guard.

'A little remodelling, that's all.'

'What kind of remodelling?'

'I don't have the details, I'm afraid, but you know, once the money is safely in your account, his intentions for the building and the land are no longer your concern.'

Abbie knew Alex meant his comment as a positive, that as soon as she had signed along the dotted line, she wouldn't have to worry about the complexities of running and maintaining a hotel in a foreign country, but his words had the opposite effect.

'What sort of business is Mr Konstantinou in?'

'It's okay, Miss Coleman, the hotel will be in good hands as he already owns a group of hotels; one in Kefalonia, one in Zakynthos, and another in Santorini.'

'So the Hummingbird Hotel will become a part of a chain?'

'Yes.'

'Oh, I—'

'Miss Coleman – Abbie, if I may – permit me to give you a little advice, as your lawyer. The property market here in Corfu is far from buoyant at the moment, especially for properties so far away from the beach. This is a very good offer, in fact, it is several thousand euros more than I had expected. I recommend you accept it; you won't get a better one, unless, of course…'

'What?'

'Unless you plan on staying here on Corfu and managing the hotel yourself.'

'No, I… no, I don't plan on doing that.'

'So what is the problem?'

'Nothing, you're right. I'm sorry, yes, it *is* a very generous offer.'

'So it's a deal? Will I draw up the paperwork?'

'Yes, please do.'

'Okay, remind me when you're leaving?'

'My flight is on Thursday afternoon.'

'I shall have everything ready for Thursday morning; you can call in to my offices on your way to the airport and sign the paperwork then.'

'Thank you.'

As soon as the call ended, Abbie's mood deflated like a pricked balloon. She didn't understand her reaction. Wasn't this exactly what she had wanted? Alex was only following her instructions to sell the hotel and get the best price possible. That was his job and that's what he had done. She could have no control over what any future owner of the hotel did to the property, she knew that, and she'd never had any intention of staying on in Corfu and running the hotel herself. This was the result she wanted, and with that amount of money she could afford to buy her dream cottage in Devon with a small garden.

So why was she so upset?

But she knew the answer. She had made friends here, become – even if it was for just a short time – part of the community, and not just that, she'd formed a connection with Nikos.

Nikos.

Why hadn't he called her? And what would he say when she told him the hotel had been sold? Maybe he would be relieved that someone in the hotel business was buying it. Maybe Georgios Konstantinou would keep it as a rustic retreat for small groups, but in her heart of hearts she knew the word "remodelling" was just a euphemism for expansion, or maybe even rebuilding altogether.

Oh God. Was this why Nikos hadn't contacted her? Everyone knew everyone else in Corfu; maybe he'd heard through the grapevine that the Hummingbird Hotel was as good as sold, and, unlike her, he knew *exactly* who Georgios Konstantinou was and what he intended to do with the place.

She checked her phone again. Still no response, and when she tried to call Nikos her call went straight to voicemail. She sighed; there was only one thing to do that she knew would make her feel better, so she grabbed her satchel, locked the hotel door behind her, and made her way to Sofia's taverna.

Chapter Twenty Five

Taverna Sofia, Ropa Valley
Flower: Iris 'Flight of Butterflies'

'Hey Abbie.'

'Hi, Rachel.'

'What can I get you?'

'Just an iced coffee, please.'

'Okay.'

To her surprise, Rachel reappeared a moment later with her frappé, as ordered, but there was none of her usual cheerfulness accompanying the beverage and Abbie noticed that the backs of her hands were splashed with specks of paint.

'Have you been painting?'

'Yes, spending time with my brushes usually helps me to put life into perspective, lifts my spirits, makes me smile, but to be honest the inspiration was totally missing-in-action this morning, which isn't surprising.'

'Why? Is everything okay?'

'Actually, no, it isn't.'

Rachel checked the restaurant to see if there were any customers requiring her attention, but it was Monday evening and trade was slow. Apart from Abbie, there was only a sun-bronzed couple lingering over their bottle of wine, and a sole diner immersed in his phone, so Rachel slumped down into the seat next to Abbie, dropped her elbows on the table, and placed her chin in her hand, her face wreathed in misery.

'What's the matter?'

As soon as she saw Rachel glance over her shoulder towards the bar where, unusually, there was no sign of Kostas polishing his cocktail glasses, she understood.

'Kostas?'

Rachel nodded.

Abbie then remembered the previous night. She had been so distracted by everything that had been going on in her own life, with Paige's confession and Savannah's news, that she had forgotten that pain-filled expression she'd seen on Rachel's face when she was watching Kostas talking to the woman with the huge gold earrings at the end of the night.

'I'm sorry, Rachel.'

'Apparently, he asked Panos if he could leave early and… and they left together on her scooter, her arms around his waist, her head resting on his shoulders, like they were… like they were a couple.'

Abbie saw the sorrow etched in Rachel's eyes and she

reached out to give her friend's hand a squeeze of sympathy. 'Have you asked Sofia if she knows who she is?'

'No, I haven't. It doesn't matter; he's single and he's entitled to do whatever he likes with whoever he likes. It's just I…' Rachel's eyes sparkled with unshed tears. 'I love him, Abbie.'

'I know.'

'It's the only reason I stayed on here. Well, not the *only* reason, I stayed to paint, and would you believe that I actually sold one of my watercolours this morning to a customer who saw me coming back from my painting session and asked to see what I'd painted? My very first sale.'

'Congratulations! That's great.'

'I suppose so.'

Abbie's heart went out to Rachel. What should have been a cause for celebration – the achievement of a long-held dream of actually making a living from something she was so passionate about that she had rejected the offer of a place in the family business – had been overshadowed by the appearance of a rival for Kostas' affections. She wouldn't admit this to Rachel, but Kostas and the dark-haired woman *had* seemed close, more than just friends, and she was once again reminded of the treacherous journey that lay ahead when you entrusted your heart to someone else.

'What will you do?'

'What do you mean?'

'Will you go back home?'

'Home? No way. Anyway, Corfu is my home now. I've never been happier than I am here; it's where I can be truly myself without feeling I've let my family down. I have a great job, lots of amazing friends, and I can paint whenever I like.

Why would I leave this gorgeous island and go back to the UK?' Rachel's mood brightened. 'By the way, have you seen Felix today?'

'No, I've been busy sorting out the hotel after my guests left this morning.'

'Well, he's had a bit of interesting news.'

'What kind of interesting news?'

Before Rachel could answer a platoon of cyclists dressed from head-to-toe in Lycra chose that moment to descend upon the taverna, so she gave Abbie an apologetic smile and drifted off to take their order. Abbie finished her coffee and then fingered her phone, toying with the idea of trying to call Nikos again, but then deciding to text Felix instead. She could do with some cheering up and Felix certainly did that, even contemplating what he might be wearing that day made her smile. No sooner had she pressed send than Felix himself appeared in front of her, resplendent in one of his fluorescent pink outfits that would have put Mr Motivator to shame.

'Hey Abbie, I assume you're not here for another yoga session?'

She laughed. 'No, I'm not, sorry. Rachel told me you've had some news.'

'Fancy a walk?'

'Oh, right, yes, sure.'

Confused, Abbie gathered her satchel and followed a surprisingly agitated Felix down the steps from the taverna's terrace and into the shade of the olive grove they had dined in the previous evening. The heat of the day was starting to wane as sunset approached and a light breeze offered some welcome relief.

'So, come on, what's your news?'

'Rachel told you my story, didn't she?'

'Yes, she—'

'And she told you that Carlie left me standing at the altar like a discarded possum?'

'Yes—'

'Did she also tell you that the guy Carlie ran off into the sunset with was my best friend?'

'Yes, she did, and I'm so sorry that happened to you, Felix.'

'It's the reason I decided to go travelling; first to Bali for a couple of months, then I spent some time at an ashram in India where I learned the importance of practising yoga every day, and then I ended up here, in Corfu, and Sofia and Panos gave me a place to stay. I'm happy here, I truly am. It's a very spiritual place. Do you feel it, too?'

'Er, I…' Abbie lapsed into silence. She wasn't sure she did, to be honest, but she didn't want to contradict Felix. She'd certainly found a degree of serenity, if that was the same thing. They continued walking in silence, passing through a field of colourful wildflowers filled with a confetti of butterflies, and onto a narrow footpath that descended towards the valley floor.

'You know, my horoscope promised that I would have an important decision to make today; a decision which would completely alter the direction of my life. I thought you were going to ask me to run a yoga retreat at the hotel.'

'Really?'

Abbie had no idea how Felix had come to that conclusion. If he'd seen it in the stars, then they were definitely having an off day.

'But nothing could prepare me for the phone call I got this morning.'

'Phone call?'

They had now reached a wide, dusty clearing with two rickety bamboo chairs, and Felix slumped down onto one of them, his forearms on his thighs, his hands dangling between his legs, his head bent. Abbie was no expert in body language, but she didn't think the news he'd received could have been at the "good" end of the spectrum.

'A phone call from Carlie.'

'What did she say?'

'That she was sorry. That she regretted what she'd done. That she and Scott are no longer together, and she wants us to try again.'

'What are you going to do?'

Felix raised his head and Abbie saw things she'd never expected to see in Felix's eyes – anguish, turmoil, anxiety, apprehension. 'I don't know.'

'Do you still love Carlie?'

'I suppose that's what I need to figure out.'

Abbie thought of asking him what the stars predicted, but she didn't want to appear flippant, so she simply smiled at him. 'I'm sure you'll make the right decision.'

'I have to walk my own path, Abbie, we all do, either alone or in tandem with our soul mate. That's the route to finding happiness, and it's what I told Nikos to do.'

'Nikos? You've spoken to Nikos?'

'Yes, this morning, after he got the call.'

'What call?'

Felix stared at her; his eyes wide with confusion.

'Have you spoken to Nikos today?'

'No, he's not answering my calls. Why? What's going on?'

'I dropped him off at the airport this morning. He's gone to Athens to see his mum and his sister.'

'Oh my God, what's happened?' she asked in alarm.

'No, no, it's nothing like that.'

A flash of indecision floated across Felix's face as he clasped and unclasped his hands, clearly trying to decide what to tell her. Then, to her relief, he sat up straight in his chair and met her eyes.

'It's the vineyard and the winery; they're struggling financially.'

'Yes, I know. Nikos told me. He's had to sell his motorbike.'

'It's worse than that.'

'How much worse?'

Her stomach began to churn as she waited for Felix's reply.

'Sadly, the business is teetering on the brink of bankruptcy, has been for a while, and he's refused to admit it to anyone – most of all his family – but his sister called him this morning to tell him that their mother had received a call offering her a huge sum of money for the vineyard and she was seriously thinking about accepting it.'

'Sell the vineyard? But it's been in his family for generations.'

'The offer is from some kind of developer – a wealthy Greek businessman who's buying up land for a new hotel complex he wants to build – and apparently he's already negotiated a deal with another landowner in the area.'

Abbie's stomach dropped like a stone. She gasped but managed to disguise her reaction by turning it into a cough and fortunately Felix didn't notice.

'Nikos is devastated, that's why he's dropped everything to fly over to Athens so he can talk to his mum and sister face-to-face, to persuade them that things will improve. But his mum thinks this is their only option if they want to avoid the stigma of bankruptcy. He's tried to make it work, tried his utmost to honour his father's legacy, but, by his own admission, he's no winemaker; he's a chef, and a damn good one at that.'

'I know, I know.'

'Maybe he'll get his job back at that fancy hotel he worked at in Paris.'

'I don't think—'

'Oh my God, Abbie, I've had the most amazing idea! Nikos can work with you at the hotel offering more of those Greek and French cookery classes! I'm sure there'll be a huge market for them if you can set up a half-decent website. And I'm happy to do a few yoga retreats, too, and Rachel can do painting classes for you – it's a perfect solution!'

Felix jumped up from his seat and pulled Abbie into his arms, picking her up and swinging her round and round in excitement. She didn't have the courage to explain to him that what he'd suggested wasn't an option, and that – while she could be wrong – the reason Nikos had received an offer for the vineyard that morning was because she'd accepted one for the hotel.

'Come on, I need to get back to my room so I can meditate on Carlie's proposal.'

Chapter Twenty Six

The Terrace, Taverna Sofia, Ropa Valley
Flower: Frothy Pink Peony

Abbie was surprised she had managed to get any sleep with so many different questions circulating through her mind, one after the other, each one demanding attention and answers she simply didn't have. However, when she woke to the familiar alarm call of the early morning chorus of cicadas, her head was clearer. She was even able to assemble her thoughts into some kind of order, and there was one question above all others that she needed to resolve before she left for home.

Why had her aunt left her the Hummingbird Hotel?

She knew that the only way she was going to find out was by asking Sofia. She knew Sofia had more to tell her about her aunt's life – in Corfu, and in California – than she had already disclosed. The issues between her mum and her aunt, although never mentioned whilst she was growing up, had dominated her life for as long as she could remember, and it was time to deal with those ever-present demons that had refused to relinquish their hold on her, even after her mum's passing, once and for all, otherwise she would never find peace.

If Sofia refused to tell her what she knew, then she would go to California and try to find someone there who had known her Aunt Liz and her husband, Greg. She certainly didn't relish that task; in fact, the very thought of flying out to the United States by herself filled her with dread, so she took a quick shower, tied up her wayward curls into a ponytail, and made her way to the taverna.

She paused halfway down the driveway to appreciate the view, fixing the splendour of the sunrise over the luscious green hillside in her mind's eye so she could enjoy it when the London, or Devonshire, skies were grey and overcast and the early morning drizzle made the daily commute even longer, and more depressing, than usual. She glanced over towards the Angelopoulos vineyard, a cloak of sadness descending as she thought of how Nikos and his family must be feeling. She'd already checked her phone several times that morning, and Nikos still hadn't contacted her, which couldn't be a good sign.

At seven thirty, it was still too early for even the most enthusiastic of Sofia's customers and so Abbie was unsurprised, and relieved, to see that the taverna was deserted, apart from its eponymous owner, sitting at a table on the terrace, filling tiny blue and white ceramic vases with flowers and herbs.

'Hi, Sofia, need any help?'

'Oh, Abbie, yes please. I'm sure you'll do a much better job than me – flower-arranging is definitely not my forte.'

Abbie took a seat opposite Sofia, selected a couple of stems of lavender and added a gorgeous fluffy pink peony, then another, and another until she'd created an attractive bouquet for the restaurant's tables in a matter of minutes.

'I wish someone around here would grow a few flowers in addition to grapes and olives. We all need a little more beauty in our lives, more colour, more fragrance, but it would make excellent financial sense, too. I'm not the only business in Ropa Valley who likes to brighten up their customers' day with a pretty floral arrangement. It really wouldn't be that hard, either – you can stick a broom in the ground here and it will grow! I've mentioned it to Nikos – have you seen that jungle of a garden at the winery? – but of course, he has enough to do with managing the vineyard.'

Abbie didn't know if Sofia had an ulterior motive for the suggestion she had just made, and if so, she was flattered that Sofia had so much confidence in her horticultural and flower-arranging abilities – it was more than she had in herself – but whatever her intention, bearing in mind she was leaving in two days' time, Abbie thought it best not to comment, so she did what she always did when faced with an awkward situation and changed the subject.

'How's your ankle?'

'A little sore still, and Panos is insisting I rest as much as possible, which is why I'm making such a mess of these flowers instead of standing by his side in the kitchen, stirring my famous *stifado*.'

Sofia smiled, tucking her neatly styled bob behind her ears to reveal a pair of stunning diamond and sapphire earrings that glinted in the sunshine. She wore a wide-sleeved, cornflower-blue kaftan, and once again, Abbie's heart gave a nip of sadness as she caught a waft of the same floral perfume her beloved mum chose to wear on special occasions.

The low hum of music emanated from the radio, interspersed by the high-pitched voice of the over-excited DJ as he introduced each new tune, and a tantalising aroma of warm bread and freshly ground coffee lingered in the air. Abbie's stomach growled loudly, and Sofia laughed, calling to Panos to bring them some breakfast, which he did with a broad smile before disappearing back to his culinary preparations.

'How did you and Panos meet?'

Sofia's eyes softened as she glanced through the open door into the kitchen where her husband was now busy slicing up an onion and tossing it into a pan, along with a handful of chopped tomatoes and fresh basil.

'Before I came to Corfu, I was an interior designer in Athens. I had my own boutique and many wealthy clients. I had a wonderful life, filled with glitz and glamour, beautiful clothes and a great group of friends who invited me to all the best parties, to dine at the finest restaurants, and to spend weekends on their yachts, which was where I met Panos. He was skippering one of those yachts, and, well, I knew right there and then that we would be together. I fell in love. He grew up here on Corfu; this is his home, just like it is Nikos' home, and the place drew him back. We settled here, got married, and had two wonderful children, and I've never been happier. Isn't that what we're all searching for, what we all dream of doing? To find the ever elusive happiness? The picture might not be exactly as we had first envisaged it, and the journey may be bumpy, but so what? It's the end result that matters.'

Abbie swallowed down her emotions; it was time to ask her questions.

'Is that why my aunt went to California?'

Sofia eyed Abbie carefully, taking her time to consider her answer.

'Yes. Liz fell in love, too, and love makes us do many impetuous things. Things that, in other circumstances, we wouldn't dream of doing. Things that hurt the ones we love, too.'

'Hurt the ones we love? What do you mean?'

Abbie's breath caught in her throat and her chest contracted painfully, but she needed to keep it together, needed to concentrate on what Sofia was saying so she could file away every detail for later dissection, and so she could steer the conversation in the direction she needed it to go, no matter what Sofia told her.

'Your aunt paid a high price for love. She forfeited her relationship with her sister, and lost the chance of knowing her niece, and I can assure you those two things left a huge void in her life, a void she filled with regret and sadness, but she never, not once, regretted marrying Greg. She loved him with every fibre of her body, and he adored her. She told me that he made her heart fly and her soul sing, which is exactly how I feel about Panos.'

'But I don't understand. How did falling in love with Greg cause her to lose her relationship with my mum?'

Sofia averted her gaze and started to fiddle with a stem of lavender, adding random stalks into the vases that Abbie had already arranged, clearly uncomfortable and hesitant about taking the conversation further.

'Sofia, if you know anything, please tell me. I need to know. I've needed to know for a very long time. Every time I asked my mum about what happened with Aunt Liz, why she lived in America, why she didn't contact us or why we didn't contact her, she would change the subject, or, when I was older and not so easily brushed off, she would simply refuse to tell me. The not knowing continues to eat away at me even now, and it affects my whole life, and my relationships. Neither of them is here anymore, regretfully, so whatever you tell me can't hurt anyone now.'

'*You* can be hurt, Abbie.'

'Believe me, nothing can be worse than not knowing.'

Sofia hesitated for a long, interminable minute, then inhaled a breath and met Abbie's eyes.

'Are you sure?'

All Abbie could do was nod. This was it, what she had been waiting for for so long, and her heart was beating so fast that she thought it might break free of her chest and sprint away into the distance.

'Greg, your aunt's husband, was your mum's fiancé when he and Liz eloped.'

A spasm of shock hit her with the force of a sledgehammer, whipping the air from her lungs and the words from her mouth. Sofia pushed herself up from her seat and hobbled to the bar where she filled a glass with ice-cold water and brought it back to Abbie.

'Are you okay?'

Abbie nodded, trying hard to process the bombshell

Sofia had just dropped. She felt dazed, numb, completely bewildered, but as the seconds ticked away, understanding began to dawn. Whilst her heart cracked with the hurt her aunt's actions had clearly caused her mum, the fact that she now knew what had happened, what had instigated the family estrangement all those years ago, gave her a modicum of solace.

With that knowledge, she could start to work on coming to terms with it, and try to look at the dreadful situation from both sides. Her mum must have felt devastated, rejected, humiliated by someone she had thought loved her – not only losing her boyfriend, but her sister, too, to a country on the other side of the world. And then there was the guilt and remorse her aunt must have felt, for the pain she had caused in the name of love.

'Liz told me that she reached out several times to your mum, hoping to make amends, but her efforts were gently, but firmly rebuffed every time. As you know, Liz and Greg didn't have any children of their own, so they threw themselves into Greg's father's organic winery business and…'

'And what?'

'Well, over the last few years, while Liz was living here in Corfu, and after she found out that your mum had passed away, with urging from me and a few of her other friends, she started to follow your progress through life on social media. She knew you were working as a florist in London, that you had someone special in your life, and she was adamant that you should inherit her beloved hotel. She kept saying that was what Greg would have wanted, and so that's what she did.'

Abbie couldn't hold it in any longer. Hot tears flowed down her cheeks as she was bombarded with a kaleidoscope of emotions; sorrow for the loss of her mum, disappointment that she hadn't felt able to confide in her when she would have understood, would have been able to offer her support; then sadness for her aunt who had left everything she had ever known behind to start a new life so far away from home in the name of love. She mourned the lost opportunity to meet her aunt after her mum had passed away, to listen to her side of the story, to have the chance to know her only living relative. She didn't know whether she would have taken up that chance, but whether she would or wouldn't didn't matter at this point, it was too late now.

After what she'd just heard she didn't know how she felt about inheriting the hotel, and she had never wanted to talk to her mum so desperately as she did at that moment. She felt drained, every ounce of her energy spent, and her demons began to raise their heads above the parapet once more. She was alone in the world, she was a member of that club no one wanted to brag about – an orphan. She had no one to turn to in times of trouble, no one to ask for helpful advice.

She pushed back her chair and stood, suddenly desperate to escape so she could nurse her thoughts in private.

'Abbie, please, I…'

Abbie saw a flash of distress, and indecision, streak across Sofia's face.

'Is there anything else?'

'No, no, there isn't but please—'

'Sorry, Sofia, I just need some time to… to think.'

She tried to offer Sofia a grateful smile but it came out more like a twisted grimace, and then dashed from the taverna, knowing that Sofia couldn't come after her, even if she wanted to. She ran down the driveway towards the hotel, her legs like jelly, her breath coming in spurts, only stopping when she reached the steps and heard the rev of a car's engine behind her. When she turned around, she saw Nikos' rusty red Peugeot skid to an abrupt halt next to her and, as he wound down his window to talk to her, relief flooded her veins.

'Oh, Nikos, you're back, I—'

'Abbie? Is it true? Are you selling the hotel to Georgios Konstantinou?'

'I—'

'I didn't think you'd do it. Not to that guy, anyway. Did Alex tell you what his plans are?'

'No, I—'

'He's going to extend; he's going to turn the place into an all-inclusive hotel! It will destroy this area, and people's livelihoods. Please, will you reconsider?'

'Nikos, I…'

Abbie had no spare capacity to think of anything other than the metaphorical grenade that had just been tossed into her life, so she simply stared at Nikos, her brain blank, completely unable to compute what he was talking about. She tried to speak, but though her lips moved, no words ensued.

'Well, good luck, Abbie. I hope you've got what you came for.'

Nikos rammed the car into gear and shot off down the

driveway, leaving a cloud of dust in his wake.

Chapter Twenty Seven

Stephanopoulos & Florakis, Corfu Town
Flower: Yellow Friendship Tulip

When Abbie woke the next morning, she felt as though she'd been hit by a ten-tonne bus. Every bone in her body ached, her head was fuzzy, like she'd consumed every one of Kostas' cocktails, and when she looked in her mirror, her hair was more akin to that sported by a scarecrow in a force-ten gale. However, her appearance was the least of her worries.

She stepped in the shower hoping that a blast of cold water would help to chase away at least some of the emotion that was scorching through her body, but of course it didn't. She dressed quickly in whatever came to hand first, and went down to the kitchen to fix herself a coffee, which she took out to the veranda. For the first time since she'd arrived in Corfu, the early morning birdsong failed to lift her spirits.

She was exhausted from spending the whole night running through what Sofia had told her over and over again – a constant tickertape of torment – trying to slot the facts she'd learned into what she already knew… which, granted, hadn't been much.

When she had come to Corfu hoping for answers about her past, never in her wildest dreams – or nightmares – had she thought it would be something like this, something so painful to all concerned. She could scarcely believe that her aunt would have been so cruel, so disloyal to her older sister, or that the man her mum had chosen to spend her life with would have left her without a backward glance.

She tried hard to see the situation from a different perspective, but her thoughts kept swerving back to her mum, her wonderful mum who had worked so hard to give her a loving home, who was a much-loved member of her tiny village community in Devon, as well as a popular teacher at the local primary school where she had many friends. She wondered how her mum had coped with the fallout, and she was ambushed by a fresh wave of sorrow for what it must have been like to discover her fiancé's, and her sister's, betrayal. She knew her mum must have moved on, if only temporarily, meeting the man who had subsequently become Abbie's father, only for that romance to end badly too - a double blow. No wonder there had been no more relationships – one heartbreak was painful enough; two in quick succession must have been soul-destroying.

What hurt Abbie the most, though, was the fact that her mum had never felt able to confide in her about any of it.

Oh, how she wished she was there now, sitting in her mum's garden in Devon next to the lily pond in the shade of the clematis-covered pergola, talking to her about the swarm of emotions she was experiencing – shock, confusion, disorientation, sympathy, and she may as well throw in the guilt she felt about having agreed to sell the Hummingbird Hotel to someone who had turned out to be a property developer, a decision which would ensure she retained no friends in Corfu.

Things couldn't possibly get much worse.

And then she remembered Nikos' reaction the previous night, and her mood sank even further. She couldn't stay there; she couldn't face the accusatory glances from people who had been so kind to her only to find out she had thrown their generosity back in their faces. But she particularly couldn't face Nikos.

She abandoned her coffee, dashed up the stairs, grabbed her suitcase from under her bed, and started to fling in at random everything she had brought with her from the UK. With some difficulty, she managed to force the lid shut and drag the case out to the landing, pausing outside her aunt's bedroom, her emotions in turmoil. She still hadn't got round to sorting through her personal belongings, but she couldn't bear to do that now. Maybe she could ask Sofia to do it.

She called a taxi and spent the next thirty minutes making sure everything at the hotel was safe and secure – no more potential fire scares – and pocketed the keys to drop off at the lawyer's office. She didn't know whether Alex Stephanopoulos would see her without an appointment, but she would have to take that chance, then she would head over to the airport and pray that she could get a standby seat on the next flight back to Gatwick.

The taxi arrived sooner than expected and she had no time to linger; no time to take a last look at the pool, or the courtyard, or the mini-vineyard – her favourite part of the Hummingbird Hotel. She handed the driver her suitcase, gave him the address of Alex's offices, and jumped into the back seat. As the white Mercedes trundled slowly down the driveway for what would be her final time, Abbie stared out of the window at the familiar rows of grapevines snaking across the hillside in parallel lines, the silvery green tufts of the olive groves, the tiny white-washed houses hugging the hillside opposite.

Her heart cracked that her sojourn in the Corfu sunshine had ended this way, but how could it have ended any differently? She had come there to find out about her family's history and to sell the hotel and she had accomplished both those things. Now, once the sale proceeds had been deposited into her account, she could get on with starting a new chapter of her life in Devon – a place that was both familiar and comfortable and where she wouldn't have to deal with any hair-dye-wielding guests.

Wasn't that what she had always dreamed of?

So why did she feel so bereft?

The taxi came to an abrupt stop and the driver pointed out her destination some fifty metres away at the end of a narrow pedestrianised street which she recognised from her earlier visit. She handed over a twenty euro note, scrambled out of the back seat, and, with her suitcase in tow, made her way to the offices of Stephanopoulos &

Florakis where she was informed by the receptionist that Mr Stephanopoulos was out visiting a client but he would be back after lunch. The young woman promised to print out all the paperwork that required her signature, and also agreed to allow Abbie to leave her suitcase in the foyer while she went in search of a much-needed coffee.

Abbie roamed the streets of Corfu Town, unable to concentrate on anything except getting through the next two hours, then meeting with Alex, signing the documents for the sale of the hotel, and heading off to the airport. She didn't think she would be able to breathe properly until she was actually on the aeroplane and heading for home. Her stomach growled its objection to the lack of attention, so she found a tiny café in a shady courtyard off the beaten tourist track, sat at one of only two tables, and ordered a Greek coffee and a croissant, the rich, dark caffeine providing a welcome boost of energy that served to clear her mind, and suddenly she experienced an overwhelming urge to talk to someone.

She picked up her phone, and paused. Who should she call?

How had she ended up at this point, with no one to turn to in her time of need? She was alone, in a foreign country, with no one to share her anguish with, no one to hold her hand.

However, despite her despondency, a familiar voice told her in no uncertain terms that she was most certainly *not* alone, and that she could do anything she put her mind to, and when she realised who that voice belonged to, she had to smile.

How had she forgotten? There *was* someone who loved

her; someone she could talk to and who would listen, and nod, and sympathise, before offering up her special brand of straightforward advice. It might not be what she wanted to hear, but it would come from the heart. Abbie selected the number and waited, her heart giving a leap of affection when she heard Emily's voice.

'Hey, Abbie, how're things?'

'Oh, Em, I don't know where to start.'

'Start at the beginning and we'll go from there.'

Abbie swallowed down hard, determined to get everything out as succinctly as possible before she crumbled into a sobbing mess.

'Okay, so, I've spoken to Sofia… about my aunt.'

'And what did she tell you?'

'She told me that the reason my mum and her sister were estranged for all these years was because my Aunt Liz… she… she ran off with my mum's fiancé.'

'Oh, Abbie darling, I'm so sorry.'

'I just can't stop thinking about my mum, how devastated she must have been.'

'I know, I know, it's terribly sad, but…'

'But what?'

'Well, this is something you've been wondering about for most of your life, Abbie, a conundrum that you were so desperate to solve that it became a sort of quest, and now you have the answers you've been searching for. There's no more uncertainty, no more "whys" or "what ifs" to ponder. What happened to your mum was heart-breaking, for *her*, but it doesn't have to be for *you*. You are not your mum's past, or even your own, Abbie, you are your future. Now you can move on, start afresh with all the pieces of the jigsaw…'

'Well, not *all* the pieces, Em.'

'Okay, maybe not, but this is a start. Now you have the facts, you can leave this sad story in the past, where it belongs, because there's nothing you can do to change things, or to help those who were involved, no matter how much you want to. All you can – and should – do, is stitch the knowledge of what happened to cause your family's estrangement into the tapestry of your life, and face your future with the conviction that *you* are the director of your own fate.'

Abbie took a few moments to consider what Emily had said. She had suspected she would receive the usual sensible, logical, straightforward advice from her friend, and that was exactly what she had got. And Emily was right. Leaving aside her rampaging emotions and looking at what she knew from the point-of-view of a casual bystander, it was true that she had spent more time than was healthy wondering what had torn her family apart, and it had had a detrimental impact on her confidence.

She had felt as though she was one of those cartoon characters who walked around with a raincloud hanging over their head, and it had prevented her from reaching for her dreams – like Emily had done with her pâtisserie, like Rachel had done with her painting, like Nikos had done when he went to Paris to train as a chef. Instead, she had always chosen the easy route; the route where she knew someone would be there to hold her hand.

Could she really do what Emily was suggesting and face the future with a new burst of confidence? To make a new life – a life she truly wanted, not merely a comfortable one –

by herself? With no safety net?

But then what was it that she truly wanted? Well, that was one thing she didn't have to think too long or hard about. She wanted to spend every day surrounded by all the wonderful flowers, and plants, and shrubs, and trees, that she loved.

'Abbie? Abbie, are you okay?'

'Yes, I'm fine. I—'

'Look, I can catch a flight over there—'

'No, no, you don't have to do that. I'm actually coming home tonight. I'm just waiting to meet with my aunt's lawyer, and then I'm going to the airport to see if I can grab a last-minute ticket.'

'You're going to see the lawyer?'

'Yes, the hotel's been sold.'

'Okay. That's great news, isn't it?'

'I think so.'

'What do you mean "I think so"?'

'Oh, Em, Nikos hates me! And so will Sofia and Panos, and Rachel, and maybe even Felix – who doesn't hate *anyone* – when they find out.'

'Why?'

'Because the guy who's buying the hotel… well, he's going to turn it into one of those awful all-inclusive complexes which is bound to have an impact on everyone's livelihoods, especially Nikos'.'

'So do you really need to sell the hotel?'

'What do you mean? Of course I do. I can't stay here; I can't run a hotel!'

'I'm sure you could, Abbie. What have you been doing these last two weeks? But I know what you mean, it's not where your true passion lies, but can't you do both?'

'Do both?'

'Maybe you've found your garden and it's just not where you expected to be. Why can't your dream garden be in Corfu? You could open it to the public, put on guided tours for avid gardening enthusiasts, or grow a whole host of gorgeous flowers and sell them to the businesses around there. Or you could offer your award-winning floral architecture to the hotels and apartments, or even put on flower-arranging classes, or host a flower-arranging retreat at the hotel. What I'm trying to say is, there are lots of ways you can achieve your dream and it doesn't have to be here in the UK. Why can't it be in Corfu?'

'You're telling me I should stay here? But I don't know anyone here.'

Emily laughed. 'Of course you do! You know lots of people; probably more than you know here in London. Abbie, home isn't a house, or a cute cottage with roses around the door, it's about people, it's about community, it's about those who care about you, who support you in times of need and who celebrate with you in times of joy, and it sounds to me like you've found that right there at the Hummingbird Hotel. Not to mention the main reason you have to stay.'

'What's that?'

'Nikos!'

'But I just told you, he hates me.'

'Will he still hate you if you're not selling the hotel?'

'I—'

'Take a leap of faith, Abbie. Give yourself a chance and shoot for what you truly want.'

'I'm not sure I can do that, Em.'

'Oh, I nearly forgot, did you check out Nikos' YouTube channel?'

'What? No.'

'You should.'

'Why?'

'He's famous.'

'Who?'

'Nikos! Keep up, darling. You know, I'm actually surprised we never stumbled across his show.'

'Show? What show?'

Abbie's head started to spin; this conversation was getting surreal.

'Nikos used to work as a chef in Paris, right?'

'Yes.'

'Well, while he was there, he uploaded weekly cookery demonstrations to YouTube – a mixture of French and Greek cuisine – and he has over half a million regular viewers. Although I'm not sure it was the cookery those people were tuning in for – that guy is seriously *hot*! Take a look at the link I just sent you!'

'I—'

'Okay darling, I've got to go, my shift starts in ten minutes. Can we talk later?'

'Sure, and thanks, Em.'

'No problem. You've got this!'

Abbie remained sitting at the table, sipping her now-cold, but still deliciously fragrant coffee, listening to the faint hum of traffic beyond the hidden courtyard and the buzz of a lone bee going about her daily task of collecting nectar from the hanging basket of pink geraniums next to the café's door, and her emotions began to calm. Talking to Emily had always had that effect and she took her time to slowly and carefully consider everything her friend had said, and then looked at what she had learned with new perspective.

Okay, maybe given time she could accept what Sofia had said; that love did spring in the most unexpected of places, and that it *did* make people do the most unexpected of things – like emigrating to another country to marry someone who was engaged to someone else. She wasn't so numbed by the shock of the revelation to realise that it couldn't have been an easy choice for her aunt.

To Abbie's surprise, as she worked through her feelings about finally finding out the truth, and thought about what Emily had said about dreams changing and taking a leap of faith, her spirits started to rise, which in turn delivered a boost to her previously missing-in-action self-belief. No one dished out confidence; you had to raise your chin, grit your teeth, and work at gathering it yourself.

Why *couldn't* she do anything she wanted?

She had no job to return to in the UK. She had no home of her own there, and no relationship to worry about, either. However, she did have *one* of those things here in Corfu – the Hummingbird Hotel – and, if she worked hard, she could potentially have a second – a means of earning a living instead of living off an inheritance she hadn't expected and, if she were honest did not want, or deserve.

But becoming a hotelier wasn't her dream; that had never been written in her stars.

And then she thought of what Emily had told her about Nikos and she couldn't resist taking a peek at his YouTube channel – she was an aficionado of cookery shows, after all – and when she saw him, so handsome, so at ease in front of the camera, so passionate about his chosen profession, she had an idea, a wonderful, amazing, exciting idea and her spirits soared.

She knew exactly what she was going to do.

Chapter Twenty Eight

The Angelopoulos Vineyard and Winery, Ropa Valley
Flower: 'Happy Days' Red Dahlia

Abbie dropped some coins onto the table and sprinted round to the lawyer's office.

'Oh, Miss Coleman, I'm sorry, Mr Stephanopoulos isn't…'

'It's okay, I've changed my mind.'

'What do you mean?'

'Just tell him I'll call him later.'

She grabbed her suitcase and trundled it to the end of the street where she hailed a taxi. Ideas sparked from one thing to the next, to the next, to the next, and her excitement mounted as she thought of what she was going to do. It was time to stop lurking in the shadows because life was easier that way. She had to trust herself, trust her abilities, and if she couldn't do that, she just had to find the confidence to take a leap of faith anyway.

She would be no worse off than she was now if her plan didn't work out, and at least she would have tried. Failure was only another way of saying a person had found the courage to shoot for their dreams and, despite the fact it hadn't worked out, they had gained valuable experience that could be taken on board for the next opportunity that came their way. She knew that Felix would have some kind of quotation that said it better, and she made a mental note to ask him so she could file it away for future use.

The taxi slowed outside Sofia's taverna to navigate the sharp turn in the road that led to the driveway of the Hummingbird Hotel and she made a spur-of-the-moment decision.

'Could you stop here, please?'

She jumped from the cab, left her suitcase at the door of the restaurant and made her way around to the terrace at the rear, delighted when she saw the very person she was looking for. Her mood edged up another notch; clearly the gods of good fortune were smiling on her, which she took as another sign she was doing the right thing.

'Hey, Felix, can I have a word?'

'Sure.'

Abbie watched Felix unfold his body from a complicated yoga pose that involved balancing on his forearms with his feet dangling over his head like a scorpion ready to pounce on its unsuspecting prey. It looked as far away from relaxation as it was possible to get, but Abbie couldn't prevent a slight smirk from tugging at her lips when she received an eyeful of his all-in-one shorts-and-leotard outfit in a vivid green and turquoise that showcased his muscular physique to its best advantage.

'First, can I ask you if you've decided whether you're going back to Australia yet?'

Felix grabbed a bottle of water and drained half the contents in one long gulp, wiping his lips with the back of his hand before meeting Abbie's eyes.

'It's been a really tough decision, so I've consulted several different sources.'

'Your horoscope? Your guru? The stars?'

'No.' Felix's forehead wrinkled in perplexity, as though she had gone mad. 'My mum, my sister, and Rachel and Sofia.'

'Oh, okay.' A giggle agitated at Abbie's chest but she managed to keep a straight face because if she wanted her plan to succeed, she needed Felix on her side. 'And what did they say?'

'All of them told me to follow my heart.'

'And?'

'And they're right. The only reason we should look back at our past is so we can see how far we've come.' Felix leaned forward, touching his toes with the tips of his fingers, then stretching out his calves and his quads, his biceps and his triceps. 'Fancy a yoga lesson?'

'Not right now, thanks. So, what *have* you decided to do?'

Abbie's heart raced. Whilst her plan wouldn't fall apart if Felix high-tailed it back to Sydney to resume his relationship with Carlie, it wouldn't be half as much fun without him.

'I have to be the priority in my own life and look for

sanctuary in no one but myself. So that's exactly what I've decided to do.'

Abbie sighed at his prevarication, but her affection for Felix expanded through her chest. She loved his quirks of character, his crazy eye-popping outfits, his love of all-things spiritual, the fact that his hair was as wild as her own, and she knew for sure that her guests at the Hummingbird Hotel would love him, too. She just wished he would get to the point before she burst with frustration.

'Felix!'

'Everything has an ending, Abbie. If we make peace with that then all will be well.'

'Which means?'

'I'm not going back to Australia. I've spoken to Carlie and she understands it's too late for us. I have no regrets. I'm staying on here in Corfu, but the Hummingbird Hotel will not be the same without you. I'll miss you, Abbie, I feel we've made a strong and vibrant connection.'

'Okay, so that's what I wanted to talk to you about. What would you say if I asked you to run a week-long yoga retreat at the hotel, or perhaps a more general well-being retreat, with meditation and mindfulness exercises, relaxation and rejuvenation with a digital detox, as well as hiking the Corfu nature trail, or doing a little pottering in the garden – which, I can assure you, is just as good for the soul as any meditation exercise? I want the Hummingbird Hotel to be a place where guests come to slow down, to escape the pressure of the nine-to-five…'

'To align their chakras?'

'Yes, that, and to take the time to smell the flowers,

listen to nature, to find serenity.'

'Sounds like fun. Sure, I'd be up for that, but I thought you were selling the hotel?'

'I was, but I've changed my mind.'

'I knew you would.'

'Really?'

'Yes, your horoscope said that today was the day for new ideas, new insights, and new visons for the future. There will be many difficult decisions ahead, though it isn't the fear of failure you should be concerned about, but the fear of trying. If you have the confidence to believe in yourself, anything is possible.'

'I think you and my best friend, Emily, would get on well.' She smiled.

'Have you told Nikos what you're doing?'

'No, I'm on my way over to see him now.'

'You do know his mother and his sister want to sell the vineyard, don't you? The offer they received is apparently very generous, more than either of them expected to get, and Nikos doesn't have the cash to keep the place going until the end of the season. Want me to come with you?'

'No thanks, Felix. I've got this.'

Once again, a surge of confidence washed through her. She had no idea if her plan would work, or whether she was being plainly irresponsible, but whatever it was, she was going to give it her all. With Felix on board, that was the first part sorted. Now she had to put in place the second part of her plan, and she had an inkling that the conversation wouldn't be as easy as it had been with Felix.

But hadn't he just said that her stars foretold success?

'Well, at least let me give you a lift.'

'No, it's—'

Felix ignored her protestations and strode to the side of the terrace where a bright yellow and black Vespa slumbered in the shade, listing to one side like a drunken bumble bee.

'What are you waiting for? Hop on!'

'Is this… is this yours?' She giggled.

'Yes, she's a real beaut, isn't she?'

Abbie couldn't think of a more incongruous pairing than Felix – barefoot and wearing skin-tight Lycra – sitting astride a bright yellow Vespa, but it was better than walking the kilometre to the Angelopoulos winery in the searing heat.

'She's certainly eye-catching. Thanks, Felix, a lift would be great.'

She hopped onto the back and, to her surprise, enjoyed the five-minute trip down the road with her hair streaming behind her like a Medusa on steroids. When they drew to a halt outside the winery, she saw Nikos' rusty red Peugeot parked next to a brand-new black Audi and her heart gave a nip of trepidation. The last time she had seen Nikos he'd screeched away from the hotel in a dark mood, and she didn't know what kind of reception she would get.

'Want me to stay?' asked Felix, as perceptive as always.

'No, I have to do this on my own. Thanks, though.'

'No problem. *Namaste*.'

She watched Felix disappear back down the road, then crossed the courtyard and rang the doorbell, refusing to succumb to the siren call of her confidence demons telling her to spin round and sprint for the hills without a backwards glance.

However, when the front door swung open, she wished she had heeded their demands as she performed an involuntary double-take when she saw who Nikos' visitor was.

'Alex?'

'Oh, hello there, Abbie.'

'I…'

Shock ricocheted through her chest, which turned to panic when she saw the distress scrawled across Nikos' face.

'Nikos, what's Alex doing here?'

Nikos opened his mouth to say something but couldn't formulate the words; Alex wasn't so tongue-tied.

'Like you, Abbie, he's taken the sensible route and agreed to accept Georgios' offer for the winery and the vineyard. A very prudent decision, if I might say so, bearing in mind his financial situation.'

Alex flashed a very white smile at Nikos, then slapped him on his back in what Abbie thought was a rather patronising manner. She had no idea why, but his gesture galvanised her into action.

'Have you signed anything, Nikos?'

She saw a streak of curiosity flash through his eyes, and his lips tweaked at the corners.

'Not yet. Why?'

'Because I've got a proposition for you.'

'What kind of proposition?'

Abbie glanced at Alex, and saw his eyes narrow, his forehead crease.

'Do you think we could talk in private?'

'Nikos, I don't think you should—' Alex started.

'Alex, thanks for your advice. I'll call you after I've spoken to my mother and my sister.'

'But I think—'

'Thanks, Alex,' Nikos said firmly.

Realising it was pointless to continue arguing, Alex strode to the black Audi and, with a roar of its powerful engine, disappeared down the driveway in Felix's wake.

'Shall we walk?' Nikos suggested, pointing towards the vineyard.

'Perfect.'

They strolled in silence between two rows of vines, coming to a stop where the Angelopoulos estate bordered the Hummingbird Hotel's mini-vineyard. Abbie turned to face Nikos, excitement and nerves tumbling through her veins in equal measure; it was so important to her to get this right.

'Okay, Abbie, what's this about?'

She inhaled a deep breath.

'I might be a useless hotelier, and an even worse cook, but I do know something about plants, and shrubs, and flowers, and growing things in general, and I think I could learn about vines and vineyards.'

'But what does that—'

'Let me say this, Nikos. You've tried to manage the vineyard, to produce great wine to honour the memory of your late father and brother, and it hasn't worked out quite how you expected. But Nikos, you are a talented chef, and a charismatic cookery course presenter.'

'So what are you saying?'

'That we should work together.'

'Work together?'

'Form a partnership, a joint venture – the Hummingbird Hotel and the Angelopoulos Vineyard & Winery – or, to be more precise, we should swap roles. I'll manage the vineyard, and my aunt's mini-vineyard – maybe we could produce a new blend of wine? – and I'm thinking of running a few wine tours, with wine-tastings. I'll also make a start on transforming that jungle over there into a fabulous garden, with tropical plants and stunning flowers that one day I might be able to supply to the businesses around here as cut flowers or as floral arrangements.'

She paused, keen to see Nikos' reaction, but his expression was unreadable, so she ploughed on.

'And you can handle the culinary side of things at the hotel; running classes, creating amazing recipes, and sharing them with our guests. So, I get to pursue my passion for plants, and you get to pursue your passion for cooking. It might not be *exactly* what we dreamed of, but dreams can change, and this way I'll keep the Hummingbird Hotel, and you'll keep the winery and the vineyard.'

She saw the surprise on Nikos' face; he clearly hadn't been expecting her to give a speech. Then his features softened and he smiled, though his smile didn't quite meet his eyes.

'It's an interesting proposition, but there's one thing you haven't factored in.'

'What?'

Nikos hesitated; the words clearly too painful to say.

'The vineyard, the winery; there's no money left in the business to keep it going. I've done everything I can to keep it afloat, used all my savings, even sold my motorbike. That's why my mother has decided that it's time to sell, she wants to get out before we get into serious difficulty. I'm sorry,

Abbie, it's a great idea in theory, but it won't work.'

'What if I told you there'd be an injection of cash into the business that would see the winery through until next year? Enough time to see if, between us, we can make this plan work?'

'But where will we get an injection of cash from?'

'My aunt left me a small legacy—'

'Oh no, I don't think—'

'Do you think this is a good idea? Do you think it will work?'

Abbie held his gaze, determined for him to see she was serious about what she was proposing.

'I think it *could* work, but I can't accept your money.'

'It's not a gift, it's an investment in a new business venture.'

Finally, she saw a flicker of excitement in Nikos' eyes.

'Please say you'll give it a go.'

'But I thought you were leaving Corfu? That you were selling the Hummingbird Hotel to Georgios Konstantinou?'

'I was.'

'So what made you change your mind?'

'My aunt.'

'Liz? I don't understand.'

'I didn't know her, but I *do* know that she wasn't afraid to take a leap of faith for something she believed in. I want to do the same, I want to honour her memory by carrying on her legacy at the Hummingbird Hotel, and Felix has already agreed to come on board.'

'Felix?' Nikos laughed.

'Yes, he's promised to help out at the hotel, as well as

run a yoga and well-being retreat, which, if successful, I hope to repeat every month going forward. I also plan to ask Rachel if she would be interested in running a few painting workshops, maybe even branching out to include some sculpture, ceramics and photography, and there are lots of other courses we can run, like creative writing classes, flower-arranging lessons, and of course, the main attraction will be classes in creating authentic Greek pastries.'

'And Parisian pâtisserie?'

'Of course.'

'And you really want to do wine tours?'

'Yes, I do, and tastings. I think it's a great way of not only bringing in some extra funds, but also promoting and selling the Angelopoulos brand. I'm actually really excited about learning about the wine-making process, but even more so about learning how to tend the vines, and creating the Angelopoulos gardens from scratch. How many botanists get to say they've done that? And in such a stunningly beautiful location?'

'Are you sure you want to do this, Abbie? It's a huge decision.'

Nikos took a step closer to her, his dark eyes boring into hers, their intensity sending a cascade of desire through her veins and out to her extremities until every single one of her senses fizzed.

'I'm sure.'

'Then it's a yes from me.' His wide smile told her that he was just as excited as she was about what lay ahead. 'Come on, there's only one way to seal this deal.'

Abbie followed Nikos back to the house, through the front door, down the corridor and out to the rear terrace where he pointed to a scarred wooden bench that faced a jaw-droppingly spectacular view over the whole of the Ropa Valley.

'Take a seat, I'll be back in a moment.'

When Nikos returned, he was carrying a bottle of red wine and two glasses, which he set down on the low wall in front of them. To Abbie's surprise, there were tears sparkling at his lashes.

'I've been saving this for a special occasion, and there's no more special occasion than today.'

Abbie glanced at the label. She immediately recognised the gold-embossed Angelopoulos name and realised what Nikos' gesture meant.

'Oh, Nikos, are you sure?'

'Absolutely.'

'But… isn't this one of the last bottles?'

'My father would have approved.'

She watched him open the bottle of wine with the deference it deserved, and her heart gave a nip of sadness for the family's devastating loss, but she saw that Nikos was grinning as he poured out two generous measures and raised his glass high in the air.

'To the future!'

Abbie smiled, picked up her glass and went to stand next to Nikos. 'To the future.'

The wine tasted like liquid sunshine, and she knew she had made the right decision to stay on in Corfu. If she could help the Angelopoulos estate produce wine half as good as this, then the winery's future would be safe.

'And there's just one more thing we need to do to seal the deal.'

'What's that?'

Nikos returned his glass to the wall, and closed the distance between them.

'A kiss,' he whispered, his voice thick with emotion.

Abbie stepped into his arms, and within moments his lips were on hers, soft, gentle, tentative, and then, as he pulled her closer, their bodies melding perfectly, filled with passion. She gave herself up to his embrace, savouring every pleasurable sensation that scorched through her body, inhaling the delicious aroma of his lemony cologne, and she knew she was exactly where she wanted to be. She was excited about what might lie ahead, and, with Nikos by her side, she knew it would be a rollercoaster of an adventure.

An adventure she couldn't wait to start.

The End

Acknowledgements

First and foremost, I'd like to say a huge thank you to my amazing editor, Laura McCallen, whose skilful guidance and eagle eye has made Abbie and Nikos' story all the more vibrant and polished. I'd also like to thank Berni Stevens for the gorgeous, summery cover – I truly wish I could spend a few hours on the Corfu beach she has so artfully portrayed.

The romance writing community continues to be a source of inspiration and support for me, and I thank each and every one of them – authors, bloggers, designers, social media gurus – for their kind words and encouragement. In particular, I'd like to thank Catherine Ferguson for her constant cheerleading and our brainstorming coffee mornings (with my favourite pineapple and coconut scones!) currently taking place outside.

And finally, a massive thank you to all my amazing readers! I have you in my mind and in my heart all the time I'm sitting at my keyboard, immersed in all-things Greek, trying to write the best story I can, hoping that I'm doing you proud.

Also by Daisy James

The Hummingbird Hotel series

Escape to the Hummingbird Hotel

Summer at the Hummingbird Hotel

Snowflakes at the Hummingbird Hotel

The Cornish Confetti Agency series

The Cornish Confetti Agency – *Caribbean Dreams*

Summertime at the Cornish Confetti Agency – *Festival Fiasco*

Christmas at the Cornish Confetti Agency – *Mistletoe Mayhem*

Tropical Skies at the Cornish Confetti Agency – *Caribbean Chaos*

Tuscan Dreams at the Cornish Confetti Agency – *Idyllic Italy*

A Summer Wedding at the Cornish Confetti Agency – *Seaside Surprises*

The Tuscan Dreams series

Wedding Bells at Villa Limoncello

Summer Dreams at Villa Limoncello

Christmas Secrets at Villa Limoncello

The Paradise Cookery School series

Sunshine & Secrets

Confetti & Confusion

Mistletoe & Mystery

Standalones:

The Summerhouse of Happiness

Christmas at the Dancing Duck

Sunshine After the Rain

There's Something About Cornwall

Lucie's Vintage Cupcake Company

If The Dress Fits

The Runaway Bridesmaid